JOURNEY'S AIM

JOURNEY RUSSO SERIES: BOOK THREE

MARY STONE

AMY WILSON

Copyright © 2024 by Mary Stone Publishing

All rights reserved.

No part of this book may be reproduced in any form or by any electronic or mechanical means, including information storage and retrieval systems, without written permission from the author, except for the use of brief quotations in a book review.

❦ Created with Vellum

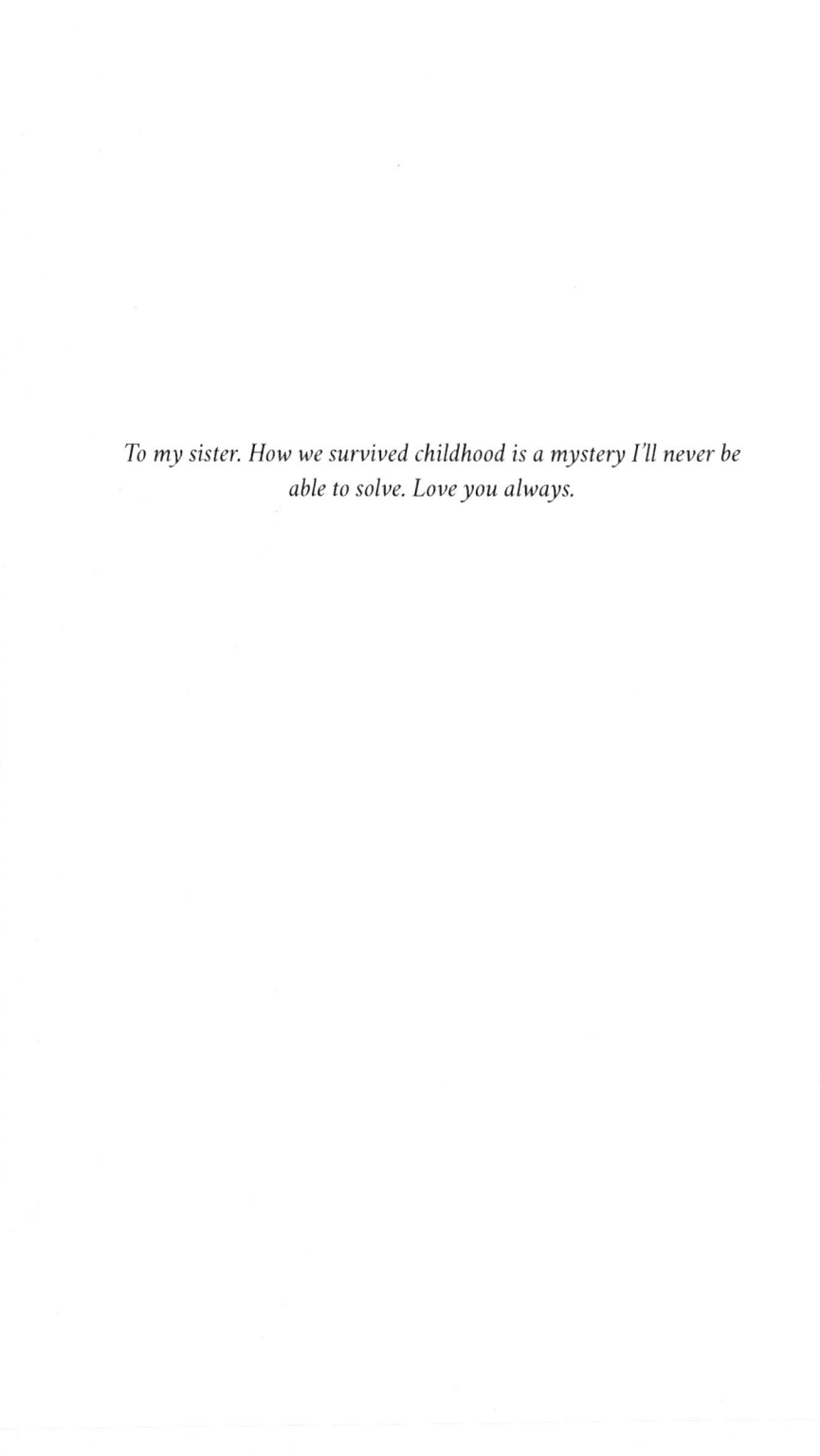

To my sister. How we survived childhood is a mystery I'll never be able to solve. Love you always.

DESCRIPTION

Ready, aim, die.

Barely twenty-four hours after tracking down a brutal serial killer, Special Agent Journey Russo is thrust into a different kind of hunt. This time, the stakes are much higher. Because the prey are innocents.

And all too human.

In less than two weeks, two families are found murdered in their homes, each victim fatally pierced by arrows. A mysterious feather left on each body serves as a haunting calling card, pointing to a new, sinister serial killer—one eerily reminiscent of the tragedy that decimated Journey's family.

As Journey and her partner track down leads on the distinctive murder weapon, a horrifying reality takes shape. Several types of arrowheads at the scene indicate four potential killers working together. Hunting together. Playing games with the victims that they're guaranteed to lose.

When a third victim is found, his heart pierced with an

arrow, the hunt is on. But can Journey and Lucas narrow down the suspects and stop the vicious marksmen before they find their next target? Or will they get caught in the killers' crosshairs?

Journey's Aim, book three of the Journey Russo series by bestselling author Mary Stone, delivers a heart-pounding twist on the pursuit of justice, making 'dead aim' a terrifying reality.

1

Daniel Reaver pulled his truck into the driveway of his two-bedroom, picket-fenced starter home, every muscle aching, caked in dirt from twelve hours of manual labor. He'd installed the irrigation system he'd worked on today himself, but the homeowner hadn't serviced it for winter, resulting in a near-total replacement. For Daniel, that meant a day of excavating, hauling, and crawling around in the mud under a blazing June sun.

Limping through his front door, Daniel wanted nothing more than to fall asleep on the couch with a cold beer in his hand, his wife at his side. He needed a shower, but he was too tired to stand. Maybe he'd head to the bathroom after putting his feet up for a while.

As he came in, he found Claudia curled up beneath a soft blanket on the couch, dozing in front of the television's bluish screen saver light. Her brown eyes fluttered open, and her lips curved into a sleepy smile.

After pulling off his mucky boots and sweaty socks and setting them next to the door, Daniel stepped close and brushed her curly, chocolate-colored hair to the side, giving her a peck on the little beauty mark on her cheek.

"Bella's asleep."

A gentle reminder to not make too much noise if he wanted to grab something to eat. Their ten-year-old daughter was a light sleeper, even with her bedroom on the second floor.

His day might have been exhausting, but life felt right. Daniel was about to collapse onto the couch, ignoring food and focusing on his wife, when the doorbell rang.

Claudia startled. "What time is it? Who is that?" Inside her kimono robe, her shoulders slumped a little. "That definitely woke Bella up."

"Shhh...I'll check it out." Despite his attempt to sound reassuring, Daniel knew late-night visitors rarely brought good news.

Thanks to his new job at the landscaping company, they'd been able to move to a neighborhood much better than the last, away from the apartment building where an elderly man's son-in-law shot him over his disability check. In their new home, they no longer ducked at the sound of bullets ricocheting off bricks or feared them coming through the windows.

These days, they could afford to shop at the regular supermarket with the government assistance they'd depended on until just last week. Daniel now parked his old truck without worrying about becoming a carjacking victim. Claudia safely walked Bella to and from school.

Daniel felt a little silly peering through the peephole, but old habits died hard. Straining his eyes against the darkness outside, he only made out shrubs hiding beneath the bright glow of the porch light's halo.

This was ridiculous.

With an irritated grunt, he flipped the dead bolt and

eased the door open. Stepping onto the stoop, Daniel spotted a single feather lying on the center of his doorstep.

What the hell?

Most feathers were old and ragged, but this one appeared pristine, with long, white, downy edges dotted with brown spots. The feather put him in mind of a bird of prey but was too clean and perfectly placed to have been discarded.

Was this a prank?

A muffled groan from inside the house caught Daniel's attention. "Claudia?" He kept his voice low, mindful of his daughter hopefully still sleeping just up the stairs. He headed back in. "You okay?"

She wasn't. Not at all.

To his horror, Claudia was in the grips of an intruder, a sinister figure clad in camo with a pig mask obscuring his features. His arm encircled Claudia's waist, his fingers digging into her flesh through the thin fabric of her kimono. Fear had drained all color from her face as the sharp edge of a knife pressed against her pale throat.

Daniel's heart raced as he raised his hands. "Please, don't hurt her." He hated how his voice trembled with fear. "Take whatever you want."

"Don't worry." The deep voice was only a little muffled beneath the rubber pig disguise. "I will."

Above their heads, something crashed to the floor in Bella's room. Instinctively, Daniel glanced up, torn between rescuing his wife and protecting his daughter.

"I wonder who's up there?" Pig Man giggled as if this were nothing but a joke. As if he weren't capable of slicing Claudia's throat with a twitch of his wrist.

Daniel had a split second to decide whether to make a break for it and race upstairs. Panicked, he looked to Claudia, who mouthed one word.

Go!

That was all he needed. He turned on his heel to rush the stairs, but he ran directly into a second figure appearing from around the corner in a dog mask. The guy wore head-to-toe camo like his pal and sported a powerful-looking curved bow strapped to his back, a quiver of arrows clipped to his belt over his hip.

Rebounding off Dog Man's chest, Daniel crashed onto his back, struggling to fill his lungs with air. Dog Man dropped his knee hard on Daniel's stomach, driving out the rest of his breath.

A third man started down the stairs. This one also carried a bow with arrows, but he wore a mask shaped like the muzzle of a buck.

Claudia shrieked, echoing Daniel's feelings at seeing Buck Man coming from the direction of their daughter.

"Hush now." Pig Man clamped a hand over her mouth. "All that noise ruins the fun."

Please let Bella be hiding in the closet or beneath the laundry. Please, Lord. Please protect our little girl.

Claudia gulped for air from beneath Pig Man's clamped palm, each gasp a horrible sucking wheeze. Daniel tried to sit up to check on her, but Dog Face had him pinned to the floor.

A second thump came from upstairs. Daniel forced himself not to look, not to draw attention to their daughter. He watched the masked men for clues, but both Dog Face and Buck focused on Pig Man.

Awaiting orders.

"Let's play a game!" Pig Man released his grip on Claudia and clapped his hands. "It's called Ready. Set. Run!" He shoved her forward. "Ladies first!"

Claudia tried to make a break for the back door, but Pig Man and Buck stayed on her heels, chasing her around the kitchen table like a scrambling pair of shadows. But Claudia didn't scream. Though her breath came in heavy gasps, she remained focused.

Dog Face grabbed Daniel by the shirt collar and lifted him off the floor. As soon as his feet were under him, the guy spun him and shoved him hard enough to send him back down to his knees. "Are you stupid? You heard the man. Run, boy, run!"

When her pursuers switched their attention to Daniel, Claudia broke for the door, leading them out into the backyard. "Save Bella!"

As all the men followed, they laughed like devils loose on Hell's playground.

Daniel did *not* want to leave his wife in the hands of these monsters, but with them preoccupied with Claudia, he had one shot—probably his only shot—at getting upstairs to his child.

Turning, he sprinted for the stairs to the two bedrooms. But as he rounded the corner halfway up, he skidded to a stop on the landing at the sight of the nightmare waiting for him at the top.

A fourth man, this one in a bull mask, held little Bella clinched in his arms, her bare feet dangling above the floor. Even though everyone always said Daniel's daughter looked small for her age, this was the first time he really noticed the fragility of her thin arms and legs.

Tears streamed down Bella's face, soaking into her favorite dinosaur nightgown. "Daddy!"

"Don't hurt her!" Wooden stairs groaned beneath the onslaught of Daniel's feet as he rushed upward, fueled by fear-induced adrenaline pouring through his limbs.

Bull chuckled beneath his rubber skin. "Think fast, *Daddy*." His last word came out in a snarl.

A second later, Bella went airborne, arms and legs flailing. Time froze as Daniel's full attention zeroed in on the child, noting the way the light from downstairs caught on Bella's loose, outspread hair as he calculated her trajectory faster than he could think.

Stumbling, he caught her, just managing to stay on his feet. Bella's nightgown ripped in his grip with her inertia, but he swung her head away from the wall before she could slip through his hands.

Bull clapped, slowly, all disdain. "Good catch. Bravo!"

Bella sobbed, shaking in Daniel's arms as he swung around to escape back down the stairs.

Find Claudia. Call the cops. Find Claudia. Call the cops.

But he pulled up short when Pig Man walked back into the kitchen, dragging Claudia by the shirt behind him. The screen door slapped sharply into the frame in their wake.

She hadn't made it far, but she'd clearly put up a fight. Mud streaked her face, and tears rent her robe. Blood dripped from her nose, and her eyes held a dazed cloudiness, as if she'd taken a punch to the face.

Fear and rage crashed over Daniel at the thought of all the ways these freaks could've hurt her.

"Announcement!" Pig Man skipped over to the foot of the stairs, Claudia barely keeping her feet in his grip. "Announcement, everyone. I believe it's time to play our last game of the evening."

Dog Face, Bull, and Buck clapped and cheered.

Daniel pushed Bella's face into his chest, blocking her view of the horror as he descended the stairs, Bull clattering down at his back. "Don't look. Close your eyes." Her warm tears bled through his cotton t-shirt as he whispered into her tangled hair.

When Pig Man shoved Claudia toward her family, she crashed into Daniel. Her hands encircled his bicep, and they stood huddled together between the stairway and living room.

In one smooth motion, Pig Man reached over his shoulder and withdrew his bow, then pulled and nocked an arrow. "This is a game called Race for Your Lives." He raised his weapon, aiming at the center of Daniel's chest, the exact spot where Bella's head rested. "Put her down."

Daniel shook his head. "Please don't—"

"No, no." Pig Man clucked his tongue. "On her feet. This game is everyone for themselves."

Bella screamed and clung tighter to Daniel's neck.

"Don't make us help you, little girl." Pig Man altered his voice to sound like an evil cartoon character, his tone dripping menace. "Daddy needs all his strength to win."

"C'mon. She's just a kid."

The poured-rubber mask remained unmoved. "The rules are the rules. If she doesn't follow them, I'll have to shoot her."

Claudia placed herself in front of Bella and Daniel, chin raised. "Don't you touch her."

"I said, put her the fuck down!" Pig Man stepped forward, putting the point of the arrow an inch from Claudia's eye. "I will shoot you. Then her. Then him." When he turned his piggy face to Daniel, his eyes seemed to sparkle as red as the devil's. "Do you want me to put this arrow through her eye, big man? Put. The. Girl. Down."

"Okay, Bella." Every syllable tasted sour, a betrayal of his duty as a father, a protector. But he had to play the game or lose his little girl and his wife. "It'll be okay. Trust me." He peeled her hands from his neck and lowered her to the floor. "Stay behind me where they can't hurt you."

She clung to his leg.

"That's more like it." Pig Man let the bowstring go slack. "All right now, we want to make this sporting, so everyone line up in the kitchen."

Bull prodded Daniel and his family into the other room.

Dog Face and Buck ranged back and forth around them, hooting and crowing like hounds baying for the hunt. Once they reached the kitchen table, Bull spun the three of them around to face the front of the house. Pig waved him and the other two over to one side of the living room.

"I'm going to count down from ten. If you make it outside through the front door, we'll let you live." Pig Man paused, letting the horror of his statement sink in.

Just in front of Daniel, Claudia struggled to stifle the terrified sobs in her throat. Her shoulders shook.

To calm his thrashing heartbeat, Daniel took in deep breaths through his nose and out through his mouth. The front door to the house stood open only a few long strides away—all three of them could easily get there in ten seconds.

"If you don't make it," Pig Man clucked his tongue again and cocked his head, "too bad. So sad."

Bull, Buck, and Dog Face copied Pig Man's taunt. "Too bad. So sad."

Daniel didn't even have time to catch Claudia's eye before Pig Man began at the top of his voice.

"Ten!"

Bella must've understood, because she let go of Daniel's leg and made like a shot for the front door, tiny feet slapping the floor.

"Nine! Eight!"

Claudia followed right behind her.

"Seven!"

Daniel glanced one last time to make sure the men weren't going to try to stop them like they had before.

"Six!"

Bella and Claudia were a few steps ahead of him, halfway across the living room. Almost free.

"Five!"

And then Bella tripped on the plush carpet and landed face down.

"Uh-oh!" Pig Man laughed. "Four…"

Claudia tripped over Bella. As she fell, she grabbed for their daughter, snagging a fistful of her nightgown.

"Three…"

The fabric gave way, tearing at the seams as she pulled.

"Two…"

Dashing forward, Daniel struggled to grab his family, all of them tangled and tripping over each other, scrambling to get up and escape.

"One!"

At the final count, Daniel straightened and did the only thing left to do. He stepped between those nocked arrows and his family, raising his arms to take up as much space as possible. As he did, he got a perfect view of Pig Man loosing the arrow a millisecond before it drove straight into his chest.

In disbelief, he looked down. A fiberglass shaft pierced the very center of him, blood already welling around the edges. In his own home. The room where, just minutes ago, he'd felt comfort and peace as he'd greeted his sleepy wife.

Pain flared through Daniel's heart as he crumpled, slumping onto his side. His daughter's desperate cries filled the house. His ears. His soul.

"No, no. You gotta watch the rest of the show." Buck's boot landed on Daniel's shoulder and shoved him onto his back.

Claudia shrieked and collapsed as an arrow pierced her back. This one from the Bull's bow.

Daniel cried out in anguish as Bella, his beautiful girl, still struggling toward the door on her own, took Pig Man's arrow between her ribs. Her screams cut off as though a switch had been flipped inside of her.

He reached for his family, but darkness spread toward the center of his vision. The walls faded from peacock blue to gray. Waves, like the crashing of an angry ocean, roared through his ears.

Pig Man strutted up and stood over Daniel. That horrible rubbery pig mask clarified in his vision for his final moment as the man bent at the waist, a clenched fist held over Daniel's face. When he opened his fingers, a brown-speckled white feather floated down toward his chest.

"Thanks for playing."

2

Special Agent Journey Russo inhaled a deep breath as she removed a photo from the manila envelope in her lap. It wasn't necessary, though. The image was still seared in her mind from where she'd first seen it in the stark, fluorescent-lit office of her supervisory special agent just moments ago.

She hadn't been able to react to the disturbing crime scene in front of her SSA, though, and she hoped to hell that she'd be able to maintain the same blank expression now.

"You good?"

The question from Special Agent Lucas Sullivan broke through her thoughts, his voice laced with concern. His brief glances, shifting from her to the road as he navigated their Bureau-issued car, underscored his worry.

Ignoring the question, Journey rubbed a shaky hand over her mouth before returning her focus to the photo of thirty-one-year-old Michael Bragg and his thirty-year-old wife sprawled side by side on their carpet. Michael was face down, but Rose lay on her back, mouth open in a permanent scream, face frozen in the terror of her last moments. Broken glass littered the floor around their bodies, while a bookcase and its contents peppered the room with debris.

With seven years as a special agent under her belt, Journey was no stranger to gruesome murder scenes. Just a couple weeks ago, she and Lucas had dealt with a sexually-suppressed murderer who'd abducted and killed seven couples, going so far as to scalp the women and wear their hair as wigs while he tortured the men to death. Yet despite the horror of that case, it hadn't fazed her this much.

At least, not on the outside.

But the picture SSA Victoria Keller had showed them of a possible serial killer's calling card resting on Rose Bragg's chest had hit Journey hard. A long, white feather with brown spots.

Though Journey didn't recognize the token, the move reminded her too much of The Chosen, a fanatical group she suspected but couldn't yet prove had murdered her family with gasoline and a well-placed match.

The head of the Pittsburgh Field Office Violent Crime Division had just gotten the call from the chief of the Pittsburgh Bureau of Police reporting they'd found two families slaughtered in their homes within two weeks of each other.

It was almost too much, too fast. The Braggs nine days ago, and now the Reavers. Two families cut down in their homes, just like Journey's parents and their friends, who they'd tried to help leave The Chosen before paying for their bravery with their lives.

Journey flipped through the rest of the images once before dropping the stack on her lap. Several minutes of road separated them from the Reaver-family scene, leaving plenty of time for her to go through the Bragg crime scene again when she felt ready.

"Hey…" He nudged her with his elbow. "You okay?"

"I'm not about to puke all over your shoes, if that's what you're asking."

"What a relief." Lucas slid his sunglasses over his stone-gray eyes. "What about this case has you so spooked?"

Nope. Definitely not going there.

Journey would tell Lucas about her family when she was ready. *If* she ever got to that point.

Knowing Lucas possessed the impressive talent of outwaiting Ghandi himself for answers, Journey decided to dodge the question instead of clamming up.

"Daniel, Claudia, and their ten-year-old daughter Bella were found this morning with fatal puncture wounds to the sternum *and* that same kind of feather Keller showed us that turned up with the Braggs."

In the briefing, Keller had given them the rundown of the Braggs' crime scene, which Pittsburgh Bureau of Police had processed just the previous week. While PBP had originally considered that one a B and E gone wrong, with a second murder using an as-yet unidentified weapon at a house only a few blocks away, this was looking like a serial killer.

Lucas turned down the radio to silence a DJ's crackling chatter. "So that's why we're taking the case. Potential serial killer with a calling card."

Clenching her teeth, Journey flipped through her pile of photos to a wider shot of two brown-speckled white feathers, one lying on each of the victims. On Michael Bragg, it sat centered on his back. On Rose, her chest. Both tips pointed to the right. The feathers rested approximately at a thirty-degree angle. Was any of that relevant?

"Could be." Her stomach twisted with a sick realization… a small thrill from processing the details of the murders of two separate families had just electrified her brain.

Maybe I need therapy.

Though she'd come to some realizations about herself the

night before—that chasing serial killers quieted all the noise of guilt and fear inside her head, which probably shouldn't have been the case—the idea of therapy hadn't quite connected until right now.

"You've gotten quiet since we received this assignment." Lucas sipped from the enormous cup of coffee she'd purchased for him that morning. His second of the day, since she'd wanted to surprise him only to find he'd also picked up coffees for the both of them. "Sure you're good?"

"Yeah." Journey tried to punch up the energy in her voice. "Weird morning. That's all."

He pulled up to a stoplight and took a moment to study her. "I hope by now I've proven myself a pretty good listener."

"I'm fine." She pointed at the recently turned green light. "Don't be a traffic hazard."

Huffing in irritation, Lucas pressed the accelerator. He didn't like being told how to drive any more than she did.

They continued in silence that way a few moments longer —Lucas obviously outwaiting her and Journey sweating— before she decided to change the subject. "Do you have any hobbies?" She loved skateboarding but hadn't gone out to the park in ages. Maybe if she got back into doing activities outside of work, she could dodge signing up for therapy.

Setting his cup back in the drink holder, Lucas considered his answer. "I spend time with Hallie. I exercise." As his answer petered out, a sheepish expression crossed his face. "I skateboard a bit."

Journey smiled. At least she wasn't the only one. "What does 'a bit' mean?"

He shrugged. "I'm a workaholic, so 'a bit' means hardly at all." He shot her another glance. "Why ask? My birthday's not 'til next month, you know."

"Oh, 'not 'til next month,' huh? That sounds like a hint to me."

A small smile played at the corners of Lucas's lips. "I'd never dream of it."

After maneuvering through a bunch of cop cars lining the streets, he pulled up to the curb outside the Reaver house. Yellow tape lined the driveway and small yard, flapping in a light breeze.

Journey's chest swelled at the sight. She wondered what Daniel, Claudia, and Bella would've been doing right now if they still lived. Going to work. Going to school. Looking forward to a weekend outing together, maybe. Now they'd never do any of those things ever again.

But Journey meant to make sure whoever stole that future from this family would face their own specific future. One behind bars.

That, after all, was the real reason she'd joined the Bureau. Not for the thrill of the chase, but for the chance to secure justice for families like the Reavers. Sure, an undeniable rush came with solving the puzzle of the crime, but the satisfaction she received knowing she'd stopped a ruthless killer outweighed the adrenaline.

She just needed to make sure to keep her priorities straight. If going to therapy could help with that, maybe she'd check out what the Bureau's health insurance offered.

3

A burly police detective met Lucas and Journey at the front of the driveway. Detective Lonnie Gutierrez was a rectangle of a man with dark skin and hair to match—a fresh buzz cut, high and tight. He extended a hand as they approached. "Thanks for coming. It's a horror show in there."

Lucas shook Guitierrez's proffered hand. "What've we got?"

While they were already acquainted with the basic facts of the case, Lucas knew the value of local nuance. Listening to firsthand accounts could unveil subtleties that might have otherwise been missed. It wasn't just about the facts…it was about the perspective, the local color, the small details that could, if they were lucky, suddenly align to form a clearer picture of both the victims and the person who took their lives.

"Triple homicide. Two parents and their kid, all dead by puncture wounds to the chest or back. Lots of signs of a struggle."

"Who called in the murders?"

"Guy's boss. Jose Garner." Gutierrez angled his head

toward a man standing on the sidewalk beside a truck sporting a lawn-care company logo with a multitude of grass-encrusted tools poking out of the bed. "We got the call at the station around ten after eight. He's still here. Heard you were on the way, wanted to make sure he caught you."

"Thanks." Journey smiled. "We'll just have a chat with him before going in."

"Let me know if I can help."

Old, dried mud crumbled off Jose Garner's work boots in flakes as he straightened at their approach from where he leaned against his pickup. Even when he stood upright, his spine showed a slight curve, a product of crouching over sprinkler systems and turf lawns for years. "You two the agents?"

"That's us." Lucas gestured between himself and Journey. "Special Agents Sullivan and Russo. Can you tell us what you told Detective Gutierrez?"

"Reaver didn't show up to work at seven. So after he didn't answer my calls, I came to check on him. Then I found…that." Garner cast a glance toward the house. A little skittish.

"What time did you find them?"

"Around eight."

At Lucas's side, Journey clicked her pen a couple times. "You always check on your no-show employees when they're only an hour late?"

"Not usually." Garner shook his head. "But what's unusual is Reaver not showing up for work. He's only been with us a couple months, but that's never happened before. Never took a sick day. He was on the fast track to becoming my best employee."

"So what happened after you got here?" Though Lucas found the overly attentive boss story a little unlikely, bosses checking on their employees wasn't unheard of.

"Nobody answered the door, even though I could see Reaver's pickup." Garner pointed with a calloused finger at the truck sitting in the driveway. "So I peeked in the front window. That's when…" Trailing off, Garner swallowed, a haunted look in his eyes. "When I saw…"

"We can see for ourselves what you saw." Journey stepped back, as if afraid the guy might heave on the sidewalk. "You don't have to described that part. Just one more question. Can you confirm your whereabouts last night?"

They didn't have a time of death yet, but Lucas could admit they might as well ask now so Garner could get back to work.

"At home with my husband."

"We'll need to speak with him to verify that."

After getting Garner's home phone number to call his husband later and passing over their cards, they let him go. His truck door slammed and his engine revved as they collected pairs of booties and gloves from a nearby forensic tech, slipping them on before heading into the house.

Inside, Lucas stopped short in the entryway. Though Journey had described the victims on the way over, the details somehow hadn't registered as he'd focused more on her change in attitude from jovial to moody as soon as they received this case.

Maybe because she saw what was coming in those pictures.

As far as Lucas could tell, every single thing in the house had been overturned. Chairs. Kitchen table. Couch. Shredded books and smashed knickknacks dotted the carpet in tiny pieces. Several bookshelves' worth.

Three bodies lay where'd they fallen, spread out across the small living room.

Hunched over Claudia Reaver's body was Journey's sister, Michelle Timmer of the Evidence Response Team. With her dyed black hair, light-blue eyes, and short stature, she bore no resemblance to Journey's tall, violet-eyed brunette. But they shared an interest in criminal investigation, just on two sides of the same coin.

No matter how much he didn't want to look, Lucas found his gaze dragged toward the child's tiny body lying next to her parents. Bella wore a torn nightgown with a dinosaur climbing a rainbow. On her back sat a white feather, roughly six inches long with brown spots.

Desperately trying not to think the name *Hallie*, Lucas knelt beside the little girl. He kept his voice low. "I'm so sorry." Bella's life had ended before it even began.

A cold, calculating fury trickled through Lucas like ice as he imagined someone doing this to his own daughter. To any little kid in the world.

As Journey crouched near Daniel less than a foot away, she shared a warm smile with her sister before refocusing on the task at hand. "These feathers were definitely meant to be noticed."

They'd been placed on all three bodies. And they matched the ones in the previous case—long and white, speckled with brown, as they'd seen in SSA Keller's photo. One had been set on Daniel's chest while the other two were placed on Claudia's and Bella's backs.

"Michelle will have fun examining those back at the lab." Journey threw a glance over her shoulder at her sister, who had stepped away to speak to a tech, before shifting to get a closer look at Claudia Reaver.

How can she consider anything about this 'fun?'

As Lucas adjusted his weight, a piece of broken porcelain or glass crunched beneath his shoe. He raised his foot guiltily, glancing around for any techs who might yell at him for disturbing the scene. But there really wasn't anywhere to step that didn't contain potential evidence. Shards even glittered in Bella's hair and over her nightgown. "I wonder how much of this destruction occurred after the family was murdered."

"I've got the same here." Journey poked a gloved finger toward a sliver of glass on Daniel's ankle. "His feet are bare, but I don't see any cuts or punctures."

Daniel's body rested between his wife and his daughter, perpendicular to them with one arm stretched toward each. While Claudia and Bella appeared to have been angling for the front door, Daniel had fallen as if coming from the direction of the living room wall.

Though they hadn't yet spoken with any crime scene techs to determine whether the victims had been moved, Lucas, assuming they hadn't, tried to picture the shot that killed Daniel. "Looks they were running for the door, but he wasn't. So he might have been facing the shooter."

Journey moved to stand at Daniel's feet, taking in the scene from a different angle. "He could've stood between his family and the killer. Maybe trying to block the assault." She held her arms out wide. Bella lay below her left hand, with Claudia slightly out of reach of her right.

Lucas stood and joined her as he, too, imagined the potential scenario. He motioned at Journey's spread-eagle stance. "Maybe Dad's here, trying to block." He turned and walked around her toward the door. "Mom and daughter are making a run for it. Trying to get out of the house."

It made sense. But judging from the chaos on display, any number of things could have unfolded in that room.

"Hey. Glad you're here." Michelle appeared alongside them, stepping carefully. "We've found muddy boot prints in the kitchen…" She pointed toward a small nook in the other room where a screen door had been ripped to shreds. "Thank all the rainy weather we've been having. There are also larger prints in the front entryway and up the stairs."

"So at least two perps?" Journey held up two fingers.

A trace of doubt wormed its way into Lucas's brain. *Wasn't Garner wearing muddy boots?*

Michelle nodded in response to Journey's question while glancing at her notebook. "Looks that way. I just got my hands on the PBP reports from last week's scene. Haven't gone through them all that well yet, but I did see they found prints there too. The lab identified both prints as likely coming from the same brand of boots, called Kenetrek Eversteps."

Lucas glanced at Journey. "Never heard of them. You?"

She shook her head.

"Not surprising." Michelle thumbed at her phone, then showed the screen. The web page displayed beautiful mountain scenery above a line of rugged footwear, obviously designed for hitting the trails.

At the sight of them, Lucas breathed an internal sigh of relief. Those didn't match the boots he'd seen Jose Garner wearing, so they hadn't just let one of the perpetrators drive off after insinuating himself into the investigation.

"A low-end pair will set you back six or seven hundred bucks."

Journey whistled. "Yeah, no, that's rent money."

"For me too." Michelle tucked her phone back into her pocket. "These prints look very similar, but we won't know, of course, until the lab confirms."

As if summoned by that common forensic refrain, Dr. Smith Simon, the Alleghany County Medical Examiner, entered carefully through the destroyed screen door, avoiding any tripping hazards as he crossed the kitchen to join them. "Agents Russo and Sullivan." He didn't offer his hand to shake, since they were all wearing gloves. "We've got to stop meeting like this."

"Sure, let me just find another job real quick." Journey snorted. "What do we have so far? Any theories?"

Dr. Simon armed sweat off his brow. "Well, I'm not ready to make any confirmed statements yet." He knelt next to Daniel's body, pointing at the wound in his chest. "But it appears our victims have been shot with arrows."

"Arrows?" Journey cocked an eyebrow. "That's a bit medieval."

"Seriously." Dr. Simon's focus was still on the wound. "The only reason I can identify even that much at this point is that the wounds on these victims bare similarities to those from the case last week. You see, yanking out a broadhead arrow tears up the wound as it exits the body, which makes it difficult to identify."

Journey nodded. "That makes sense. But arrows, huh? Who uses that in this day and age?"

"I need further study for comparison to the other victims but, yes…arrows. See, arrows are designed to cut vital organs. And unlike a bullet, they don't crush or tear tissues, nor do they mushroom or fragment on impact."

"Time of death?"

Dr. Simon gently lifted Daniel's shirt with his fingertips. "The lack of fraying around the incised wound indicates the arrow was pushed all the way through. Whether before or after death, I can't say until we move the bodies. I'd estimate time of death occurred somewhere between nine and eleven last night based on liver temp, rigor mortis, and lividity. And from what I can see here, there were two different arrowheads used. Just like at the last scene."

"Two arrowheads, two shooters." Journey exchanged a glance with Lucas.

He shrugged. "Different arrows fit on the same bow. They're not like bullets."

Journey's lips thinned at that. One archer using multiple types of arrows would complicate the investigation.

"Each body has penetration and exit wounds similar to

what we saw with the Bragg couple last week." Dr. Simon's sharp tone pulled their attention back to his report. "Based on my research since then, the wounds on Daniel and Bella Reaver appear to be a combination of incision and puncture. Probably a fixed-blade broadhead hunting arrowhead with three blades."

Whipping out his phone, Lucas did a quick search for such an arrowhead. He found websites offering arrowheads with beveled steel points above three sharp triangular blades set perpendicular to the shaft. He shuddered, imagining how it must have felt to be shot with one of those. Even worse to have them pushed all the way through.

He hoped they were dead before that happened.

"The other," Dr. Simon turned toward Claudia Reaver's body, "is similar around the penetration point, though this only had two blades. That's probably another broadhead arrowhead type."

Lucas gestured toward the front door, then faced the opening where the kitchen and living room met. From where they stood, the back door was in plain sight. "We've been speculating that the family was attempting to flee. Makes sense for one or more people besides the shooter or shooters to have blocked the exits, creating panic as the family tried to escape."

"Certainly plausible." Dr. Simon raised his big, bushy eyebrows—his whole style always put Lucas in mind of Doc Brown from *Back to the Future*. "Let's also consider these bruises." He directed attention to a line of purple splotches along Claudia Reaver's ribs. "I'd venture a guess to say these were inflicted during the struggle prior to the shooting. But again, we won't know for sure until lab work comes back."

Lucas's gaze fell on the broken dining table and scattered chairs. He tried to imagine the frenzied scene…screams, glass shattering, and the frightened parents scrambling to escape with their daughter.

But an itch niggled at the back of his mind. He couldn't shake the memory of the glass scattered over the bodies after their deaths, as if the house had been wrecked to obscure the investigation.

"Someone was definitely playing games with this family." When his gaze shifted to little Bella Reaver, his stomach turned. For a moment, he saw his own daughter's face in Bella's, even though Hallie was fifteen now. "Maybe even with us."

At his statement, the team fell quiet.

"If you guys are done here, we need to get these bodies loaded." Michelle stretched her arms over her head as she returned, breaking the spell.

As if she'd summoned them, a team of medical personnel, their badges proclaiming them as members of the Allegheny County Office of the Medical Examiner, pushed the first stretcher into the house.

Journey patted Lucas on the arm. "Shall we go talk to the neighbors and let these guys work?" She glanced from him to the body of Bella Reaver, seemingly having noticed his reaction to her presence among the victims.

Lucas straightened his spine, annoyed with his own lack of professionalism. Still, he didn't want to stick around and watch little Bella zipped up into a body bag.

"Yeah." He slapped his notebook against his palm. "Let's go."

4

At the house next door, the lawn had been mowed recently, but weeds still pushed their way up through the grass. As Journey approached the two concrete steps up to the porch of the redbrick rambler, a raised chunk of sidewalk caught her toe. Wheeling her arms, she stumbled forward, just managing to regain her balance.

Though Lucas held his hands up to catch her, he smirked at her clumsiness. "Been walking long?"

Forcing herself not to rub her sore toe, Journey strutted the rest of the way up the sidewalk like a runway model. "Just started today, actually. See how good I am?"

At the door, however, she blew out a breath.

Focus. There's a killer with a Robin Hood fetish on the loose. Maybe even with a Little John sidekick.

When she knocked, flakes of cracked white paint stuck to her knuckles.

"Not interested." A man's voice came from inside the house. "I already go to church."

Journey sighed, aiming her next words at Lucas. "It's the suits again."

If she'd been thinking at the beginning of her FBI career, she would've started a tally of how many times she'd be mistaken for a salesperson peddling everything from magazine subscriptions to religion. The addition of Lucas, with his meticulous attention to his look, only enhanced the effect. Still, she couldn't remember this ever having happened with law enforcement swarming the street.

"Be more fun if they'd start taking us for *Men in Black* agents." Lucas leaned a muscular shoulder against a brick support column. With his black hair slicked back and his jaw shaved clean in a James Dean style, he already looked the part. He just needed his sunglasses.

"Yeah, I bet people would just line up to get their memory wiped." Journey herself carried more than a few memories she wouldn't mind having removed with a flash. She raised her voice a little louder. "Sir, we're with the FBI. We'd like to speak with you about an incident that occurred next door."

"I told you yesterday." The man's grumbling voice had moved closer now. "My doctor says I can't eat cookies no more."

At that, Lucas snickered. "If the FBI thing doesn't work out, you'd kill it as a Girl Scout."

Journey flipped him the bird behind her back.

"Sir, I'm Special Agent Journey Russo with the Federal Bureau of Investigation. I have my partner here with me. We'd like to speak with you, please."

At last, the door cracked open, revealing a pair of milky eyes peering at them from beneath overgrown gray eyebrows within a pale face. An odor of microwave dinners and stale cigarette smoke accompanied him.

Wondering whether he could read the smallish print, Journey held her badge up for his inspection. "Are you aware there was an incident last night with your neighbors, the Reavers?"

"The who?" Now the man pulled the door wide and stepped onto the threshold, his hunched form dominating the doorway.

Lucas pointed at the house next door. "Daniel and Claudia Reaver. They have a ten-year-old daughter."

Journey watched as the old man's face contorted with confusion before finally settling into a grimace of recognition. She shifted her stance, stepping forward and holding out her badge once more. "Can I get your name, sir?"

A beat passed before the man responded in a gruff tone. "Alfred Casal." His sunken chest puffed. "Twenty-seven sixty-three South Twenty-Third Street."

Journey blinked at Casal's *ma'am, yes, ma'am* attitude. It was like she'd asked for his rank and file number.

"Do you live here alone, Mr. Casal?"

He nodded curtly. "My wife died in 2017."

Now Lucas straightened from his leaning, setting a casual foot on the lowest step. "We're talking to everyone on the street. Did you happen to hear anything unusual last night?"

"Nah." Mr. Casal shook his head. Deep furrows etched across his forehead. "Pretty quiet night. I watched the ball game and went to bed."

Journey scribbled *no noise* into her notebook. "And you were alone last night?"

"Don't got no one else." His chest deflated. "But I manage all right on my own."

"Just to confirm…" Lucas glanced at Journey, then back at Mr. Casal, "you were inside all night?"

"Except to smoke between innings, yeah." He put two fingers to his lips. "Stepped out where you're standing now for a few smokes during the evening."

Lucas nodded. "What time was that?"

"Between seven and whenever the game ended. Had one more smoke and went to bed after."

Journey hadn't watched, but that was easy enough to confirm. She guessed that unless play went into extra innings, the game probably ended around ten o'clock.

Which matched with the estimated time of the murders.

Lucas must've made that connection, too, because his tone darkened. "See anything while you were outside smoking?"

"A stray dog."

"A dog?"

"Yeah." Mr. Casal's rheumy eyes lit up. "Streaking down the middle of the street like its life depended on it."

"One of the neighbors' dogs?" Lucas raised an eyebrow. "Belong to the Reavers, maybe?"

"I guess it was a neighbor's dog." Mr. Casal shrugged. "Don't know if the Reavers have one, but there was definitely a dog. Hey. Remind me, I gotta get more cigarettes."

"Right." Journey put the pieces together—his wandering mind, the overgrown stubble, and from what she could see over his shoulder, a house in desperate need of a deep clean. She jotted down his comment, along with a note that he might benefit from a visit from elder care social services. He took better care of himself than some young people she'd met, but she'd rather be safe than sorry.

They thanked him for his time and handed over business cards. Then they headed for the house across the street from the Reavers' place, an outlier in the neighborhood. Neatly trimmed yard. Fresh paint. Even a welcome mat that looked new.

This time, Lucas took the lead and knocked.

A petite woman in her thirties with dark skin and bright eyes opened the door. When they introduced themselves, she gave her name as Natalie.

"I've been watching out my window all morning." When Natalie crossed her arms, Journey spotted a cell phone in her hand. "I asked one of the officers what happened, but he wouldn't tell me anything. So I've been scrolling the news sites." She held up the phone, as if to prove her point. "I'm sorry. Would you like to come inside?"

Natalie's small house featured much the same plan as the Reaver home, with a living room and a combined dining room and kitchen on the main floor. Stairs leading to a second level. Back door off the kitchen. Journey and Lucas sat side by side on the couch in Natalie's living room while their host took the side chair.

"I know whatever happened over there has to be serious, or there wouldn't be so many cop cars."

"We're not at liberty to discuss an active investigation," Lucas locked gazes with Journey for a moment, "but we'd like to ask you about anything you may have heard or seen last night."

"They're new on the street, but the Reavers are nice. Friendly. Did a fight happen?" A little gasp escaped Natalie as she clasped her hands before her. "I saw on the news there was a murder just up the road last week. Did someone kill them? I mean, do we have to worry? Is there someone loose in the neighborhood?"

"Regarding last week's incident, the police are increasing patrols in the area." Journey held up a palm to forestall further speculation. "But in the meantime, just be aware of your surroundings. Keep your doors locked, even when you're at home, and only open up if you recognize the person on the other side."

When Natalie looked unconvinced that would be nearly enough precaution, Journey couldn't blame her for her skepticism. No one moved into a house expecting their neighbors to get murdered.

"Going back to my partner's earlier question. Did you hear or see anything unusual last night?"

"No. Nothing." Natalie shook her head. "I asked my husband this morning how he slept, and he said fine. We're both heavy sleepers, though. And we have a white noise machine. I gave it to him for Christmas. It blocks out almost everything."

Lucas flipped the pages of his notebook. "Your neighbor, Alfred Casal, mentioned seeing a dog running down the middle of the street around ten p.m. Do you know if the Reavers had a dog?"

"I've never seen or heard one." Natalie flipped her phone end over end for a second. "Do you mean Alfred in the house next to the Reavers?"

Journey nodded.

"Yeah." She hesitated, but then pressed on. "I'm not sure you should take much of what he says as fact. He's got dementia. A few weeks ago, he marched across our lawn as I was getting out of my car and told me to get out of his driveway."

In her notebook, Journey double underlined her note about social services for Mr. Casal. She'd make that call back at the office.

Meanwhile, this was another house without a viable lead. Her jaw clamped in frustration. Though canvassing the neighborhood played a key role in the investigation process, the odds of finding witnesses when those in the homes closest to the scene had nothing to offer shortened with every house farther away.

After confirming Natalie's whereabouts at ten o'clock the night before with her husband, Journey and Lucas spent the rest of the morning knocking on doors. But like the first two, no one had seen or heard anything.

Before leaving the scene, Journey and Lucas reconnected with the PBP detective, Lonnie Gutierrez. During their search, a news van had showed up. One of Gutierrez's officers now had the thankless job of keeping the media crew off the property.

Frowning in the direction of the van, Journey nodded at Detective Gutierrez. "Word's out, I see. Been able to locate next of kin yet?"

"Well, that's the odd thing." Gutierrez let out a weary sigh. "There doesn't appear to *be* any next of kin, except for Claudia Reaver's mother, who suffers from Alzheimer's and lives in a facility nearby. We've spoken to her, though she didn't appear to understand. Her father is deceased, as are both of Daniel Reaver's parents. Both were only children."

Lucas frowned. "That's bad luck. How about the Braggs?"

"Michael's parents are both dead. His brother's in prison and doesn't know anything. We haven't been able to find any information about Rose Bragg's father, but her mother's last place of residence was a halfway house in Seattle. Wherever she is now, she's not there."

"Yikes. Well, appreciate it." Lucas stepped forward and extended his hand. "We're heading back to the office, but before we go," his gaze shifted back toward the Reavers' house, "can you tell us anything about the neighbors interviewed at the last crime scene? Anything worth following up on?"

"I'd love to tell you otherwise, but we turned up a big nothing burger over there." Disappointment dragged Detective Gutierrez's features downward. "Nobody's seen or heard anything."

That news did not surprise Journey in the least.

"Keep us in the loop if something turns up." Lucas flashed a smile.

"Will do."

Once in their car, Journey leaned forward in her seat, biting her lip as she mulled over everything they'd learned. "A bow? Arrows?"

"Interesting choice of weapon." Lucas hummed from the driver's seat as he drove them out of the neighborhood. "I've been wondering about that too. That's a whole different skill set, using a bow rather than a gun."

"Precision is key." Journey tried to think back to the one time she'd tried archery in gym class. "A steady hand too. I'm having a hard time picturing how to get off a successful shot in the middle of struggle and chaos."

"Also, bow shots are silent." Lucas's eyebrows furrowed together as they headed for the highway. "Nothing for the neighbors to hear."

Journey stared out the window a few moments longer before finally settling back against her seat. Soon as they got back to the office, she planned to dive into research and learn everything she could about the bow and arrow.

She rubbed the gold ace of diamonds pendant at her throat. With any luck, the use of such a unique murder weapon might help them narrow down their killers before they struck again.

5

As they drove, a quick internet search for archery supplies flooded Journey's phone with results. "Looks like all the big sporting-goods chains carry bows."

There were five stores within ten minutes of their location. But after thinking about the boot prints Michelle had found, Journey narrowed her search to stores that specialized in archery only.

"Wait. Here's something interesting." She clicked a link for a small shop located only a few blocks away from the Reavers' home. "There's one not too far from here. Durham's Hunting Supplies. They specialize in quality bows for hunting and competition."

"There's a boutique for everything nowadays." Lucas chuckled.

"Does a thousand dollars seem expensive for a bow?" Journey clicked on the link, expecting to find something made of solid gold for that price. "When did bows get wheels?"

"Sounds like a compound bow."

"That's what the description says." She enlarged the image on her screen. "What happened to the recurve bow? It was a classic. Why did they have to make it all weird-looking?"

"Easier to draw. Especially for a hobbyist."

"A hobbyist with a lot of money and probably not a lot of muscle?" Journey reviewed her notes before adding that thought to them. "If they can afford six-hundred-dollar boots and still drop a grand on a bow, plus who knows how much else on accessories, they would definitely be the type to buy from a specialty store."

"Let's go see how the rich hunter shops." Lucas pulled over as Journey rerouted their destination. Durham's was four minutes away. He swung a U-turn.

Price tags with multiple dollar signs still ran through Journey's head. "What does a person with that kind of money gain from breaking into a lower middle-class home like the Reavers'?"

"Nothing material. Something personal, maybe? A vendetta?"

"Could be." Journey scribbled a note to herself to check for any connections between the two murdered families. "Daniel worked as a landscaper. Maybe the other family had some kind of service job that shared a client."

"Blue-collar workers." Lucas nodded. "Might be something to follow up on."

"Already wrote it down." She raised her notebook, then smiled at herself for mirroring Natalie's earlier action with her phone.

After a few silent moments of driving, Lucas glanced at her and cleared his throat. "Have you ever seen a bow murder in any of your cases?"

He hadn't worked in Violent Crimes as long as Journey. Though he'd started his career in VCU at the Anchorage field office, he'd transferred to White Collar after just a year. Back then, a domestic abuse case drove Lucas out of the VC when his colleague flipped out and killed his wife and child. Neither Lucas nor the rest of the team could stop him.

In much the same way, Lucas's dad had murdered his mother. If not for Lucas's uncle arriving in time to save him, Journey would've never gotten the pleasure of partnering with him. She didn't know all the details, but he'd told her enough.

Trauma doesn't care about the calendar, doesn't just disappear with time.

At that thought, Journey narrowed her eyes at the side of Lucas's head consideringly. How had he overcome such a haunting past enough to return to VC? He still got sick during visits to the medical examiner's office, yet he fought through every time to keep doing this job. Had therapy played a role in his choice? Or something else?

If anyone would willingly answer such questions, Lucas would.

Journey flipped open her notebook and wrote that idea down. She wasn't ready to ask him just yet. That conversation could come later.

Baby steps.

"Hey…Earth to Journey." Lucas nudged her with his elbow. "Did you hear me?"

"Um, so, let me think."

What was he asking about…? Cases involving bows. Right.

"I haven't personally taken a case like that, but I remember seeing something similar in ViCAP."

Since the Bureau's Violent Criminal Apprehension Program database was an excellent resource, she tended to keep an eye on the cases that popped up there. Always having one ear to the ground had once helped her solve a serial killer case that crossed the state line from New Mexico into Texas back when she still worked as a beat cop in El Paso.

"If I remember correctly, the case was about a year ago. In Illinois. A twin brother and sister were both killing campers. Sister used a crossbow to kill one victim while her brother slit the throat of the other with a machete."

Lucas scowled. "Good grief. Of course they hunted in pairs."

"Yeah. It really stuck in my memory because they scalped their victims after killing them. I noticed when I was wrapping up my report on Phillip Ramsey, since he also scalped his victims. According to what I remember from the database, their childhood was pretty bad. Their older brother testified that they tried to poison him when they were kids." Journey glanced at her partner. "Those two can't be our killers, though. They're behind bars."

One other aspect of the case she didn't mention was that the agent who brought the murder twins down had also helped Journey bring Michelle home after her then-boyfriend kidnapped her. That, more than anything else, made the case memorable for Journey.

"Could our killers be siblings or copycats?"

"Until we learn more," Journey shrugged, "we have to stay open to just about anything."

"Same story. Different day."

A wave of negative energy flowed through the car.

"Hey. Earth to Lucas now. Where'd you go?"

"Still here." He sighed. "I just hate the beginning of a case, when there's so much to untangle and the way forward isn't quite clear. Always waiting for *further analysis.*"

"I hear that. But we're about to do our own 'further analysis,' so we're not just waiting."

They were on their way to finding useful information

about bow hunting. Anything to help identify those responsible for murdering two families was a win.

Silence descended until Lucas broke first. "This is going to sound like a stupid question."

"My favorite kind." Journey smirked. "What cha thinking?"

"You got to wonder sometimes...how some of these criminal partnerships get started." Lucas cleared his throat. "Like...how does that conversation go? 'Hey, I see you like shooting things. Let's commit a murder together.'"

Journey wanted to laugh. Even with his question rooted in reality, he'd couched the thought in silliness. Truth was, though, she'd experienced a bit of that kind of encounter firsthand.

"It's easier than you might think." Though her voice remained steady, memories of the cult flashed through Journey's brain like lightning bolts. "Some people can be talked into believing or doing just about anything. Just takes the right words and a little desperation."

She'd spent several months undercover investigating The Chosen, a cult based in and around the Pittsburgh metropolitan area but whose tentacles spread across the U.S.

During that time, Michelle had gone missing, with Journey none the wiser until the case also nearly ended Journey's life. At The Chosen's insistence, she'd taken out a life insurance policy and named the cult as the beneficiary. The ink had barely dried on the contract before The Chosen put a hit on her.

Guilt and fear twisted clawed fingers around those memories.

"Right. I'm sure you saw a lot during your time undercover." Lucas had brought down one of The Chosen's fraudsters, Bryce Faulkner. But they hadn't really known each other back then. He took a turn into a strip mall parking lot. "Do you think this could be cult related?"

"I'm not saying this is…"

I'm praying it isn't, in fact.

Journey unbuckled her seat belt, ready for any action that didn't involve dredging up old memories. "But I wouldn't write it off just yet."

6

Durham's Hunting Supplies occupied the largest unit in a small strip mall. Not exactly a superstore, but with one step inside, Journey could tell the shop did brisk business.

Merchandise was easy to find on uncrowded displays without a single clearance sign to mar the view. Money walked in with this store's clientele, and there was plenty to keep it there. A quick glance at the price tag on a women's camo jacket made her cough into her fist.

Twelve hundred dollars! No thank you very much.

A salesperson in tailored but rugged canvas pants and a well-ironed, button-down shirt approached. "How may I help you today?" Gray streaked his dark hair, so Journey put him in his late forties. Though, with the sun damage and creases in his ruddy face aging him up, he might've been a little younger.

"We're Special Agents Sullivan and Russo. FBI." Lucas pulled his badge from his pocket. "Is there a manager we can speak to?"

The man scoffed. "What is this about?"

From his tone, Journey wondered if this wasn't his first visit from law enforcement.

"We'd prefer to discuss that with a manager." Lucas pocketed the badge.

"You're talking to him." The man shook his head as if in disbelief. "I own this place. My name's Jed Durham. I'll have you know, I follow all city, state, and county regulations for firearms sales. I carry a few high-end hunting rifles. No pistols. Nothing your average criminal can afford."

"We're not interested in your firearms, actually." Journey kept her tone light to avoid riling the man any further. He clearly took pride in his store and the merchandise he sold. And they'd come to learn, not intimidate. *Catch more flies with honey*, as her grandmother used to say.

She held out her hand to shake.

He took it.

"Mr. Durham, we're investigating a crime in which a bow was used as a weapon. And we really need an expert on them. We were hoping you could help us with some useful information about the various bows available and their capabilities. Have you been in this business long?"

"Oh." That seemed to work. "Years and years. What do you need to know?" The customer-service smile returned to Durham's face. "What kind of bow was used?"

"We're not entirely sure yet." Lucas offered a sheepish smile. "Maybe you can help us understand the different types you've got."

"I suppose I can give you some introductory information."

"And perhaps the type of people who might want to use such a weapon."

Durham's expression soured again at Lucas's addition. "Don't you go thinking my customers, or the people who prefer to use a classic hunting weapon like this, are some kinds of monsters."

"No, sir." Journey shot a look at her partner that hissed *shut up*. "We're just trying to get a feel for things."

"Good." Durham gave a firm and decisive nod. "My customers are people, just like you. They might have the means and interest to pursue the sport, and hunting is a big part of that, of course, but none of my customers would use their rig on another person. I want that understood."

Journey caught Lucas's eye and presumed they were both thinking the same thing. Whenever someone insisted they, or their associates, were innocent as fast and emphatically as Jed Durham just had, there was usually something to suspect.

"Let's start with the bows." Journey took charge of the conversation and pointed at a wall display featuring several of the bows she'd been looking at in the car. "The compound bow. Is that what those are called?"

"The bow is a tool that's thousands of years old, and its effectiveness has stood the test of time. Most people are familiar with the recurve." Durham pointed away from the display Journey was looking at. His finger slashed across to the side wall, where more traditional bows were displayed. "Those are your Robin Hood-style bows. Harder to draw, rely on manual sights, but still a favorite among enthusiasts. The kinds of folks who like to feather their own arrows personally."

Those were the ones Journey had trained with during her archery classes way back in high school.

"Now, the compound bow obviously looks different. Most notably because of its rigging. All the extra cables and cams. Those wheels and pullies, you see. They give the bow an added mechanical advantage, allowing the shooter to pull more draw weight than with a recurve bow."

"The draw weight is how hard it is to pull back on the string, right?" Journey's arm flexed at the memory of drawing a recurve bowstring. The first time hadn't been as easy as experts made it appear.

"And hold back." Durham mimed pulling a bowstring. He lengthened his spine, held one arm straight, then pulled his other hand slowly back from it. "A traditional bow will give you a smoother-looking draw because it gradually increases in weight as you pull. Let's say you're shooting a fifty-pound compound bow versus a recurve."

Again, he took his stance, but this time he lifted his straightened arm and kept the other arm bent. Then he lowered the straight arm and only pulled back slightly with the bent arm 'til his curled fingers hovered near his ear.

"With the compound, you might only hold back fifteen pounds once you're at full draw. But with a fifty-pound recurve or longbow, you're holding all fifty of those pounds. The big advantage of compounds is they're easier to hold drawn for longer, which means more time to aim and fire precisely."

"Better aim would be important for hunting at longer distances." Not a scrap of a hint entered Lucas's voice as to his true intentions with that comment as he scribbled in his notebook. Journey approved.

"Correct." Durham pointed at Lucas. "The overall design of a compound puts all that potential energy into the arrow as it's released. Many of the compound bows you see here," he waved a hand at the display, "can shoot over three hundred feet per second with a relatively light arrow. Hell, even with a heavier hunting arrow, they can still get up to two fifty or better."

"What about closer distances?" Journey considered the different bows, trying to picture how the killer would have been standing during an attack inside a house.

Durham's brow furrowed. "Like target shooting?"

"Sure. Let's go with that." That wasn't at all what she meant, but he didn't need to know.

Durham scratched his head. "The bow was traditionally a short-range hunting tool. You might manage to fire an arrow three hundred or so yards off, but the accuracy range for most is somewhere in the range of thirty to forty yards. That's if you want full penetration with the arrow. Now, like I said, the compound bow with all the bells and whistles will make your job easier with a stationary target. But talk to any recurve enthusiast, and they'll tell you the relationship they have with their bow is what makes them an excellent archer."

That was a bit of useful information, which Journey made sure to note. "So if you're closer to your target and there is a risk of it moving, you'd rather have the recurve than the compound?"

"And when it comes to a moving target, the fancy stabilizers and sights," he motioned to a showcase of add-ons for the bows, "aren't going to make up for the skill you need to execute that clean shot. Especially if the reaction time is what's needed."

Based on Durham's explanation, it seemed Journey and Lucas were looking for an archer with years of practice. Possibly an older hunter.

"Yeah, recurve is what I take hunting." He smiled as if he were talking about his child. "See…what you have to understand here is the difference in how that bow makes you work for your shot. The compound is beautiful. And it has its purpose. Don't get me wrong. But it's much more rigid and mechanical. It's a perfectionist's weapon that has more in common with shooting a rifle. The recurve bow, on the other hand…well, that weapon is all about the archer."

"What do you mean?" Lucas wore a confused expression.

"Mastering the recurve bow is about the challenge and time you invest to get a feel for the weapon. Everything from your stance and the way you hold the arrow to your aim and your strength makes the bow work."

Once again, Durham mimed a smooth pull of a bowstring, this time stepping around and turning, making the motion look like a dance as he lined up his imaginary shot.

"The farther you draw the bowstring, the heavier the draw weight becomes. But assuming the archer has a solid and steady grip on the bow and can accurately aim at the target, they're more likely to hit that buck." He let his invisible arrow fly with a crooked grin.

Journey jotted down *recurve bow* and underlined it three times. If their archer had accuracy inside a chaotic house, it sounded like that was the bow he would've used.

"You want to have a look at any bows in particular? Get a feel for 'em?" Durham motioned toward the display of recurve bows.

"That's okay. Maybe another day." Lucas waved away the offer of a product tour. "Let's talk about the people who own or use them. I assume you know your customers well. You're in a great position to tell us whether you've had any clients who struck you as suspicious."

"No." The joy that'd been building on Durham's face drained away. "Absolutely not."

"Take a moment to think about it." Journey raised her notebook and pointedly hovered her pen above the page. "We've got time."

While she faced off with Jed Durham, Lucas began picking up merchandise, looking at price tags, purposefully putting things back slightly rumpled and out of place. Nothing intimidating, just enough to send a type A personality like Durham into orbit.

"Fine." He grabbed a plaid shirt from Lucas's hands and refolded it correctly. "I have some guys who've been coming in for a few years. At first, they struck me simply as enthusiasts. Lately, however…"

Journey waited a beat for him to regain his train of thought, but when he didn't pick back up, she cleared her throat. "What's been different lately?"

Durham shook his head. "They're not killers."

"Okay. That's good to know, but not what I asked." Journey had only described the investigation as having to do with a crime, not a murder. "If something has a professional like you concerned, I'd like to know what it is."

"They seem a little too excited." Durham looked at his feet.

"About?" Lucas leaned forward.

"All of it. They act like kids at Christmas whenever they come in here." Now that the bag was open, Durham was letting all the cats out. "The tradition in this sport is about the challenge. A clean shot is the result of well-executed skill and sportsmanship. But even though they've been customers for years, they act like they're buying toys. There's just no respect for the power they hold in their hands." He frowned, but the expression looked almost like a pout to Journey.

There was more he wanted to say. Journey could tell. She waited for him to get there.

"And the equipment…" Again, he motioned toward the wall of bows. "They've got the money to buy the latest and greatest." He rambled off technical specifications like arrow grain weights, field point bullet tips, and vibration dampeners that sounded important, but Journey really didn't know what they all meant. She wrote down everything she could to research later.

Lucas reeled him in. "How many of them did you say?"

"Three." Durham held up his fingers. "Though one of them always pays. Very high-end items."

Why was Journey not surprised to hear him add that last detail?

"We need their names." Lucas wasn't asking now.

"I don't like handing out customer information." Durham's refusal was hollow as he sighed like a defeated man and walked over to his desk behind the counter. After a few clicks of his mouse, and with no further prodding, he gave up his customer's name. "Walter Albright is the one who pays for everything."

Journey recorded the name in her notes. "And the other two?"

Durham shook his head. "Don't remember them calling each other by name."

"I think we're done here, then."

"Thanks for your help." Lucas handed over his card. "If you do notice any strange behavior in your clients, please keep us in the loop. No matter how insignificant it may seem."

"My customers are good people." Jed Durham took the card and tucked it into his back pocket. "But I'm a law-abiding citizen, so I'll do my part if I see something that needs reporting."

7

Journey opened the passenger door the moment Lucas hit the unlock button on the key fob. "Thoughts?"

After sliding into his seat, Lucas turned the key in the ignition but left the car idling. "I get the sense that Walter Albright's name sprang to mind long before Jed Durham gave it to us."

Journey had noted the same. Durham struck her as cagey. He clearly felt a love of archery, but the minute the questions turned to his customers, his cooperation waned. "Think he's intimidated by Albright?"

"Could be." Lucas nodded. "Sounds like he spends a lot of money there."

"Like maybe Albright is propping up his business?" Journey crossed her arms and leaned back in the seat. That wouldn't have surprised her. Money was such a powerful force, it led even the best people into dubious moral territory. In her line of work, Journey'd seen the results more times than she wanted to admit. "If Jed Durham or his shop were in financial trouble, Albright could hold an inordinate amount of sway."

"I'll look into it when we get back to the office." Lucas pulled out his notebook and dashed out a reminder.

Journey freed her phone from her pocket. "I'll see what I can find out about Mr. Albright."

"Meanwhile, coffee." Lucas backed the car out of the parking space. "I need to refuel."

"Ditto."

Their GPS pointed them to a neighborhood shop a mile away. Loyalty to good coffee was one of the first things the new partners had bonded over, and they knew each other's orders by heart. Lucas drank dark roast with two sugars, no cream. Journey liked hers black, extra hot.

Lucas went inside to order while Journey stayed in the car, seeing what she could pull up with simple internet searches and taking notes on Walter Albright.

The man was almost too easy to find. Most businesspeople kept their web presence under wraps, but Albright was like an open book. That meant he was less likely as a suspect, as criminals usually brushed their trails clean.

On their website, the investment banking firm he worked for listed Walter Albright as the senior vice president. Journey suspected the accompanying photo was several years out of date. His social media profile showed an outdoorsy forty-two-year-old man with unkempt hair wearing an orange hunting vest.

Yet the investment banking firm featured an image of a clean-shaven man with firm skin and a crisp, short haircut. It was entirely possible the investment company Albright worked for just didn't update their executives' biographies often. Or he was one of the lucky ones who could go from the rugged outdoors to the boardroom without missing a beat. Either way, Journey had an idea of the man they were going to speak with.

Lucas reappeared at the car door holding two cups. "Find

anything?" He slid into the driver's seat and handed a steaming cup of liquid energy over.

"Albright was easy to locate. Home address is about three miles from here. Apparently works in investment banking. Building isn't too far from here either." Journey lifted the steaming cup to her lips, gingerly blowing on it before taking a careful sip. She closed her eyes as the hot liquid made its way down her throat.

"Should we stop by the home or office?" Lucas arched his eyebrow.

"One sec." She dialed Albright's office phone number and asked to speak with him.

"I'm sorry, but Mr. Albright isn't available." The woman on the phone sounded young. "May I ask what this is regarding? Perhaps I can connect you with someone who can assist you in the meantime."

Describing someone as not available could mean different things. Maybe he was in a meeting, out to lunch, sleeping with his mistress, or just not taking calls. Journey made a snap decision on what to ask for next to get past the young secretary screening her call. "Can you tell me a better time to reach him?"

"I'm afraid he's out of the office today." Keyboard clicking in the background accompanied her overly cheery voice. "Do you need immediate assistance?"

Journey needed confirmation that he was, in fact, not at work. "Yes, please. I need to discuss my..." *What do people call investment bankers about?* "Portfolio."

A moment later, a fresh voice came on the line. "Angela Davidson. How can I help you?"

"Oh, excuse me, Angela. I thought I was being transferred to Walter Albright. Can you connect me, by chance?" Journey crossed her fingers that would work.

"Walter?" The new woman's tone was brisk, like she had

better things to do than deal with errant phone calls. "I think he's out of the office today. Sending you to his assistant."

After a click and a moment of elevator Muzak, a third woman came on the line. "Walter Albright's office. He's not in today. I can take a message."

To cover all her bases, Journey went ahead and left a request for Albright to call her back.

"He's not at the office." She exhaled, her shoulders slumping as she disconnected. "Let's drop by his house."

Lucas jumped to attention and swiped Journey's notebook to get the address she'd written down.

The GPS guided them through rows of affluent-looking homes with pristinely manicured lawns, towering hedges, and large pools guarded by pool houses. A little more wealth oozed from each house they passed than the last until they finally arrived at Albright's McMansion perched atop a hill.

The neighborhood screamed new—*look at me!*—money.

Albright probably paid someone to maintain the landscaping. He might've been an outdoorsman, but that didn't make him a gardener. The rounded curves on his hedges were too pristine for someone who mowed the lawn on weekends.

Must've taken hours of clipping to look that smooth.

Despite the weekday morning, the surrounding homes showed signs of life—gardeners at work, expensive cars coming and going, and dogs barking. Albright's house featured all the bells and whistles to match the affluence in the neighborhood, including four security-company signs posted at various points on the property.

But something about the house felt strange. Nothing stirred. Thick curtains shaded all the windows, almost as if Albright were trying to hide something.

Lucas parked at the end of the sidewalk. "Ready?"

Journey didn't have time to answer before he slipped out

of the car. While Lucas strode up the stone-lined pathway, Journey crept along in his wake, keeping her gaze on the various windows, searching for movement as she approached.

When Lucas rang the bell, no one answered.

It was Thursday. Most businesspeople would've been at work, but Journey had already confirmed that wasn't the case for Mr. Albright. His assistant hadn't mentioned him being out of town, just that he wasn't in the office.

Journey glanced anxiously at the windows again.

Where was he? And what could he be up to?

8

I claimed the leather couch by the stone fireplace in the back corner of the cozy bungalow nestled within the confines of the country club. It wasn't a true hunting lodge, but the interior was rugged enough, with mounted deer and elk heads looking down on us from every angle.

The Lodge was our home base, our own private clubhouse where we could gather in safety and solidarity.

No one ever challenged my right to it, or my right to lead the gang of hunters I'd created. They wouldn't be playing at all if it weren't for me, and this sport was addictive.

We learned firsthand out in the forest.

Buck, my second in command, took the most comfortable leather chair for himself. The other two, lesser in skill and experience but not in dedication, lay stretched out on the floor.

The air was thick with the unspent energy of our latest conquest. I smiled at the thought of the terror those animals must've felt in their final moments.

We'd been up late and deserved some R and R. But our work wasn't done yet.

Bull propped his dirty boots up on the leather chair opposite his own, as if no one had ever taught him any manners. It made me twitch, but I overlooked the sloppiness. No reason to ruin the buzz.

"Listen up." I leaned in, elbows on my knees, meeting each of their eyes one by one. "We've entered a new phase of the game. Yesterday marked a milestone. Bull made an important shot for our team." I lifted my glass. "To the joy of the hunt, and the sweet taste of the kill."

"Cheers!"

"That dude actually thought they could get away." Buck laughed. "He turned around to look at us, and I was like… what are you doing? Door's the other way, dumbass."

"Dumbass!" Bull laughed so hard his whole body rocked.

I'd assigned him that mask for that very reason. It was his namesake, because he could be as raucous as a mechanical bull at a backwater bar.

Buck was long-legged and quick, and Hound was as loyal as an old dog.

"Chick was fat too." Buck continued to laugh. "I wanted to shoot her in the belly just to hear it go splat."

I rolled my eyes. "You can add it to your bucket list."

"Hell yeah!" Their voices echoed throughout the bungalow.

Here, we were powerful, owners of destiny, men on a mission.

"You get it now, right?" I reached for my trusty bow—my fingers kept gravitating to the string. Too bad I didn't have an arrow. "Humans are a much more satisfying prey than lower animals."

I closed my eyes and saw him, the father who'd believed he and his family could escape. He'd looked straight at me. Knew I was the one who would decide his fate. He'd felt my power, but it was too late for them. There was no stopping us, and he'd known it.

Pure fear and hopelessness were in his eyes. The prey's recognition of its apex predator.

I relived the memory of drawing back on the bow's string, the arrow nocked and ready, waiting for my target. I was calm, patient.

Three. Two. One. Release.

Thud. The sound was crisp. A perfect shot to the heart.

Bull writhed on the couch like he had a woman riding him. "It's just like busting a nut, man!"

"Bullshit." I shook my head. Bull's energy wasn't the only reason I'd assigned him his mask. "It's about more than just your dick. A kill sets the whole body on fire, every nerve tingling with electricity." My vision was never as clear, my reflexes never as quick, as the moment just before release.

"To Crécy and Agincourt." Buck raised his fist with the shout.

Crécy and Agincourt! Our motto honored the battles that changed warfare forever, ushering in the modern world. The bow and arrow linked the ancient and the new.

"It's their eyes." I drew two fingers across my brow. "They're the first to show death. Like a brilliant burst of life for a millionth of a second and then...nothing. Nothing at all. Gone, baby, gone."

"Gone, baby!" Bull propelled himself up onto his knees. "I took the lady. It was almost too easy once she tripped over the girl."

Buck agreed. "Hardest part is waiting for a clear shot."

One of our team wasn't in the same celebratory mood.

"Hound, why the silence?"

He was sitting, knees up, head hanging. When he didn't answer, Bull nudged him with the toe of his boot.

"Fuck off!" Hound grabbed Bull's foot and gave it a good

twist before smacking it out of his space. Then he looked at me. "I didn't know there was gonna be a kid."

"A kid? Are you fucking serious?" I had to laugh. "What? You get chased on the playground when you were young or something?"

"Ring around the Rosie." Buck picked up on my sarcasm and ran with it. "'Oh, no! They're after me!'"

"'Help me!'" Bull cackled as he joined in.

I waited, letting Hound's humiliation sink in before I added my two cents. "Let me guess…you cry during movies too. You just love the part when the guy and the girl finally get together after all that time pining for each other—"

"You all are assholes. You know that, right?" Hound rolled his eyes and hugged his knees tight to his chest. "I'm not a pussy. It just feels wrong to kill a kid, is all."

I understood. "You think she was just an innocent little girl? 'Why did she deserve to die?' Am I right?"

Hound shrugged and gave a half nod. "Yeah. Sort of."

"Because maybe she would've grown up to be totally different from her parents. Would've made it all the way through high school. Maybe even gone to college for a year or two? Got a job where she didn't come home stinking like her dad? Didn't have to take two showers a day. Could save enough money to actually buy a house instead of having to rent. Or would she be another statistic, poor, leeching off the system, and popping out more babies doomed to live one emergency away from becoming homeless?"

I knew Hound was listening, because he hadn't bothered to interrupt or try to defend himself. Still, I could see there was more convincing to do.

"Tell me, should we have waited for her to pop out a few welfare brats or turn eighteen before removing her from that future?"

The room fell quiet as I waited for his answer. Hound looked confused.

"I'm asking a serious question. What would be the point of waiting? What would that prove to us when we know people rarely escape their economic fates? The statistics don't lie. You're born into your social class, and you die with your social class. And she was born to be a welfare queen."

I had the numbers on my side. I'd studied them. Taken comfort from them.

"Hound, these people are all animals. They're just a few evolutionary steps up from surviving in the wild."

I waited silently until he looked at me.

"You're missing out on your chance to truly understand what it is to kill one. You're depriving yourself of the most fucking awesome part of the game…the high."

"I don't know." The look on Hound's face said he wanted to believe but needed one final push.

"Buck? Bull? Back me up." I had set up the play, but it was my teammates who would deliver the victory.

"We're hunters, dude!" Bull thumped the couch for emphasis. "The predator shows no compassion for its prey."

Buck threw his body into his answer as well, shifting his weight side to side with each question. "Does the lion feel bad for killing the gazelle? No. It's in his nature. It's the balance of things. Or how about baby gazelles? Does he wait until they're all grown up before hunting them?"

"No!" Bull snorted.

Buck shook his head. "Most predators target the young. You know why? Because they're weaker and easier to kill."

Hound slowly lifted from his protective huddle. "But those are animals."

"And so are you." I stared Hound straight in the eyes. "So tell me. Are you the lion or the gazelle?"

"I'm the lion, dude. Yeah. Fuckin' Richard the Lionheart."

"Then grow a pair. Because you're in my pride. You're stuck with us." I raised my voice a couple of octaves. "Together forever."

"We're fucking liii-onnns!" Hound's voice was clear now.

Buck and Bull tackled Hound, and the three of them rolled around like cubs on the floor.

"Hey." I clapped, finally calming them. "The predator celebrates after a kill, but then he must rest and prepare for his next attack. We will be hungry again soon."

"I'm hungry now." Hound pushed the others off him. "I want a chance at a takedown."

"Then let's get a plan together." Though last night's kills and the work to cover our tracks had taken it out of me, seeing Hound's enthusiasm was worth the effort it would take to set up our next hunt.

9

Journey and Lucas were climbing back into their Bureau-issue Ford when the Allegheny County Office of the Medical Examiner called with word that Dr. Simon had some information for them. They headed straight over and were escorted back to his office.

"I've finished examining all three victims in the Reaver family murder." Dr. Simon turned and grabbed the exact report he needed from the teetering piles covering his desk.

His messy office, filled with stacks of books, case files, and papers—all at imminent risk of toppling—really sealed the Doc Brown mad-scientist vibe. Amazingly, he never seemed to lose track of anything.

"As I told you back at the scene, I wanted to compare them with my notes on the case from last week. And as I suspected, the wounds are consistent."

"This case is turning out much harder than your average shooting." Journey crossed her arms. "I hate to say it, but anything you can give us across both incidents will help a lot." Two families killed within two weeks was tragic, but any patterns or similarities between the crimes were crucial for bringing those responsible to justice.

Dr. Simon leaned forward in his chair, an eager look on his face. "Forensic analysis of this type is challenging, given the rarity of these cases and the variety of arrowhead types." He flashed a mischievous smile before tapping on his computer mouse.

At Journey's side, Lucas clenched his fists, seemingly bracing himself. He always struggled with this part of the investigation.

"The primary wounding potential of an arrow depends on the shape of the arrowhead." An image appeared on Dr. Simon's screen showing a small circular wound with perpendicular slices on opposite sides labeled with Claudia Reaver's name. "Based on the size of the wounds, there were two types of arrowheads used. Those used on Claudia was a fixed, broadhead, two-blade arrowhead. They cut through the skin, similar to wounds inflicted by sharp instruments, such as a knife blade."

Journey leaned in, intrigued. "And the other type?"

"Similar. Fixed, broadhead, three-blade arrowhead." When Dr. Simon clicked his mouse again, the picture changed to the wound in Daniel Reaver's chest. "Based on our measurements, this same type of arrowhead also killed Bella Reaver."

A knot formed in Journey's stomach. Her heart sank at the thought of the pain the family must have endured.

"In the previous case, the two-blade arrow was used on the man, Michael Bragg. A three-blade broadhead arrowhead on his wife, Rose Bragg."

Journey frowned. That didn't fit any pattern. No correlation between arrowhead size and the size of the victim.

Dr. Simon continued to click through a slideshow of each

arrow wound in the two cases. "Gunshot wounds lend themselves to easier wound path determination because of the difference in appearance between the entrance and exit wounds. The same cannot be said of arrowhead injuries. In general, entrance and exit wounds are identical, even after the broadheads transected multiple ribs as it passed through the body. This is true of the arrow fletching as well. The flexible construction of the fletching allowed them to bend within the wound path and not impart any distortions."

Journey and Lucas exchanged a look of disbelief.

"Remember how I said anything you could tell us will help?" Journey raised her eyebrows.

"Being unable to determine the shooting trajectory doesn't." If anything, Lucas looked a little greener than he usually did in this place.

"It certainly makes things harder." Dr. Simon allowed them a wry smile. "But I believe in you. The penetrative arrow trauma is dependent on the draw weight of the bow, the distance the arrow is shot from, the type of arrowhead used, and the type of tissue encountered. We can apply what we know of the scene and the arrowhead used to make informed calculations. But without more information, nothing will be definitive."

"Please." Lucas ran a hand down his face, muttering into his palm. "Only gun shooting cases from now on."

"Hey, I do have *some* good news for you." Dr. Simon gestured in a sweeping motion with his hands, as if he were drawing an invisible line on the air. "The wider, three-blade arrowheads appear consistent in their trajectories. I studied the tearing, or as some refer to it, the *splitting*, of the flesh at the site of the wound, as well as the wound's depth and the angle of entry."

Journey wasn't squeamish about much, but she was human, and the way he painted a picture of the victims' flesh splitting sent a shiver up her arms. Sweat also appeared on Lucas's temple at the M.E.'s choice of words.

"My data suggests these broadhead arrowheads were propelled with similar speed and force, likely shot by a single archer. That being said, I can't discount the possibility that multiple people of equal height, estimated at six feet, could've fired those arrows that killed Daniel and Bella Reaver and Rose Bragg."

He paused for a beat while Journey frantically scribbled notes into her notebook. She'd be given a copy of the M.E.'s report, but writing all the info kept her from imagining arrows piercing a ten-year-old girl.

"Now, as for the two-blade arrows…they are less consistent. The calculations lead me to believe that two people of different heights fired the shots that killed Claudia Reaver and Michael Bragg, but we're less able to draw conclusions here in terms of the perpetrators' physical statures. Likely, they are between five-ten and five-eleven. Keep in mind, however, that this difference could be the result of distance as much as the height of the shooter."

At the scene of the Reaver murders, Journey and Lucas had suspected more than one perpetrator almost immediately. Everything Dr. Simon had just reported confirmed their assumptions. Two different arrowheads, three different trajectories. And at the scene, at least two different sized boot prints.

With every finding, this increasingly looked like the work of a deadly team.

"As for time of death…" Dr. Simon shuffled his papers until he found what he sought. "As I told you at the scene, they killed the Reaver family between nine and eleven p.m. Michael and Rose Bragg were killed between eleven p.m. and midnight."

"Interesting." Lucas looked up from his notes. "After dark but not the middle of the night."

"Bedtime." Journey jabbed her pen on the page with a flourish and underlined the word for emphasis. She looked up at Dr. Simon, raising her eyebrows in anticipation of his response.

Dr. Simon lifted both palms. "I'll leave that bit of the investigation up to the two of you."

"Anything we can look for to help lock down those heights?"

"Not really." Dr. Simon's gaze met those of Journey and Lucas. "We need a bit more information from the evidence team on scene to make final determinations."

They thanked him and made their way back into the corridor. There was one thing Journey could do, something she'd learned from Jimmy Aguilar, the first FBI agent she'd ever worked with on a serial killer case—leverage her contacts.

Journey paused just outside the office door, pulled out her phone, and dialed Michelle.

"Hola, Gitana. ¿Qué pasa?"

"Hey. We just met with Dr. Simon about the similarities between the scenes. Any chance the evidence team has pinpointed where the killers were standing when they took the kill shots?"

"Yeah, we've got a good idea."

Pivoting on her heels, Journey gestured for Lucas to keep up. "Scrap the plans for heading into the office. We're going back to the crime scene."

10

It was after two p.m. by the time they returned to the Reaver house. The commotion on the block had settled down, but the yard remained a festival of busy law enforcement and fluttering yellow police tape. Obviously, cordoning off the scene was a necessary procedure, as was scouring the area, but the whole fiasco also made for a giant advertisement to anyone driving by.

Something terrible happened here!

After Journey and Lucas showed their badges to the PBP officer on the front stoop, slipped on booties, and stepped inside, Journey followed her sister's voice to the living room, Lucas trailing behind her.

"Oh, hey." Michelle stood to greet them. "This is what I wanted to show you. The carpet here has been helping to tell us the story of what happened in this room."

Lucas glanced at his feet and toed the pile. "Seems pretty new."

"Yep, but I suspect it's a weaker polyester. It's far less durable than nylon or wool, which in this case is good for us. You see here?" She pointed at a bloody area where the knap looked mottled. "That was the first spot I pinpointed. The spot where Daniel Reaver's blood spread."

"But you knew that, anyway, didn't you?" Journey had seen for herself the victims' bodies lying in these locations just a few hours earlier.

"Yes. But it helped lead us to several conclusions. For one, it told me this was where he fell, so he wasn't moved there. We knew he'd likely been shot here…" Michelle showed on her own torso where the arrow entered the victim's chest, "and he was found lying on his back. But we didn't find any other places in the carpet as matted as this one, which also told us *how* he fell. Remember, the arrows went all the way through all of the victims' bodies. There were both entrance and exit wounds. But you see how the blood spreads almost like a perfect fan?"

A dark red half-moon spilled across the carpet, outlining the left half of Daniel's now-absent body.

"From his clothing, we know he bled primarily out of the left side of his chest. And knowing the way he fell tells us which direction he was facing when he was hit, which was toward the person who shot the arrow."

Though Michelle made the explanation sound simple, Journey knew the process was more complicated than what she'd just described. Her sister's powers of observation never failed to amaze her.

Michelle was practically beaming. "All that led us to these beauties."

They followed her to one side of the living room where more small areas had been taped off and marked with evidence flags.

"Got some more of the potential killer's boot prints." Michelle placed her feet next to them and mimicked the killer's stance.

Lucas followed her with his eyes, retracing the presumed

path between Daniel and his killer. "Anything different from the boot prints you'd already found in the kitchen and outside?"

"Same boots, better story." She knelt and waved them over to join her. "And another example of where the vulnerability of these carpet fibers helps us. Despite being fairly new, the polyester didn't spring back into place the way a higher-end fiber would. And that gives us far more detail for our assessment. Whoever shot Daniel likely dug the heels of their boots into the carpet before making the shot. Since the impression still remains, it's also likely that the shooter was a heavier, or larger, individual."

Crouching, Michelle lifted a Mylar sheet that was shiny on one side and black on the other. "With the aid of this light, you can see the prints we pulled from this space." She shined a tiny flashlight at a low angle on the dark side of the sheet, and a dusty boot print appeared.

"Do you know the size?" Journey grabbed for her pen.

"Ten." Michelle stood. "We've also identified prints from size nine and eleven boots. Meaning that there were at least three individuals present at the time of the murders. But we found significantly more size-nine prints. That could be attributed to a fourth person who was also wearing the same boots or one perp who moved around more than the others."

All speech left Journey at the horrifying prospect of four potential killers. A wave of nausea crept up her throat, but she swallowed it down. She had a job to do and couldn't let emotions stand in her way. If she wanted justice for those killed, she had to focus.

Journey pointed at the first set of flags marking the boot prints. "Any chance this guy was at the other scene last week?"

"Good question, and quite possibly." Michelle gave her a smile, seemingly knowing that was what Journey had hoped to hear. "A few members of the team got access to last week's crime scene. They came back reporting they found the same indentations."

That was the kind of fantastic forensic work Michelle was known to deliver. Journey flipped back to the notes from their conversation at the M.E.'s office. "Dr. Simon concluded that Daniel and Bella were shot with three-blade broadhead arrows, while Claudia was shot with a two-blade broadhead."

Michelle nodded, her liquid-blue eyes bright as Journey and Lucas connected the dots.

"So from what you've laid out here, the perpetrator with the size-ten boots also uses a three-blade broadhead arrowhead, while whoever he's working with uses two-blade broadheads." She glanced at Lucas, remembering how he'd postulated multiple arrows from the same archer. "Probably."

"Correct."

Lucas caught Michelle's gaze. "And out of the five murders, he's possibly committed three of them."

"Also correct."

He gestured toward the door. "Time to see if Walter Albright has returned home yet?"

"Right behind ya, partner."

11

Lucas pulled up in front of Walter Albright's McMansion and, before stepping out of the car, leaned toward the passenger window for a better view. A man who looked similar to Mr. Albright's photo was sitting on the expansive front porch.

"Finally, a sign of life." In the passenger seat, Journey narrowed her eyes at the scene.

"Hope that's iced tea in his glass and not something stronger." In Lucas's experience, alcohol, especially in a glass as tall as the one in the man's hand, often made for messy interactions.

They stepped out and made for the sidewalk. Lucas expected some sort of acknowledgment. That was what most people would do when a stranger approached their home. This man, however, remained still and quiet, almost as if expecting them.

"Walter Albright?" Lucas fished for his badge in his pocket. "Beautiful afternoon to sit outside."

Still nothing from Mr. Albright. Not even a nod.

"I'm Special Agent Lucas Sullivan with the FBI." Lucas

strode closer and raised his badge. "I'm here with my partner, Special Agent Journey Russo."

"Fine." Walter Albright uncrossed his legs, placing both feet on the porch decking. "What do you want?"

This is how it's going to be?

It wasn't the first time Lucas had dealt with a resistant person, and it wouldn't be the last. But something about the wealthy made them especially prone to rudeness. He'd learned that lesson well during his time in White Collar.

Lucas cleared his throat and started again. "We're investigating a murder."

"Jed sent you." He said it as if he knew exactly why they'd come and how they'd gotten here.

"We stopped by his store." Lucas nodded. "He gave us your name."

"Timid little weasel." Walter Albright took a lengthy drink from his glass and chuckled. "Well, let me save you any more trouble. I only kill animals."

Lucas studied Walter's posture. He was trying to look nonchalant, sitting and sipping his tea. But the crossed legs and the shifting back and forth made Lucas wonder if he wasn't so calm on the inside. "How about your companions?"

Walter raised his chin and sneered. "And by companions, you mean…?"

"The men who accompany you to Jed's store." Lucas cocked his head slightly and looked at Journey, who theatrically flipped to a fresh page in her notebook with an exaggerated flourish of the wrist. "How about their names, then?"

Walter shifted in his seat. "Bill Wheeler." He pedantically spelled the name with elongated pauses between each letter. "Carson Steele." He enunciated the second name in a clear tone. "Like the metal, but with a silent e at the end."

"Anyone else?" Lucas rubbed his chin thoughtfully. "You ever have tagalongs?"

"Occasionally." Walter shrugged nonchalantly as he crossed his arms. "But they rarely stick around."

Lucas waited for Journey to finish scribbling, formulating where to take the conversation next. Albright was giving answers, but all too easily. He sensed something else, something more he was holding back.

"I'm curious." Lucas leaned in, putting a foot on the bottom porch step. "I don't hunt myself. But I have a lot of family who do. What is it about hunting that appeals to you?"

Walter rolled his eyes. "Don't give me that *I don't hunt* BS. What do you think you're doing here right now? Sniffing me out. Assessing the possibility of taking me down."

This was a game of deflection, but hardly the first time Lucas had encountered it.

Journey smiled. "Aw, come on now, Mr. Albright. You know our work is different. And we're here to listen to you. So tell us. Why hunt?"

"I am a primal man." Walter Albright sat up straight in his chair and gave the first unvarnished answer, as if he'd been waiting for the chance to speak to the pretty brunette.

Journey leaned against the porch rail. "Primal, huh?"

"Yeah." Walter Albright fixed his piercing gaze on Journey. "It's the thrill. You get that, standing there with your gun and your drive to find your suspect."

"I do like getting the bad guy."

Walter's face lit up like a man possessed. "It's the rush that comes with knowing you have power. The satisfaction of domination."

His enthusiasm sent chills down Lucas's spine. It reminded him of his father, who enjoyed "dominating" his mother with his fists every chance he got.

"The ability to survive using little more than the same

skills inherited from our Neanderthal ancestors. Modern society has made us soft. This house here?" Walter Albright motioned toward the grand house and porch. "This doesn't send my heart racing. I had money, so I bought it. But what do I get from just sitting here, day after day? I've become slow, sloppy. Like I said, soft. And that's saying nothing about the bottom feeders."

Journey took a step back from the porch rail. "And hunting?"

"Hunting connects to the part of me that evolution never wiped out. And without those primal instincts, we'd be nothing but prey ourselves." He slapped the arm of his chair as if to drive his point home.

"Uh-huh." Journey kept her voice flat as she hooked a thumb toward Lucas. "Like my partner here, I've known plenty of hunters, and I've never heard one of them explain the sport like you just did."

Albright rolled his eyes. "Really?"

"They talk about the skill, sure. The pride, maybe. But mostly, they talk about enjoying the outdoors, connecting with nature. Maybe eating what they kill."

"Which is a hunter-gatherer instinct." Walter scoffed. "Nature has a hierarchy. It strives to maintain balance. Humans must kill to keep the rest of the animal kingdom from growing out of control. We must kill or be killed."

"So is that just your fancy way of saying that you eat what you kill?" She sounded as if she were close to mocking him.

"Of course I eat what I kill!" After a moment, he gathered himself and tried to strike a calmer pose. "In fact, I'd be happy to let you taste some of my bear jerky. It's from an Alaskan grizzly I took down last summer."

Lucas and Journey looked at each other before declining in unison.

It was clear to Lucas that Walter Albright's patience was

waning. And despite his revulsion for the man, there were questions he still needed to ask before concluding what he suspected was just their first round together. "Can you tell us where you were yesterday evening, around nine or ten?"

"Here. At home." Walter appeared unfazed by the inquiry. "And alone. I live by myself and don't tend to entertain."

"Anyone who could verify they saw you here? A neighbor, maybe?"

Albright frowned. "Not unless any of them were staring at me through my window as I watched a movie."

Judging merely from the pleasantry of this conversation, Lucas suspected Walter's neighbors had as little to do with him as possible. "How about last Wednesday, May thirty-first? Shortly before midnight."

"Hmm. That, I'm not sure. But I was probably here then too. Like I said, I'm a bit of a homebody."

"And your hunting companions? Happen to have their addresses? Obviously, we'd like to speak with them too."

"But of course, you should. Turn over every rock, as they say. Though I can tell you, they won't have anything of substance to add to your investigation. Nor do they have anything to hide." He pulled out his phone and scrolled until he found their contacts, then held them up for Journey to copy into her notes.

"Just curious." Lucas locked eyes with Albright. "We stopped by earlier today. Around noon. Rang the doorbell, but you didn't answer. Called your office, too, but they said you were out today."

"And here I am now, out of the office, sitting on my front porch." He smirked. "Before this, I was at the Lodge eating lunch. I was there with Bill, in fact." He motioned toward the notebook in which Journey had just recorded Bill's information.

Journey leveled a sharp look at him over the edge of her notebook. "How long did you stay?"

"A few hours, at least." Walter shrugged. "It's our go-to, I suppose. Good whiskey. And there's a back room that's quieter than the bar up front. Better for conversation."

"One last question, Mr. Albright." Lucas turned as if ready to walk away. "What's your shoe size?"

Albright lifted his sandal-clad foot. "I wear a ten."

"Good to know." Lucas nodded. "Same size in boots?"

"Maybe half a size up. Why?" Albright's eyes narrowed.

"I'll bet you buy top of the line, am I right?" Lucas turned toward Journey. "What's that expensive brand we saw back at Durham's?"

"Kenetrek Eversteps?" Albright filled in the blanks before Journey could answer. "Those are the kinds of boots you buy if you're trying to prove you have money to burn."

"Which it seems you do." Journey waved her hand toward the house.

"What I choose to spend my money on is my own business."

"So that's a no?" Lucas asked. "You don't have a pair of size ten, top-of-the-line Kenetreks?"

"You seem a little too interested in the kind of footwear I own. Almost like you're trying to accuse me of something. I think we're done here." Albright waved his hand as if shooing a fly. "Have a nice day."

In the car, neither agent spoke until they'd turned off Albright's street and were out of view.

"Cripes, that dude has one hell of an attitude." Journey blew out a long whistle. "Privileged much?"

"Right?" Lucas glanced at her. "The whole time, I had the sense he was putting on some sort of show. Like his entire persona was practiced. He was aware of how he wanted to be seen."

"You think he knew we were coming?"

"I wondered the same." He shrugged. "I suppose Durham could've tipped him off."

"You mean Jed the timid little weasel." Journey smiled, then fell into silence as she reviewed her notes.

Lucas couldn't stop thinking about the one man he'd spent much of his life trying to drive out of his head. His father. The man who'd beaten his mother repeatedly until the day he shot her to death.

It was Albright's excitement over the idea of a predator dominating his prey that had resurfaced those memories. The need for power that, in both cases, led men to kill.

12

"Bill Wheeler lives about a mile west of here, and Carson Steele is about a mile and a half farther west of him." Lucas's voice broke Journey's concentration as she reviewed her notes. "Which house are we heading to?"

"Albright claimed he had lunch with Bill Wheeler. Let's drop by for a visit there first."

Lucas nodded and tightened his grip on the wheel as they continued driving. Journey thought he might be reacting to more than Albright's attitude. But the case held all her attention, because without anything to justify requesting a search warrant yet, she and Lucas were stuck investigating on their wits and charm.

Eventually, he glanced over at Journey with an inquisitive expression. "I find it interesting they can both skip work on a random Thursday afternoon."

Journey laughed, her eyes dancing as she looked over at him. "Sign me up for that job. But only if you work there with me."

Five minutes later, they pulled into a neighborhood similar to Albright's, with nineteenth-century mansions.

Lucas parked at the curb of a blue Victorian with red trim and shut off the engine.

When they rang a doorbell that sounded like Big Ben's Westminster bells, a man with a scruffy brown ponytail and deeply tanned skin opened the door. "Yes?"

"Bill Wheeler?" Journey withdrew her badge and took one step forward to meet Bill's gaze as she introduced herself and Lucas. "We're investigating a recent murder involving a bow and arrows, so we're speaking with avid bow hunters in the area. May we come in?"

Wheeler furrowed his eyebrows in confusion as he scrutinized them both before glancing back into the house, seemingly debating what to do next. "I'm sorry?" He shook his head in confusion.

"We were just speaking with your hunting companion, Walter Albright. He gave us your address."

After a moment of hesitation, Wheeler stepped aside and cleared his throat. "Yeah...sure. Come on in."

He led them into a brightly lit sitting room at the front of the house with a bay window that ran from floor to ceiling. The decor was modern but somehow complemented the old style of the house, with its heavy wooden trim and built-in bookshelves, old and new existing in harmony.

Through the entrance to the dining room, Journey made out several hunting specimens mounted on the long wall. A sleek animal with curly antlers stared back at her, something she suspected she'd see on an African savanna. Was that a gazelle? A kudu?

A visit to the National Zoo in Washington, D.C. was the closest she'd ever come to a trip to the Serengeti, and it had been a while since her last tour.

At Wheeler's gesture, Journey sat in a gray leather wing chair. Buttery leather molded to her form, not even emitting a single squeak.

Lucas took a spot on the sectional couch. "May I ask what you do for a living, Mr. Wheeler? Albright mentioned you enjoyed a long lunch together, and now you're both home on a Thursday afternoon."

"Bill." Wheeler paced until he finally dropped onto a small side chair upholstered in zebra stripes. "I go by Bill."

"Great. Bill it is then." Lucas flashed a smile. "Vacation day for you?"

"Yeah." Wheeler nodded. "You could say that. I'm in finance, but I'm waiting for the deal I'm working on to gel. It'll get crazy again once that happens."

"So the hours ebb and flow?" Journey took in Wheeler's physicality as he twitched in his chair, trying to appear nonchalant.

"Mostly flow, I guess." He jumped up and strutted toward a beverage cart in the corner. "I try to squeeze in time off when I can get it." He poured himself an amber-colored tumbler of something that looked strong. "Can I get you anything? I have bottled water in the fridge."

Journey and Lucas shook their heads.

Wheeler took a large swig of his drink, his Adam's apple bobbing with each swallow.

Watching the way he squirmed at their presence, Journey caught herself eyeing him more like potential prey than a mere person of interest. "Albright says you hunt together often. Indicated you both have quite an enthusiasm for the sport."

"We're traditionalists." He pronounced the word as if he'd just learned it.

"What does that mean, exactly?" Lucas leaned in. "Traditionalists?"

"It's, uh…" He scratched the back of his neck. "You know. Like, honoring the way humans have always survived. The hunt as ritual."

Ritual. Journey recorded the word immediately. She didn't recall Albright using that term.

"Or maybe that's the wrong word." Wheeler winced. "More like…honoring our connection to our ancestors. No matter how much humans have evolved, the instinct to hunt has never been erased."

Journey noted the difference in both men's attitudes. Albright had thrived on being called out during conversation, but Wheeler seemed to shrivel under it.

"Looks like you travel all over the world." Lucas pointed toward the taxidermy animals on the wall.

"Africa. Alaska. Russia." Wheeler stood taller and puffed out his chest ever so slightly while tilting his head proudly toward the trophies. "Big game, mostly."

"One of the murders we're looking into occurred last night." Journey speared Wheeler with a hard stare. "What were you doing around ten o'clock?"

"Yesterday?" His neck turned crimson. "I was on my way home from a camping trip. Got back late…like, after midnight."

"Was anyone with you?" Lucas leaned forward, seemingly also having clocked the skin-color change.

"No. It was a solo trip." Wheeler stood and rummaged through his pockets. "I think I've got a gas receipt here." He shifted his weight, and deep creases formed across his brow as the seconds passed with no receipt to show. "Shit. I paid with cash, so I guess I didn't get one."

"Where were you camping?"

"Oh. Wait." He snapped his fingers and grabbed a slip of paper from a table against the living room wall. "Here's my permit."

Journey took the paper and gave it a quick once-over. The dates lined up. Monday, June fifth through Wednesday, June seventh. He'd paid fifteen dollars per night. It was proof he'd reserved a space, but unfortunately for Bill Wheeler, not proof he'd stayed there. "Mind if I take a picture?"

He raised his palms. "Go ahead."

Journey clicked a few shots with her phone, front and back, and returned the page. "Thanks. How about Wednesday, May thirty-first? Do you recall what you were doing that evening?"

"Um." Wheeler raised his phone. "Okay if I check my calendar?"

The guy asked permission to do everything. Journey wondered how he closed financial deals large enough to afford the house he lived in. "Go ahead."

Wheeler thumbed through his phone. "Uh, right. Here it is. Wednesday the thirty-first, I met Walter for drinks at the Lodge." He lowered his phone and made eye contact with each of them. "It's a place close to here. The whisky selection is unbeatable."

"Want to share that address?" Lucas asked. "I love a good Irish whiskey."

"In that case, there's an incredible Midleton you've got to try." Wheeler's face became animated. "But it's expensive. It'll cost you a Benjamin."

Lucas didn't bat an eye. "Remember what you were drinking on the thirty-first?"

He paused and shook his head. "Sorry."

"Any credit card receipts?" Journey scanned his face for hesitation. "Or anything that would back up your whereabouts?"

"Walter likes to pay." Wheeler's neck flushed even redder as he averted his gaze and retook his zebra seat.

Journey noted with some excitement that Albright hadn't remembered what he was doing on the thirty-first. But she had to be careful how much she prodded. She and Lucas needed enough information to go for a warrant, but she couldn't push Wheeler too hard and risk scaring him off as a potential suspect before they reached that stage.

"Not a problem." She kept her tone light and flashed him a reassuring smile. "Just one last thing. Your shoes." She pointed toward the brown suede loafers on his feet. "What size do you wear?"

"Eleven?" He raised his foot, as if he wasn't certain.

"Is that a question?" Lucas tapped a finger against his closed notebook cover.

"No." The redness crept up to Wheeler's cheeks, and he dropped his gaze to the floor momentarily before collecting himself again. "No. I just didn't expect you to ask me, is all. Yeah. An eleven. Happy to show you." He pulled off a loafer and tried to hand it to Journey.

"No, that's not necessary." Journey laughed. The last thing she wanted to lay her hands on was his sweaty shoe. "But with your permission, we'd love to look through your other shoes. Do you keep them together somewhere?"

It was a shot in the dark. Journey and Lucas hadn't come with the backing of a warrant, so Bill Wheeler didn't have to comply with a request like that.

"My shoe closet." He launched himself from his chair. "Follow me."

He wasn't kidding when he'd called it a shoe closet. Down the hall, he opened the doors on floor-to-ceiling cubbies, each with its own transparent door and each containing one pair. It was bigger than Journey's master closet in the bedroom of her apartment.

They pulled out a few pairs and made a show of examining them. Each was, in fact, a size eleven. There were a few sets of boots, but they weren't Kenetreks.

"Thanks." Journey closed the closet. "I think that's about all the questions we have for you right now." As they turned for the front door, she pulled out her card. "We're heading over to your friend Carson Steele's place."

"I wouldn't bother going to Carson's today." Wheeler took the proffered card. "He's upstate. Solo trip. Sort of like me."

What was with all these hunting buddies taking the same days off but heading off to camp alone?

"He does it a lot." Wheeler nodded vigorously, as if the faster his head went, the more reason they'd have to believe him.

"Okay." Journey did her best to sound friendly. "Can you have him call us when he gets back?"

"Sure."

At the front door, Lucas reached for the doorknob, then stopped. "Hey, that just got me thinking. Do you all happen to feather your arrows together?"

Bill stopped nodding and stared. "Obviously. An arrow can't fly without fletching."

"Right, of course." Lucas nodded, keeping it casual. "It's just, we're novices, so we've been doing a bit of homework, and it seems a lot of the more avid hunters like you guys prefer to feather the arrows themselves. You know, instead of settling for the off-the-shelf stuff."

"Fletching is a time-honored skill." Bill looked straight at Lucas. "If you're a traditionalist, like us, you learn how to do it. Feathers connect us to our ancestors."

"Huh." Lucas arched a curious eyebrow. "Never thought of it that way. Thanks."

As they left, Journey could feel Bill Wheeler's gaze on her back the whole way down the sidewalk.

"Another interesting fella." She brought Carson Steele's address up on the GPS. "I assume we're not taking Wheeler at his word about Steele being out of town?"

"You assume correctly." Lucas hopped in and started the car.

When they got there, Steele's place wasn't as grand as the homes his buddies lived in. His was an average two-story Pittsburgh block house. White, brown trim, black shingled roof, just enough yard to have earned a cold beer after mowing it.

"Looks dark." Journey leaned toward her window, studying the scene. Nothing moved. A couple of newspapers lay piled on the front step.

Lucas opened his door. "Only one way to find out."

They rang the doorbell and knocked several times. Journey even peered in through the shutters. All was quiet inside.

"All righty then." Lucas looked at his watch. "The Lodge doesn't open for a couple hours. But we could head there early and ask the staff about a few of their customers?"

Journey nodded. "Yes, sounds like a plan to me."

13

Journey and Lucas arrived at the Lodge just after four p.m.

They stepped through the heavy wooden doors, their heels echoing on the polished marble floor. Rich smells of cigar smoke and aged whiskey drifted from every direction.

A young woman with long blond hair and pink cheeks met them at the host stand.

"Hi, there, I'm Alicia. I'm sorry but we don't open for dinner until five thirty." Her soft voice was little more than a whisper.

Journey smiled and pulled out a badge. "Actually, we're here to ask you a few questions about two of your regular customers, Bill Wheeler and Walter Albright."

She placed a hand over her heart. "What do you want with Walter and Bill?"

"Can you confirm they were both here for lunch today?"

Alicia nodded slowly, like she was thinking about it. "I was working the lunch shift, and yeah, they were here together. They even ordered the private room in the back… four hundred dollars minimum. It was a relatively slow day, so it kind of surprised me that only two people would book that room. But there was some noise coming from back there, so I thought maybe they had friends join them."

"What sort of noise?" Lucas tilted his head in a way that reminded Journey of a curious puppy.

"Just, you know. Hooting and hollering." Alicia shrugged. "Like they were celebrating something."

"Did you go back there?" Journey looked over Alicia's shoulder, hoping to get a glimpse of where the private rooms were. "Happen to see if any friends had joined them?"

Alicia shook her head. "No. We had a server call in sick, so I was in the weeds having to cover all her tables, even though it was pretty slow. I think they just went to the bar to get their drinks. But I don't think anyone else left with them."

Journey made a mental note to confirm later. "How would you describe Bill and Walter? Not physically, but their demeanor. What are they like as customers?"

"Big spenders." Alicia scoffed, rolling her eyes. "They strut around with this sort of gross energy. Like, *pay attention to me, and I'll make it worth your while*. Typical finance guys. Drink often, spend a lot, tip like they've got something to prove. Not that I'm really complaining."

"Do they treat you well?" Lucas's face scrunched in obvious concern. "Besides the tips, I mean?"

"I guess." Alicia's gaze dropped to the marble underfoot, as if considering her words. "They leer at me sometimes. Which I don't like. I'm not a piece of meat. But then again, they've never tried to grab at me, which is a hell of a lot more than I can say about some of the other creeps Jerry's had to throw out of here."

"Jerry?" Journey didn't recognize the name.

"The owner. He loves Bill and Walter. Mostly because their money-to-asshole ratio is so high. Like today, as I said. It's slow, but they come in and spring for the private room.

Then, instead of hassling the staff for one-on-one service, they head to the bar when they need drinks."

Putting it that way, Bill and Walter seemed like a bar owner's dream customers. "I can see why Jerry would like that."

"Yeah. He even adorned the walls with some of their trophies. You know, to make them feel more at home and keep them coming."

Journey caught Lucas's eye. "Can we look back there?"

"Sure, I guess?" Alicia glanced around the bar and hollered toward a burly blond lumberjack of a woman who was stocking glassware. "Watch the door for me, will ya? I'll be right back."

The back room was cozy. A fireplace. Open space for a crowd to mingle. Trios of overstuffed leather chairs in a few of the corners.

Alicia beelined to the wall of honor Jerry had installed and pointed at a photo plaque. "This is Walter, Bill, and their friend, Carson. He's in here a lot too. But I can't think of who this other guy is."

Journey moved in to examine the last face in the photo. No one had mentioned a fourth hunting companion. "Would the bartender know?"

Alicia leaned in. "Um, yeah, he might. Let me check."

While she was gone, Lucas pulled out his phone and snapped a picture of the plaque. It read, *Allegheny County Team Archery Competition First Place*. In the accompanying photo, Steele and Wheeler looked happy and victorious, while Albright looked vaguely annoyed. The unidentified fourth man was older than all of them, with thinning gray hair. Sun damage and age crisscrossed his face.

The logo for the competition was a long, white feather with brown spots engraved at an angle into the brass plaque.

It was angled in a similar fashion to the feathers left at the scenes.

Lucas must've spotted it, too, because he nudged her with his elbow and nodded toward the logo.

Alicia returned, flashing a thumbs-up. "Okay, he's not in here as often as the other guys, but his name is Harold Cubbins. Same deal…drinks only high-end labels, tips well. Once left the bartender a hundred-dollar bill."

Journey raised an eyebrow. "Must be nice."

"Yeah. Next time he comes, I'm definitely putting him in my section."

The two of them thanked Alicia for her time, handing her their cards before heading to the parking lot.

Journey stopped in her tracks and turned to her partner. "I'm going to guess that, like me, this is the first you've heard of the Allegheny County Team Archery Competition."

"First time ever." The car lights flashed as he pressed the key fob.

"Two more things to look into. The origins and sponsors of the competition, and the fourth man in the photograph. And we need to check the numbers on Durham's business."

Lucas slid behind the steering wheel again, which was fine with Journey. She wasn't in the mood to drive, anyway, and maybe he sensed it. Her fingers itched to scour the internet.

He started the engine but left the car in park until she determined their destination.

"Darn." Journey scrolled through the website she'd found. "I located the archery range where the competition is held, but it's closed for the day."

"Tomorrow morning it is, then."

14

We entered the Allegheny National Forest north of Marienville on Route 66. No matter the weather, every time I passed through Marienville, I thought the same thing—this was one depressing little burg. Even in the gorgeous misty evening sun, like today.

We were almost at the cabin now. My eyes remained on the road.

I remembered playing it cool the first time I saw the address for our destination.

A cabin on Route 666.

This was a few months ago. Bull had popped his head up between the front seats and snatched Hound's phone out of Buck's hand.

He read the address. "Wait, no way. Is this for real? Six-six-six?"

I rolled my eyes. "It's just a road number, dude."

"It's the devil's number…that's, like, quite the coincidence."

Bull had acted like a juvenile asshole the entire ride. Bouncing all around, excited to shoot something. I remembered thinking, *I admire your spirit*. We'd all been excited, and totally beginners. And that first time went so well, we decided to go out to the forest thrice weekly ever since.

That was how we all got so good.

We were well over one hundred visits in, yet Bull was still just as excited as ever. Hound, however, had barely spoken since we left Pittsburgh. He was in the back seat beside Bull, who was shifting in his seat like a fidget spinner, drumming on his thighs, putting his head up in between us in the front. I only knew Hound was back there 'cause I could hear him breathing.

It disappointed me. Hound wasn't only with us because he was our connection—our *in* to the cabin and to The Chosen—he was one of the gang.

He was clearly still upset by the death of the girl. And it struck me that, if he wasn't as excited as the rest of us were, well, that was a failure of leadership. My failure. I had to rectify that.

I cleared my throat and looked at him in the rearview. "Hey, buddy…Hound!"

That jolted him out of his thoughts, and he looked back at me. "What's up?"

He was listless. I hated to see it. "You good?"

"Yeah, I'm straight."

That wasn't good enough. "Are you a fucking lion?"

He caught my eye in the rearview again and smiled. "Yeah, man, I'm a fucking Lionheart."

Bull shook Hound's shoulders. "Crécy and Agincourt, bro!"

Hound shoved him off but laughed as he did so.

"That's what I like to hear."

Buck nodded at a turnoff ahead. "Slow down. We're here."

By the time you got off 666 and turned onto Kings, it was

heavy forest. But soon after you turned into that winding dirt driveway…man, the sky wasn't even visible through the foliage.

It was like plunging into dusk, every time.

My hands gripped the wheel as a familiar rush of excitement coursed through me.

After a few minutes of driving through the tunnel of trees, we emerged into the clearing. In the middle-right of the field was Aaron Harris's hunting cabin. At the far end of the field to the left, quite a bit away from the cabin, was the target range where we trained.

The clearing looked even more ramshackle than usual. The earth was scorched—like a battlefield after being carpeted by heavy artillery. Aaron must've been testing explosives or something.

I slowed as I approached the cabin. That was when I noticed the new white truck next to Aaron's beat-up blue rust bucket. "Hey, Hound. Aaron say anything about getting a new ride?"

Hound stuck his head between the front seats. "Not to me, dude. But that doesn't look like his style."

I had to agree. I felt the slightest twinge of trepidation.

Aaron Harris lived off the land out here in the wilderness. Some distant relative of Hound's, he'd taken us under his wing when we asked him if he'd teach us how to hunt. We started off on the stationary targets, then quickly progressed to tracking wild animals out in the forest. We always went back to the targets, though, becoming proficient from greater and greater distances.

He'd taught us more than that. Every single one of my prejudices he'd confirmed. It wasn't enough to get angry at the people who leeched off the system, he'd said, you had to do something about it. Or else you weren't worthy to be called an American. You weren't worthy of your heritage.

That was what being in The Chosen had taught him. He'd learned that, and much more, from its leader, Connor Leopold. I'd never met the man, or even seen him, though I had listened to some lectures of his on YouTube.

I parked behind Aaron's blue POS and killed the ignition. "All right, let's go, guys. Let's see what he's got in store for us today."

The driver door had barely shut behind me when I heard a whistle from the cabin. Aaron emerged, gaunt and wearing his usual flannel, but he wasn't alone. Behind him was a tall guy, pretty young and well-built, but with a blond fucking ponytail. Aaron held the door open for him as he passed.

I didn't know what it was about this guy—maybe the way he walked, almost gliding like some sort of Buddha wannabe —but the second I saw him, I thought he looked like a douche.

Ponytail and Aaron approached. Aaron shook Hound's hand and nodded at the rest of us. "How's it hanging, boys? I want to introduce you all to someone very special."

Ponytail beamed. Then he brought his palms together in front of his chest and nodded to each of us. "May God bless you, my children."

His smile must've been contagious like the plague because Aaron was grinning like an idiot. For a guy who barely cracked a smile when he took down a ten-point buck, this was weird. "Meet Connor Leopold, leader of The Chosen."

I froze, unable to believe this freak was the same guy who'd captivated me with his words.

Meanwhile, Leopold hesitated for a moment, as if expecting us to lay prostrate on the ground in front of him. When we didn't, he beamed again and spoke, again, in that same high-pitched, whiny voice. "Aaron's been telling me all about your progress. And I have to say, I'm very impressed.

You." He clapped Buck on the shoulder. "Why don't you show me what you can do?"

Buck looked at me, shrugged, and grabbed his gear from the trunk of my car. "From here?"

Aaron nodded. "I'd say that's about fifty yards."

Buck nocked an arrow to his bow. "Piece of cake." He let it fly.

Thwump.

The arrow quivered in the target. Bull's-eye.

Leopold whooped and clapped his hands. "Amazing! Simply amazing. You'll be a grand soldier in God's army."

Now it was Buck's turn to grin.

Leopold switched his attention to me. "But you…I can tell you're the force to be reckoned with around here. You have that energy about you. I know, I have the same energy myself."

Something about his gaze made me clam up. I pulled my shit together. "I, uh…I guess."

Those bright-blue supervillain eyes seemed to be looking straight into my soul. They wouldn't let up. "Aaron tells me you're looking to do something big. That makes sense. A good soldier must prove himself in the field. But tell me, how far are you willing to go?"

I shifted a bit on my heels. "Well, I think our crew proved we'll do whatever it takes."

He smiled. "What you've done has been enough to bring me here in person. I don't do this for everybody."

Aaron chimed in. "He most certainly doesn't."

"Follow me." Leopold walked toward Aaron's truck.

When we'd all gathered around, those evil eyes stared through me once again. "Are you ready?" Leopold flipped back the tarp covering the bed of Aaron's truck.

Underneath was an old military munitions case. He opened it. Inside was filled with black powder.

"Do you know what this is?" He scooped out a handful and held the pile under my nose.

The acrid but familiar smell filled my senses. "Gunpowder."

"Show us what you can do with it. And don't keep me waiting."

Now it was my turn to smile. "Yes, sir. We'll start right away."

15

Greg Thompson had woken up at the crack of dawn, determined to make the most of his well-earned day off from fixing toilets and leaky pipes. Not that he was complaining. After so many years of unemployment, having a steady paycheck was like a dream come true. His epilepsy had prevented him from holding down a job, but by a miracle, his doctor had finally found the right mix of medication to let him live his life.

First, he'd taken a leisurely jog around the neighborhood before cooking an omelet on the stove, which he ate in the backyard accompanied by an extra-spicy Bloody Mary. It felt great to choose whatever he wanted to eat and not have to take whatever the food bank gave him.

After ticking off items on his long list of overdue errands and a trip to the basketball court to meet up with his buddies for some pickup games, Greg headed home.

As he approached his modest—he preferred to think of it as *cozy*—single-story house that he'd recently managed to rent, bittersweet memories of Sarah overwhelmed him.

She'd been gone less than a week, but to Greg, it felt like an eternity.

Sarah had often accused him of being shy, boring, and increasingly agoraphobic.

Though her words hurt, Greg always brushed them off. He enjoyed going out and had plenty of friends. But now that he had a space of his own, he wanted to enjoy it. Living in a house was so much better than the shelter, which was where he'd lived before meeting her.

It was as if, now that he was getting his life together, she didn't want anything to do with him.

Plus, she never understood that their desires just weren't compatible. Or rather, she never gave his interests the time of day. She preferred indie films in run-down art houses, but Greg opted for comedies at home with a bowl of popcorn and a cold beer. She chose ballet, while he dribbled and shot hoops. She enjoyed sitting at cafés for hours. He overflowed with energy after ten minutes.

Opposites might've attracted, but keeping such relationships alive took far more effort than either of them could manage.

Greg fumbled as he put his key into the lock, overcome with a mix of emotions from the argument that had taken place days prior, when Sarah left him. Her note still sat on the gold-speckled linoleum kitchen counter, right where he'd found it.

I hope you find a way to be happy.

He pushed open the door and stepped inside the living room. His shoes squeaked on the hardwood floor of the entryway.

The room was just as it had been when Sarah said goodbye, except for the empty beer bottle left on the coffee table. He wanted to forget her, but he also wanted her back. He ached for another chance with her or maybe just some closure to make sense of it all. Basketball and beer weren't enough to distract him from the ache in his heart.

He slipped his shoes off and eyed the couch. Nothing left to do but grab a cold beer, kick up his feet, stream a few good movies, and pray it might dull the pain.

Maybe he'd even toast Sarah. Hold up his bottle and wish her well. He loved her. Still did. They just weren't meant to be together.

A text message buzzed on his phone, and he fished the device out of his pocket.

Dude, you left your gear bag at the court. I grabbed it. I'll drop it off tomorrow on my way to work.

"Shit."

Thanks, he texted back.

Greg headed for the kitchen, hoping there was at least one bag of popcorn left in the cupboard. Surprise had him stumbling to a stop a second later. Through the doorway to the kitchen, he could see every cabinet hung open.

His mind spun in confusion. *Did I do that?* He hadn't been in a hurry to get out of the house earlier. Plus, he was never that much of a slob. The unsettling sight raised a whirlwind of questions. Could there be a burglar in the house, or something even more sinister. A poltergeist?

As his thoughts spiraled, a sharp, unmistakable crunch sliced through the silence, accompanied by an eerie chuckle. A surge of adrenaline ignited Greg's body, propelling him forward despite the mounting dread.

He needed to find a weapon.

There, on the other side of the kitchen, was a tall person wearing a pig mask that he'd scrunched above his nose. He was eating one of the green apples Greg had bought at the grocery store the other day. The rest still sat in a wooden bowl in the center of his kitchen table.

Besides the mask, the guy was dressed in head-to-toe

camo and had a large hunting bow strapped to his back. He swallowed a bit of apple. Greg could see his smile. "Hi. I'm Pig."

Every sliver of peace—albeit a mournful peace—evaporated from Greg's system.

Still, this was his house, and he wasn't helpless. Weapons lay everywhere. The knife block on the countertop glinted in the dim light coming from the window. The cast-iron skillet rested on top of the stove.

"What do you want?" Greg's voice came out low and gravelly. His brain spun with ideas, priming his body to fight. He could spray disinfectant into Pig's eyes. Shove a chair into his gut or drop it over his head. He just needed to reach one thing and use it.

"What are you willing to give me?" Pig took another bite of the apple as if he didn't have a care in the world.

Is this a robbery, or is this fucking guy trying to negotiate?

"I don't know. Electronics? My laptop?" Spittle flew from Greg's mouth. "My girlfriend took all her jewelry when she moved out."

"No, silly." The guy in the mask snorted and sprayed flecks of half-chewed apple into the air as he barked a laugh. His mouth hung open mid-chuckle, revealing yellow spots of pulp clinging to his lips. Greg couldn't take his eyes off them as he fought against the bile climbing his throat.

"Just tell me what you want, man." A bead of sweat inched down Greg's temple as he plucked the fob to his Honda Civic from his shorts and dangled it in the space between them. "You want my car? Take it. I won't even call the cops."

Pig bobbled his head as if considering the offer.

"Take the fucking keys and get out."

"I'm not interested in your things." Pig's shrill giggle seemed to echo through the small room until it drowned out everything else. "I want you to run." He yanked down his mask and threw the apple at Greg. Hard. It exploded on the wall behind him.

Greg didn't need to be told twice. When he attempted to turn, his feet locked together, causing him to stumble back a step. Reaching out to get his balance, he searched the room, desperately seeking something, anything. He mentally calculated the distance between himself and the knives, but Pig was blocking the path.

"Run!" The pig came at him, oinking and rubbing him with the broad side of his chest.

"Get the fuck out of my face, man!" Greg shoved him, and when Pig stumbled back a step, he grabbed a heavy ceramic utensil jar from the counter and raised it above his head. "One more step, I dare you."

Pig didn't move.

Greg hoped the bastard was considering his options.

Pig inhaled deeply. "Oh, *fellas*! A bit of assistance in here, please."

Three large figures appeared through the glass sliding door that let out to Greg's backyard. They tromped into the kitchen and spread out around the counter. Like Pig, they wore rubber animal masks. A dog, a deer, and a bull.

Greg stood rooted to the spot in shock with the realization they outnumbered him.

One of Pig's masked friends, the bull, sucker punched Greg in the gut.

The ceramic pot crashed to the floor as he doubled over, gasping for breath.

Pig stared at Greg through narrow slits above the snout. "Why haven't you run yet? I told you that's what I want."

The other three began chanting. "Run! Run! Run!"

"I promise you," Pig's voice purred inside the rubber, "it's so much more fun this way."

Greg stood frozen, unable to move or speak as Pig approached him.

The other men circled around.

Pig leaned in close, his face inches from Greg's. "You. Are just a filthy. Stupid. Animal." His voice sliced through the air like a razor. "Say you're a filthy, stupid animal!"

"Fine." Greg's voice emerged barely above a whisper. "Whatever. I'm a filthy, stupid animal."

"That's more like it." Pig reached over his shoulder, pulled the hunting bow from his back, and nocked an arrow.

"Don't!" Desperate, Greg shoved at the wall of men surrounding him. They parted, giving him an escape route.

"Run! Run! Run!"

Greg dashed for the sliding back door and made it into the backyard.

Panic set in as he realized there was nowhere else to run. The wooden fence at the back of the lot was his only choice, but it seemed impossibly high. Not one to give up easily, however, he made a break for it.

He reached the wooden slats and leaped just as the *thwump* of the arrow being fired reached his ears.

Greg barely felt the arrow strike. And then another. It happened so quickly. His limbs went weak. The tang of blood filled his mouth. He lost his grip on the fence and went into a freefall.

He just wanted to feel the earth one more time—his freshly mowed lawn would be a small measure of comfort. But he was held up, stuck, suspended like a butterfly on display.

As his world faded, all he wanted was to kiss the grass, and Sarah, one last time.

But neither were meant to be.

16

Lucas had woken up early enough Friday morning to squeeze in a workout and a hot shower before heading out. It was only seven thirty, but he was glad for the head start. A full research sesh into the financial records of Durham's Hunting Supplies was calling.

Hallie was at her mom's house this week. Divorce was messy, but he was thankful they had a functional relationship as parents. This meant he didn't need to stick around to get her breakfast and off to whatever summer camp or team practice she had lined up for the day. He had some extra time on his side, for once.

As Lucas pulled into the field office parking lot, he spotted Journey's sister stepping out of her older model Mustang. Michelle worked on the second floor in forensics and shared Journey's same all-out work ethic. As a single man—he'd had a string of short-lived romances prior to transferring to VC—it was hard for him not to notice that they were also both rather painfully attractive. But he was a professional and could switch that part of his brain off when he was at work.

"Hey, Michelle." He locked his Jeep and jogged to catch up with her.

She walked like a woman on a mission and looked deep in thought. "Morning."

"You hurrying in for a meeting or something? Don't want to keep you."

She stopped short and turned to face him. "Your perps are more likely to have started with a smaller crime before moving on to a double and triple homicide, right?"

Apparently, they were skipping the small talk. She might've been even more intense than Journey, which was hard to imagine. "Yeah." Lucas appreciated the way their brains locked on to a challenge and didn't let go. "That would fit the typical profile for serial killers. Start small and escalate."

Michelle nodded, then continued speed-walking into the building. "Yesterday, I spent the whole day digging into recent crimes scenes in and around Pittsburgh. There were plenty of reports to consider, but I was looking for anything that had *feather* or *arrow* as keywords."

Judging by her tone, Michelle sounded frustrated by what she'd dug up. Or hadn't. He trotted ahead to open the door for her. "So I take it you didn't find anything?"

The corner of her mouth twitched upward. "Actually, I did." She paused in the entryway, transforming before him as she spoke. Her eyes lit with resolve and determination. "But not until last night."

"Up late, I take it?" Lucas raised an eyebrow.

"You know how it goes." A wry smile crossed her lips, and she nodded. "I couldn't sleep, so I got up and pulled out my laptop and found a case for a man named Antonio White. He was killed about two months ago."

Lucas was more familiar than he wanted to admit with the kind of late nights Michelle had. Insomnia was an old friend of his, but it often provided great cleaning opportunities. He was enjoying this chance to learn more about Michelle, but the sesh was calling him. "A burglary with arrows?"

"Not quite." Michelle winced. "The M.E.'s report indicated that his throat had been ripped, and it was messy. They think there were two stabs, but it's hard to tell. It kind of looks like the weapon went in one way and then was wrenched out."

"Wow."

"Right? There were bits of fiberglass evident in the wound, so it probably wasn't a knife."

"What kind of weapon would you bet on?"

"A bolt of some kind. An arrow. The attack feels clumsy or unintentional, but the killer got an artery…across the left carotid. Probably killed White by pulling the bolt out." She drew an imaginary arrow out of her throat.

Lucas rubbed his forehead, taking a moment to visualize the scene of the crime. Stabbing and then ripping? That was strange. If the killer severed the left carotid, he might've been right-handed. "Does the report say anything about the position he was in when he was killed? Or any conclusions about the assailant?"

Michelle grinned. "M.E. found bruising on his left shoulder, clavicle, and left rear of his neck, which indicates the perp was likely restraining him from behind, locking an arm up through his left armpit and grabbing the back of his neck. Want me to show you?"

She got on her tippy-toes, and her hands moved up and around as if she were grabbing someone in a bear hug.

"No." Lucas took a step away. "I got it."

This was Journey's sister. His partner's family. It would be weird to get that physically close to her.

But a tiny, traitorous part of Lucas's brain wished he'd let

Michelle give her demonstration on him. He pulled in a breath to ground himself.

Michelle shrugged, going flat on her feet again. "If the perp's left hand was busy restricting White's movement, the knife was in his right hand and the killer was stabbing blindly."

"He didn't have a clear view of where to aim."

"Exactly. And if he'd killed someone that way before, he'd be more likely to know how to do it."

Lucas nodded. "Huh. I get where they came up with the theory that he was inexperienced."

"Right?"

Michelle moved toward the stairwell, which Lucas could've predicted. Journey almost never took the elevator either. He'd been surprised when he first noticed that quirk, since Journey was basically as far from a gym rat as one could get in the FBI. When he'd asked her about it, she'd responded obliquely.

"If it's good enough for Cary Grant, it's good enough for me."

Further questioning revealed that the old Hollywood star had been a favorite actor of her and Michelle's grandmother —and that his only form of exercise was always taking the stairs.

"But that's not the best part." Michelle slapped her hands together in excitement.

"I'm waiting on the punchline with bated breath." Lucas chased after her up the stairwell.

"Police found a feather on White's chest."

It was Lucas's turn to stop in his tracks. "Long, white, with brown spots?"

"No. We're not that lucky. It was small and downy."

"Huh." Odd. But also, entirely possible the similarity was coincidental.

Michelle sprinted the last few steps to the second floor

and waved him up. "If you're interested, I'm heading to my desk now to call Lonnie Gutierrez, the PBP detective from the Reaver murders. I want to see if he'll put me in touch with the forensic team that analyzed the Antonio White scene."

A minute later, they were at Michelle's workspace, dialing the number from the detective's business card.

The line picked up after the first ring. "Detective Gutierrez speaking."

Michelle introduced herself and explained the reason for her call.

"You'll want to talk to Penelope Ackers, the original crime scene investigator." Detective Gutierrez still sounded just as weary as he had the day before. "I'll shoot you over to her."

The line clicked, rang briefly, and clicked again as Penelope Ackers answered.

Lucas had to chuckle. It wasn't often that an investigation got so lucky as to have everyone available and answering their phones on the first try.

Michelle introduced herself and Lucas before diving in. "Detective Gutierrez recommended we speak with you about the Antonio White murder. We understand there was a feather found on his body. We're investigating two similar crime scenes."

"You got a case number?" Ackers didn't sound as if the name struck her.

Michelle recited the PBP report ID, and Lucas could hear the investigator shuffling papers and clicking her mouse on the other end.

"Okay, yeah. Got it. My notes say he was killed after having just woken up in the middle of the night. Body found in the kitchen in his underwear, broken drinking glass on the floor. Might've gotten up for some water."

Michelle scribbled as she listened. "Any notes about the feather?"

"Yeah. There was a decorative pillow on a chair in the adjacent room with a small tear in one seam. A few feathers poking out of the side that appeared to match the one on his chest. Typical down filling. Officers deemed it coincidental."

"You didn't happen to analyze it, did you?"

Penelope *hmm*ed. "Weren't asked to, no."

Michelle glanced at Lucas, raising an eyebrow as if to say, *Got any more questions?* When he shook his head, Michelle asked Penelope to send over the file and thanked her for her time.

As soon as she hung up, Lucas headed toward the door. "We gotta talk to Journey."

17

Journey was just pulling into the field office parking garage when her phone rang, Michelle's name flashing across the screen. She tapped the button on her steering wheel, connecting the call through her speakers. "Hey. Morning."

"Are you close?" Michelle spoke rapidly, her words tumbling out before Journey could ask what was going on. "Lucas's heading to the parking lot."

"Why do you know what my partner's doing?" Journey was used to reading between the lines with her sister. Michelle hadn't said hello. That meant she was chasing something important. "Did you find something?"

"Lucas knows." Michelle was teasing now.

"I just pulled into the garage." Journey spotted Lucas stepping out of the stairwell and heading toward their FBI-issue Ford. "Hang on. I see him."

"He'll fill you in. Have fun." Michelle disconnected the call.

Journey parked, jogged over to Lucas, and hopped into the passenger seat. "Okay. You want to tell me what's going on?"

Lucas pulled out of the parking space. "We're headed to the site of a murder that occurred two months ago. Victim's name is Antonio White. Michelle's digging through the PBP case notes while we do a little footwork."

"Key points?" Journey arranged herself and her gear as she listened.

"All right." Lucas pulled up to a stoplight and looked at her. "There was a feather found at the scene."

"Arrow to the chest?" She arched a hopeful eyebrow.

"No." Lucas shook his head. "Different method of killing than the other two scenes. Killer did a butcher job on the victim's throat."

"What kind of butcher job on the throat?"

"Looked torn, apparently. Like someone shoved an arrow into his throat and ripped it out."

Journey suppressed a wince as she imagined what the crime scene must've looked like. "An arrow was jammed in his throat and ripped out?"

"My thoughts, and Michelle's, exactly." Lucas grimaced.

"That's messed up."

"Antonio White might be our first victim. Starter jobs are often the messiest. This one has potential. Arrows. Feathers. Although the feather could've come from one of the throw pillows. We can't hit the archery range until it opens, so we might as well check this out."

Lucas was right. That definitely sounded like it could be linked to their current assignment. "You said Michelle found this case?"

"Yep." Lucas smiled reassuringly before turning back to his driving.

"She has good instincts." Journey was so happy to be working in the same field office as her sister. "If she thinks there's something here, we better check into it."

"On it." Lucas nodded and gestured toward the GPS. "But

there are lots of differences. The Reaver and Bragg families lived within a half mile of each other. Antonio White lived about as far out as you can get without crossing the Pittsburgh city limits."

Out of the window, the trees kept whizzing by. The morning sky was gray but bright, with shards of orange and yellow peeking through the muck.

Journey's mind flitted around the case. The distinct change in location could be coincidental. Then again…

She opened her notebook up and flipped to the page on which she'd sketched a rough map of where Walter Albright and friends lived. She added a rough location of the victims' houses.

The map was messy. She'd need to be more precise before drawing any meaningful conclusions, but one thing still stood out. The Reaver and Bragg residences filled in more of the lopsided circle around Durham's Hunting Supplies.

Could Jed Durham's store be a literal nexus to these crimes?

They pulled up to a small, single-story house at the end of a street walled off by trees. Not so much a cul-de-sac as a dead end. Were the perpetrator on foot, the foliage would've provided excellent cover.

But the dead-end street wasn't ideal for a getaway. It forced whoever entered to do a U-turn, or even a 3-point turn, to escape the narrow road. From the look of things, neighbors parked in driveways or in their garages, not curbside.

This was the sort of street where a lack of traffic announced the comings and goings of everyone who traveled it.

A strange car would have definitely stood out.

Journey spotted curtains moving in the front window of

the house next door to Antonio White's. "We've been spotted."

"That makes it even more interesting that none of the neighbors claimed to have heard anything the night of the murder."

"Or…you know…since the murder, everyone is on high alert."

In contrast to the neighbor's attentive household, White's house looked abandoned. The overgrown grass stood pocked with gangly dandelions going to seed. And, as expected, all the windows in White's house were dark.

Once they exited the car, Lucas stood on the lawn and peeked through the glass. "Police report said the man lived alone. And given that there's still a prominent blood stain on the tile, it's probably abandoned."

Journey knocked on the door three times, not expecting an answer. Nothing stirred.

"Try the neighbors?" Lucas nodded toward the house next door. "They saw us drive up, so maybe they saw something the night of the murder."

When Journey knocked there, a middle-aged woman in sweatpants and a stained, oversize t-shirt promptly answered the door.

"Sorry to bother you this morning, but—"

"I saw you parking." Her words weaved together in a clumsy slur. "In front of Antonio's."

"Yes…" Journey was taken aback, but she smiled politely.

"I noticed you looking through his window." A strong odor of alcohol wafted off the woman.

"It's good when neighbors look out for each other. I'm Special Agent Journey Russo with the—"

"I suppose you're here to mock me too." The woman swayed where she stood, then leaned against the doorframe as if needing the support.

"Of course not." Instead of continuing to introduce herself, Journey pulled a card from her pocket and handed it to the woman. "Why would we be here to mock you?"

"Because the last cops did when they talked to me." The woman coughed, and Journey got a blast of vodka-soaked breath to the face.

Journey backed up a step and took a cleansing breath to help maintain her professional composure. "May I ask your name, ma'am?"

"Mel Rucker. Call me Mel." She pointed at Lucas's notebook. "Should be in there. I told the cops all I saw."

Lucas looked up and smiled. "We're with the FBI, ma'am."

"What are the Feds doing about Antonio?" Mel Rucker's face contorted into an expression of disbelief. "He wasn't important."

"How well did you know Antonio?"

Mel shrugged, her loose shirt slipping on her bony shoulders. "All right, I s'pose. He was an electrician, kept to himself a lot. Not someone who would interest the FBI."

Journey ignored the misconception that you had to have some kind of title to earn the attention of the Bureau. Still, she and Lucas shared a quick look at the mention of White's profession. Another blue-collar worker.

"We're helping the police investigate his murder."

"Mm-kay." Mel swayed again, clinging to the doorframe. "If you say so."

"What did you mean when you asked if we were here to make fun of you?"

"The cops from before." Mel swatted the air with her hand and scoffed. "Came to ask me what I saw the night he died, so I told them."

"Would you mind telling us?" Lucas held his pen ready.

"I looked out the window and swear I saw a dog out in his yard." She smiled at Lucas and then Journey, as if she'd just delivered key evidence. "Problem is, Antonio never had no dog!"

Frowning, Journey scribbled in her notebook. "Was the dog barking? Is that what drew your attention?"

"Nah." Mel swatted the air again. "I get tired of looking at the TV all day and night. Sometimes, it's nice to look outside." She hooked a thumb at her chest. "I'm retired. You know how it is."

Journey didn't. The grandparents who'd raised her were almost busier after they retired, volunteering and helping at church and driving elderly friends to appointments. "But this dog was outside Mr. White's house? Can you tell us what it looked like?"

"Nope." Mel shook her head too hard and stumbled back a little. "Dark outside, and the thing was running too fast. Just saw its head." She smacked the wooden frame. "I may be getting old, but I know what a dog looks like."

Journey thought of the old man who lived next door to the Reavers, Alfred Casal. He'd sworn he saw a dog running down the middle of the street the night they were murdered.

"Which direction was the dog running?"

Mel pointed toward the woods. "Across the yard and into the shadows."

Lucas captured the information, then took a breath and looked directly at Mel. "This may be an uncomfortable question, but we need to ask. Had you been drinking that night?"

She laughed so hard she snorted. "Did the day end in a *Y*? Then, yeah, I had a few drinks. I enjoy my cocktails. But it doesn't change nothing. I know a dog when I see one, and I saw one running across Antonio's yard." Again, she pointed toward the trees.

"Could it have been one of your other neighbors' dogs?" Lucas met Mel's heavily lidded gaze. "Maybe one got loose?"

"Nuh-uh. Only two dogs on this block, and they're ankle-biter size. Both of 'em are yappers too. I'd have heard them." Mel appeared as convinced she'd seen a strange dog as Alfred Casal had been.

Journey cleared her throat. "Okay. Do you know what breed? Or could you describe its appearance?"

"I dunno...brown? Big?"

"So, not our neighborhood ankle-biter friends?"

"Right."

"Got it."

She and Lucas took turns running through their list of questions. Nothing Mel said shed any new light, but her information would land on the murder board all the same.

Journey thanked her for her time. "You have my card. Please call if you remember anything else that might help."

"Sure thing. Maybe I'll invite you over for a cocktail party." Mel shut the door, and Journey heard her cackling as she moved deeper into the house.

Heading across the street to try another neighbor, Journey and Lucas exchanged wide-eyed glances.

"Vodka for breakfast." Lucas blew out a whistle. "Not exactly a reliable witness."

Journey shook her head. "Alfred Casal, the elderly neighbor next door to the Reavers, told a very similar story."

"Huh?" Lucas tapped his pen on his notebook. "Oh, yeah. You're right."

Despite several attempts, none of Antonio White's other neighbors were home. They decided to move on. Lucas held up the car keys. "Next stop, the archery range? You wanna drive?"

"Nah." Journey walked around to the passenger side. "I want to call Michelle. See what exactly the police report said about Mel Rucker."

As soon as they settled into the car and pulled their doors

closed, Lucas punched in the address for the range while Journey dialed her sister on speakerphone.

Michelle answered on the first ring.

"Can you look at the PBP report for us? See if there's anything further mentioned about Antonio White's neighbor, Mel Rucker?"

Michelle took a moment before answering. "Nothing. Just the time and date of when they spoke to her."

"Okay." Journey couldn't exactly blame them. "I guess I'm not surprised. She indicated they didn't take her seriously. Thanks." She hung up and turned to her partner. "It's probably a wild-goose chase, but I'm wondering if maybe the dog is involved in these murders somehow."

Lucas squinted in thought. "A skilled retriever can be helpful on a hunt."

"But why bring a retriever to a murder?" That part she couldn't put her finger on. "None of the victims displayed bite marks."

"Maybe a dog with a keen sense of smell. Able to follow a scent trail."

A hunting dog could be a potential link, but it was weak. "I like that. Then again, the witnesses who saw a dog both claimed it was running away from the scene."

"I don't know if it's important." Lucas rubbed his forehead. "Let's keep it on the backburner for now."

"Okay." Journey turned her gaze out the window. "Onward to archery."

18

Gravel crunched under the Ford's tires as they navigated through a set of rusty gates, passing construction crews ripping off the siding from what was presumably the main building of the Forest Cove Archery Club. The place looked like it was getting a facelift.

Journey spotted a second crew erecting a new building from the studs up. And, at the edge of the competition field, stood a newly built grandstand with flip-up seats similar to those seen in major-league stadiums. Meanwhile, a temporary fence had been posted with a sign that read, *Pardon Our Dust While We Create a New and Improved Club*.

She took in the sight as Lucas drove closer, her knowledge of archery limited by what she'd learned since the Reaver killings and seen during high school archery—people shooting paper targets attached to straw backstops in an open field. Here, however, there was also a concession stand with brass-handled bar taps.

"I don't know what I was expecting. But it sure wasn't this."

Lucas threw the Ford into park. "Best guess as to where we'll find the owner?"

His name was Mark Forester, and Journey's research told her he'd opened the range in 1984.

Outside, the grounds were a symphony of construction sounds—saws whirring, nail guns firing, and workers shouting directions to each other over the din. The tang of mildly singed sawdust filled Journey's nostrils. Her attention shifted to a small trailer tucked away beneath tall trees at the edge of the property.

The trailer door opened, and a woman holding a clipboard stepped out. She made her way toward the new building going up.

"How 'bout we start there?" Journey pointed.

Lucas shaded his eyes with his hand as they approached the trailer. "Who knew there was this much money in archery?"

Journey climbed the three narrow, steel steps and knocked. The sound echoed inside, tinny and hollow enough that she worried her knocking wouldn't be heard above the noise.

A tall, older man with a gray beard and suspenders opened the door. "May I help you?"

"Good morning, sir." Journey smiled. "We're hoping to speak with Mark Forester. Can you direct us to where we can find him?"

"I'm Mark." His smile filled his face. "What can I do for you?"

Journey glanced past him into the trailer, hoping it might provide a quieter place to talk. Two desks crowded the space, but there were also two empty folding chairs. "We're with the FBI. May we come in?"

Mark's expression went from *ain't life glorious* to *the devil just came to town*.

"Yes, by all means. Please." He ushered them inside.

Journey and Lucas stepped through, and he closed the door, directing them to the folding chairs. The construction noise was still loud but no longer pounded against Journey's skull.

She introduced herself and Lucas properly before launching into the reason for their visit. "We're investigating a recent murder, and, in the course of our work, we became aware of the Allegheny County Team Archery Competition you hold here. Specifically, we're interested in what you can tell us about last year's competition."

Mark's face went white as a sheet, and Journey worried he might be at risk of having some sort of health emergency. He was in his seventies at least, maybe pushing eighty.

He flopped into the desk chair closest to him. "Well. Excuse me if I sound startled, but I'll tell you what I can." He swiped a palm across his brow. "Let's see…we've held the competition since 2010. It's gotten larger, and more competitive, every year. Last year's was the most successful yet."

Lucas nodded toward the door to indicate the activity underway outside. "Looks like business is good."

Mark turned wide eyes on him. "The growth is completely legitimate, if that's what you're wondering. I've owned the range since 1984, and some years we barely made it, financially. But with bow hunting on the rise and Olympic competition getting more attention, the sport has exploded in recent years. Our competition draws archers from all over the United States to compete for the Owl Prize."

Really? Journey found this conversation more interesting than she'd expected. "That's the name of the competition?"

Mark motioned to a poster with the club's logo at the top. A long, white feather with brown speckles. "We named it after the snowy owl, a hunter noted for its lethal accuracy. Seemed appropriate."

Journey blinked at the same time that Lucas nudged her in the ribs. This was the precise kind of feather found at the crime scenes. "Interesting. But why choose that feather for your club's logo?"

As Mark gazed at the logo with a fond smile, more details about his office jumped out at Journey. An owl-engraved ceramic penholder. A line-art poster hung to one side of a white owl in flight, its pale feathers dusted with speckles. A quiver of arrows resting in one corner with imitation snowy owl fletching peeking over the rim. The man had a fixation.

"Snowy owls are unique in many ways, but I find them most similar to human hunters. They hunt during the day, catch ground prey, and detect prey by sight more than sound. Also, have you seen them? They're gorgeous!" He waved a hand at the line-art poster, his eyes getting brighter. "Plus, even though they're among the largest true owls, their feathers are almost silent until they hit the ground. I saw this cool documentary once—"

Make that hyper-*fixation.*

Lucas caught Journey's eye and shook his head, thinking the same thing as her. This guy wasn't their killer. He just liked archery and owls.

Journey waited for Mark to wrap up before posing her next question. "Could you provide us with the roster of all the participants from last year?"

"Of course." He turned to wake up his computer.

Lucas held up his palm, pausing him. "You can get that for us when we're done speaking."

At the interruption, poor Mark's panicked demeanor at their visit returned. The sweat he'd just wiped from his brow started up again in force. "I guess I don't understand what brings you here, though. Did something happen at the event I'm not aware of?"

"No." Journey was tempted to reach for his wrist to check his heart rate. "We'd actually like to ask you about the team who won last year's competition. Walter Albright, Carson Steele, Bill Wheeler, and Harold Cubbins."

"Walter, Carson, and Bill carried the team. Harold is newer to the sport. Not really competition ready." Mark attempted an overly wide smile. "Though he visits the range often, and there was that thing Walter said."

Journey made a note of it. "Which was?"

Mark raised his hands. "Said he was 'one of them.'"

"Team effort." Lucas nodded. "I get that."

"Can you tell me?" Mark leaned in, lowering his voice. "Have those guys gone and done something terrible?"

Journey caught Lucas's eye and raised an eyebrow. "Would it surprise you if they had?"

Mark rubbed at his pant legs with his palms. "Well, now, I don't know how to phrase it exactly. But I suppose you might say they're unusual. They have a sort of dark presence about them."

"A dark presence?" Lucas leaned in, too, matching Mark Forester's body language.

"Yes. I like to consider myself an optimist. The community here brings me pleasure, and I enjoy a bit of healthy competition. Archery goes back thousands of years, you know. Spans every continent. There's a certain beauty to the skill it takes. But those guys…"

They waited quietly for him to continue.

"Let's just say that they can really shoot. They don't take the competition lightly." Mark shook his head. "It's not *friendly* with them, if that makes any sense."

Journey could see him drawing that conclusion about

Walter Albright at the very least. "Can you give us an example?"

Mark thought for a moment. "The year before last, they came close to winning, but Carson had a poor final round, and they ended up fourth. Walter lit into him like I don't know what. And when we held the final ceremonies, they refused to shake the hands of the winning teams. Very poor sportsmanship if you ask me."

Journey scribbled as Lucas took the lead on questions. "Do the others come here often? You said Harold has been coming regularly."

"I suppose a few times a month." Mark scratched his chin. "Though not as often since we were forced to ask them to leave once."

"What happened?"

"They're drinkers." Mark held up his hands as if asking them to hold their judgment. "Which, I'm no saint myself, but they were getting sloppy. Careless. And that can't happen when you're holding a deadly weapon." He motioned toward Lucas's waist where a holster would be. "My guess is you know that yourself."

"I do." Lucas nodded.

"Now, I'm seventy-seven, so compared to me, you're a boy. But even by your age, you know how to mind yourself."

"Yes, sir."

Mark nodded at Lucas's show of respect.

Journey tapped her pen against her notebook. "How did they react when you asked them to leave?"

"They didn't raise hell, if that's what you're wondering." Mark sighed, shaking his head as he looked toward the floor. "Sometimes, they just have a tendency to get a little carried away. I keep an eye on them now."

"But they've been back since?"

"I'd expect they'll be coming even more now as this year's competition gets closer." He smiled wistfully, as if lost in his own memories for a moment. "They'll need to defend their title."

"You've been very helpful." Lucas pulled out a card and handed it to him. "Thank you."

Mark's face finally recovered its natural pinkish hue. "I suppose you'll be wanting that roster of names I promised."

"Yes, sir." Lucas smiled. "And a full roster of your members, if you're willing."

"Happy to." Mark clicked around on his computer for a minute, and the printer whirred to life.

As they waited, Journey stood and examined a set of blueprints hanging on the wall. "If you don't mind me saying so, you're over retirement age, but these look like you're building a whole new future."

Mark's body puffed with pride, and that ear-to-ear smile finally returned to his face. "My granddaughter is slowly taking over operations. Whole new generation of archers coming along, many of them women. Couldn't be happier to leave the club in her hands."

Journey recalled the way her own grandfather talked about her and Michelle. "You must be very proud."

"You don't know the half of it."

Five minutes later, they were back in the sunshine heading to the car, printouts in hand.

Lucas held up the keys and jangled them. "Yes? No?"

"You drive. I want to skim these names."

He mocked a scowl. "I may just be a 'boy,'" he air-quoted, "but even I know you prefer to drive."

"Sorry, young man. Not today." Journey climbed in and shut the door, eager to thumb through their new information. The list was thick and heavy in her hands. Who knew archery drew such a crowd of people willing to pay for membership?

Mark Forester hadn't been exaggerating. Participants came from all over the U.S. to compete in the Allegheny County event. They'd have to sift through the names to separate the Pittsburgh-area archers from the nonlocals. Even with the reduced search area, contacting just the Pittsburgh archers would take a while.

Lucas was about to start the engine when his phone rang. "It's Keller." He held up the screen before putting the call on speaker. "What's up?"

"More like, what's *down*? And the answer is another victim. Murdered with a feather left at the scene."

19

Lucas only had preliminary information about the latest murder. Even though this was a single man, there were remarkable similarities to the other cases. The victim died via a puncture wound to the sternum. Another feather had been left at the scene. And this new victim's address fell nearly equidistant from the hunting supply store as the Reaver and Bragg homes, according to Journey's rough map.

He pulled up to the curb and parked. Just like yesterday's scene, the street swarmed with patrol cars and official Allegheny County vehicles. After getting out, he and Journey flashed their badges to the PBP officer charged with keeping the lookie-loos away.

"Special Agents Sullivan and Russo." Detective Lonnie Gutierrez waved from several yards away and marched over with the efficiency and authority of a drill sergeant.

Lucas chuckled to himself. That buzz cut of his was so on-brand.

"Thanks for connecting us on the Antonio White case. We were just over there." Journey extended her hand.

Detective Gutierrez took it, then dropped his head in a

solemn gesture to the victim. "I wasn't at that one, but I've been told it was gruesome."

"Took a peek through the window." Despite what he'd seen, Lucas wished they'd gotten inside to poke around. "Judging from the bloodstain in the kitchen, I'd say it probably was."

Gutierrez grimaced. "Find anything new that wasn't in the PBP report?"

"We're investigating a few leads." Journey's face betrayed nothing as she withheld the idea that the dog his fellow officers scoffed at might not have been a figment of a drunk woman's imagination. "What can you tell us about this scene?"

Detective Gutierrez turned and led them toward the house. "Similar chaos inside as the previous two. Broken glass and dishes, shelves, and furniture overturned. There was something else too. An apple had been smashed against a wall. Like it'd been thrown or something."

"We should check that for DNA."

He gave Journey a look that said, *of course*.

Lucas elected to ignore that. Detective Gutierrez was good but also maybe a bit overworked right now. Lucas knew Journey didn't want anything missed. Neither did he. "What about the victim?"

"Punctures to the sternum and matching holes in the fence in the back, plus a feather on the body, resting on his forehead. In this case, the victim, Greg Thompson, lived alone, though we've been told he was fresh out of a long-term relationship with a live-in girlfriend. He worked as a plumber. Seemingly average life. Group of friends he played basketball with regularly."

Lucas's ears perked up. "A recent breakup?" He didn't see how Greg Thompson's ex could fit into their overall picture yet, but too many murders turned out to be scorned lovers for them to ignore this.

"Yeah, that's what the friend told us. Kid who discovered him." Gutierrez pointed at a twentysomething woman talking to officers in the driveway. "Isabel Yost."

She matched height with the officers around her. Dark hair tied up in a messy bun, she wore a pair of cotton canvas work pants and a polo shirt bearing the name of a local heat and air-conditioning company.

With Greg Thompson working in plumbing, that made for another blue-collar victim. Like Daniel Reaver, who was a landscaper. Lucas wished he'd remembered to grab the Braggs' file at the office that morning to check what kind of work Michael and Rose Bragg did. He'd gotten too excited about the Antonio White scene and headed straight for the parking garage to meet Journey.

At his side, Journey's interest had also sharpened. "We'll talk to her, then head inside." She turned to Detective Gutierrez. "Anything else we should know?"

"Not if you're getting Isabel's story from her."

At their approach, officers nodded and stepped away from Isabel Yost. Lucas made the introductions. "Can you walk us through what happened this morning?"

Up close, Isabel was tall enough to look Lucas right in the eyes. Redness tipped her pale, swollen nose, but she didn't show any other signs she'd been crying. "Came over on my way to work this morning to return a gym bag Thompson left at the basketball court last night. When he didn't answer the door, I called him. Heard his phone ringing around back."

She choked back a fresh sob, swallowing hard, and Journey pulled a packet of tissues from her pocket and handed them over. Isabel blew her nose before continuing.

"When I headed around to the backyard, I hollered for him, but he didn't answer, even though I heard his phone. So

I opened the gate and found him back there by the fence. Looked like he'd been shot." She took a deep breath. "Then I called the cops."

Detective Gutierrez had probably mentioned it already, but Lucas reminded himself to let the forensic team know Isabel had entered the scene. "We'll need you to leave a sample of your DNA before you go."

"They already got a swab."

Journey glanced up from her notebook. "Can we take a look at your phone to see the calls you made?"

"Sure. We texted last night, too, so you can look at those." Isabel pulled her phone from an oversize side pocket of her cargo pants, pausing to swipe something off the screen before handing the device over. "Sorry. My boss calling me."

"We won't keep you much longer." Lucas smiled as Journey flipped between apps.

Tilting the screen, she showed him the conversation at around eight p.m. and the calls just after eight thirty that morning, then handed the phone back over. "We heard something about an ex?"

Isabel's expression darkened. "Sarah. That bitch really broke Thompson's heart. Just when he was getting his life together." Her fists clenched at her sides. "He told me how happy he was not having to get food at the food bank anymore. Next thing I know, she's dumped him. Like she only wanted him when he was dependent on her."

Lucas raised an eyebrow at the *protective big sister* vibes rolling off Isabel in waves. "How long ago was that?"

"I think about two weeks ago."

At that, Lucas's interest in this potential lead fizzled. Two weeks was plenty of time to cool off. Plus, the girlfriend had dumped him, not the other way around.

"Did Thompson mention if Sarah had any interest in archery?" That was Journey—thorough to the end.

"I don't think so?" Isabel's expression turned confused at the question. "Yesterday during the game, he said they were incompatible because she's into artsy-fartsy stuff and he's not. My words, not his."

Now the ex-girlfriend angle looked even less likely. Still, Lucas asked for Sarah's last name and Isabel's contact info, then handed over his card. "Let us know if you think of anything else." He'd have the forensic techs pull Sarah's phone number out of Thompson's phone—if he hadn't deleted it in a rage—and follow up with her later if he thought they needed to.

They parted ways with Isabel, letting Detective Gutierrez know before heading in. At the front door, they stopped to slip on booties and gloves.

Once inside, Lucas noted that this house, like the Reavers', was a starter home, though this one was a single level. Bedroom through the living room to the back. Kitchen to the right of the front door. Just about every one of Thompson's meager possessions strewn somewhere on the floor.

When Lucas heard Michelle's voice, he expected the way Journey responded like a magnet and gravitated toward the kitchen at the side of the house.

"Funny seeing you here." Even the sunlight coming in through the window over the sink couldn't outshine Journey's face at the sight of her sister.

"I've been told I'm drawn to the macabre." Michelle squeaked with every movement in a full bunny suit as she collected samples at the counter. "Stop back by after you've seen the victim in the backyard. I've got something you need to see."

"Will do." Journey gave her a thumbs-up. "You know how much I love a good teaser."

They stepped out the sliding door in the kitchen to a

backyard hemmed in by a wooden fence. A PBP officer directed them to the southwest corner, between the fence and the one-car garage.

Evidence flags marked a dozen or more footprints between the house and the body of Greg Thompson, who lay on the ground at the foot of the fence with two bloody holes in his chest.

A member of the forensic team, Mark Lebeau, stood measuring the distance between the body and the fence. He wore his flop of dishwater-blond hair slicked backward over a shaved back and sides. A few strands had come loose, and he kept blowing them out of his face while he worked.

Stepping carefully, Journey knelt next to the victim. "What do you know so far?" Greg Thompson lay on his back, his left knee bent, right leg twisted at a sharp angle. Another snowy owl feather, like those with the Reavers and the Braggs, rested on his forehead. Old blood marked where the puncture wounds had welled up and dribbled down his shirt.

"Based on the height of the marks in the fence, we believe he took the arrows to the back while trying to climb. Penetrated all the way through his body. Would've pinned him like a beetle to a corkboard before they removed the arrows."

Lucas scanned the backyard, building a visual tale of Greg Thompson's attempted escape. "He run from the direction of the house?"

"Yes. You can see a pattern of footprints in the grass consistent with the size of his shoes and calculated length of his stride." Lebeau let his tape measure roll up with a snap before gesturing toward the house. "We estimate the shooters were standing there in front of the patio, thirty feet away. Despite the distance, they landed two perfect shots to the sternum."

Lucas whistled. "Whoever's doing this has some seriously good aim."

"'Shooters' plural?" Journey leaned close, examining the wounds. "A three-blade broadhead and a two-blade broadhead?"

That earned her a sharp look from Lebeau. "We think so. Based on Dr. Simon's autopsy of the Reavers." He joined them and crouched, pointing at one of Greg's wounds. "You can see the triple-blade marks on this one. But the other," he shifted his gloved fingers to hover above the hole right next to the first, "only has two marks."

"So." Lucas drummed his fingers on his thigh, wishing anything new had come to light. "Possibly two shooters, or possibly one shooter with different arrows. Still."

"Yeah." Lebeau clambered back to his feet, massaging his knees. "But at least multiple perps, even if there's still the question of who took the shots. The footprints appear to match those found at the other two scenes."

At least that was something.

"Any word on time of death?" Journey stood and scanned the yard.

"Still being determined, but the M.E.'s best guess is between eight and nine p.m. last night."

"That would line up with the time of the texts from his friend."

Also scanning the yard, Lucas considered the distance from where they stood to the flag marking the footprints next to the patio. "I can't get over those shots. The skill it must've taken."

When Journey glanced at him, he suspected she was thinking the same thing he was. A first-place, trophy-worthy shot.

After examining the rest of the yard, they returned, as promised, to Michelle in the kitchen.

"Hey." Journey nudged her. "We're back."

"Good. Take a look at what the perpetrators left us."

There, across the gold-speckled linoleum countertop, a large swatch of dark powder spilled across the widest stretch in the shapes of letters.

Game over.

20

"They wrote this message in what I suspect is gunpowder. In fact, judging from the smell and texture, it might be a homemade variety. Juiced up and extra explosive." Michelle motioned from left to right with a finger, then pointed at a smaller image sketched into the pile. "And they drew a hunting arrow."

Journey leaned in for a better look. "That's new. And why did they leave it at this scene?"

"Okay." Lucas straightened, then moved back a few steps, as if giving himself some distance to think. "Just for argument's sake, let's assume the same perpetrators were involved in the murder of Antonio White, the two Braggs, the three Reavers, and now Greg Thompson. That's four attacks in two months, three of which happened within the past two weeks. And now, presumably, a threat of explosion? Why the sudden escalation? And why the change of M.O.?"

Journey paused to consider. "If our timeline works, then Antonio White is the first victim. Maybe they didn't intend to kill him. A B and E would make the most sense."

"And there's a history of B and Es in the area around the time of White's death."

"So maybe their breaking and entering was interrupted, and White confronted them. Then got an arrow to the neck. And they got a taste for death."

"But why gunpowder now? That's associated with guns, almost the antithesis of archery."

"Maybe they've become dissatisfied with the number of people they're able to kill with one attack." Journey shrugged. Though she was throwing out theories, they all seemed connected by such thin threads. "An explosion, assuming that's what the powder represents, would accomplish that."

Lucas grunted, albeit agreeably. "Could be they're still looking for their signature. Or if it's a group, maybe one of them came up with what they thought was a bright new idea. Leaving messages."

Journey hooked a thumb toward the counter. "With gunpowder?"

"Nah." Another special agent with a graying goatee and spiky hair walked into their conversation. "Gunpowder wouldn't send a strong enough message to imply blowing people up."

"You're just the man we need." Lucas sounded relieved to see Kurt Booker from the Pittsburgh field office's Behavioral Analysis Unit, though Journey had to wonder who'd requested his presence, since neither she nor Lucas had. "I'm sorry to say."

"Really?" Booker laughed. "People usually hate it when I show up, because it means some seriously disturbing shit has gone down."

When Kurt Booker had consulted briefly on their recent West Virginia case, he'd impressed Journey with his ability to connect seemingly unrelated behaviors.

Michelle, however, rolled her eyes. "Hooray. Someone

who's expert enough on gunpowder to judge its potency without the hassle of testing."

Uh-oh.

"Not an expert." Booker's smile didn't fade. "But I've encountered the use of gunpowder in a number of cases. And if, as you said, this stuff has been super-juiced, it would align with the profile I've been developing for your unsubs."

"What have you come up with?" Lucas moved into the space between Michelle and Booker.

"I suspect we're being toyed with." Booker pointed at the counter. "The way I look at the message, I'm drawn to the fact that they kept it vague. If they really wanted us to understand their message, they would've made sure we had sufficient information to do so. *Game over*, however, is nebulous. I'd even call it an indication of reckless arrogance because, to me, it screams, 'We want to make you dance.'"

Reckless arrogance. Journey immediately recalled Walter Albright's smug face.

"Think about it." Booker gestured toward the counter. "What can investigators do with that message, really? Nothing."

Journey had to agree with him on that. They could test the powder, investigate Thompson's murder, analyze the scene…but this message could mean so many things, it might as well mean nothing. "We'd be running around in circles."

"I got a little bit of the same vibe at the Reavers' house." Lucas threw an apologetic glance toward Michelle. "Like they trashed the house after the kills to throw us off. But when you said earlier that gunpowder didn't send a strong enough message, what did you mean?"

"It's too easy to acquire. Makes them look less than serious." Booker shrugged, then fished around in his pockets, pulling out a receipt and examining it before folding a crease down the middle. "In fact, I've been tossing around a theory that these could be teenagers." He dipped the paper into the edge of the pile, scooping up a tiny speck of powder. "Teenagers who want to give us the impression that they're older."

"What?" An earlier theory came back to her. The time of death for the Reaver and the Bragg deaths were both around "bedtime." Perhaps their unsubs had a curfew.

"Sounds counterintuitive, I know." Booker smiled. "The crimes seem calculated. And yet, examined together, they're rather unsophisticated. The unsubs have made several big moves just days apart. That suggests impulsivity, which is often characteristic of young people."

Michelle pointed at the sample of powder in Booker's hand. "What're you doing with that?"

"Testing." Booker grinned. "Follow me." He turned toward the front door.

"Wait, what?" Michelle grabbed for him, but he skirted her grasp. "Tell me you're not gonna do what I think you're gonna do!"

Booker marched on as the three of them followed.

Though Journey and Lucas stopped to drop their booties in the entryway, Michelle plowed after him onto the front stoop, bunny suit squeaking. "You have no idea what you're holding in your hand. Or what it may do when it combusts!"

Booker marched to the far corner of the front yard, a few feet away from the curb. "Clear the scene, please!"

"Wait!" Lucas pointed at the PBP officers, who looked at Journey and Lucas for explanation. "Any news crews around?"

"No, sir."

Michelle, meanwhile, stayed on Booker's heels. "I'm telling you—"

Booker turned abruptly, holding a hand out. "Back up."

"Or what?"

"Or you might get hurt." He carefully placed the receipt and black powder on the grass.

Michelle stopped in her tracks. "I am strongly advising you to rethink this plan."

Booker backed up about three feet. "Your concerns are noted." He raised his voice and looked toward Journey and Lucas. "The two of you? Please note her concerns."

Lucas shook his head. "I'm not a part of this."

Though Journey knew only too well the dangers of being irresponsible with fires—she'd lost her parents because of it—the impromptu demonstration might just tell them something.

Booker returned his attention to Michelle. "Back up, please." He pulled a matchbook from his pocket, lit one, and used it to light the rest of the pack. When Michelle didn't move an inch, he flashed her another warning glance, then hollered, "Incoming!" and tossed the ball of fire on top of the gunpowder.

Michelle stumbled back, covering her head as the yard exploded. Clumps of dirt blew skyward, coating her bunny suit as they fell.

"Holy shit." Lucas shook his head, as if trying to clear his ears. "That's gonna wake the neighbors."

An acrid smell entered Journey's nostrils and settled on her tongue. She tried to swallow it away.

Meanwhile, the PBP officers began applauding.

Booker took a bow but looked genuinely shocked. "Gotta be perfectly honest, guys. That was more powerful than I expected."

Journey stared at him for a second. Did he…? She pointed at her own eyebrow. "Um, Kurt? I think you…" She motioned, as if wiping the hair from her face. "I think you lost part of an eyebrow, dude."

He gingerly dabbed at the bare spot. "Oh, Jesus, you're right."

Journey caught Lucas's eye. "That was so stupid."

"No kidding, right?"

"What the hell!" Michelle shouted. "Do you know how reckless that was?"

"Are you okay?" Journey jogged over to her sister.

Meanwhile, Michelle stormed toward Booker, who'd turned to make his way back to the site of the explosion. "Talk about underdeveloped brains!"

Booker ignored Michelle's distress, choosing instead to lean over and examine the hole in the ground. "That's at least eight inches deep."

"You are a *lunatic*!" Michelle stomped her foot. Her fist clenched at her side, as if she were tempted to slug him. "A professional lunatic!" She stomped one last time, then stormed off down the street, but not before raising her special finger in the air. "Brain damaged, compulsive, and juvenile!"

Journey waited for her sister to leave before joining Booker at the hole. "You've got to be way more careful."

"Oh, really?" He sounded skeptical.

"Yes, really. Now I've got to go see if she's okay."

As she stepped away, Lucas shook Booker's hand, grinning like a fool. "You're an idiot. But you're welcome at my crime scenes anytime."

When Journey caught up to Michelle stomping down the middle of the quiet street, her sister pointed an accusatory finger. "Do not try to rationalize that stunt to me."

Journey raised her hands in surrender. "I wouldn't. That was reckless and unnecessary."

Michelle waited a second, testing her resolve. When Journey didn't argue, she blew out an exasperated breath. "Don't ever include me in that kind of stunt again!"

The way Journey saw it, Michelle had taken part entirely of her own accord. But she kept that opinion to herself. "Pinky swear."

After one last, exasperated sigh, Michelle began peeling off the dirty bunny suit. "What's next for you and Lucas?"

Journey hooked a thumb back toward the front yard and the car. "We're heading back to Walter Albright's to see where he was between eight and nine last night. And then on back to the archery range."

The accuracy of those kill shots had her thinking about a certain first-place archery trophy.

21

Lucas convinced Journey to drive so he could process what they'd learned at Greg Thompson's house. Booker's explosive experiment had been entertaining and supplied potential insight into the killers they were searching for, but he needed to think more about Booker's suggestion of adolescent rather than adult suspects.

"Hey, Ace." Midmorning sunlight glinted off the gold ace of spades necklace he'd caught Journey fiddling with more than once. He felt the nickname suited her. "What did you think of Booker's theory about teenagers?"

She grunted. "I can see where he's coming from, but I just don't see kids having access to the kind of money they'd need. Nor would they have the time to develop the necessary skill to execute such precise shots."

"I don't know. Plenty of minors have access to mommy and daddy's credit cards. And plenty of parents are too checked out to pay attention to what's being bought. They just pay the bills." Lucas had seen a lot of that during his decade in White Collar, including sums that made him, for the most part, physically ill.

"Guess so." Journey drummed her thumbs on the steering wheel. "But remember, Jed Durham at the shop said one guy always paid for the others. That's triple the spend."

"Except that one guy was Walter Albright."

"Right." Journey put on her blinker at the next turn. "I guess they could have a rich mom or dad's credit card to play with."

When they pulled up to Albright's home a few minutes later, they could see from the street that someone was inside. Someone tall and broad like him was talking to Albright in front of the bay window, although his visitor had his back turned so that Lucas couldn't get a good look at him.

"I'll start the conversation." Journey unclipped her seat belt. "He seemed more cooperative with me yesterday."

"I'll follow your lead." Lucas nodded and stepped out of the car.

Walter must've spotted them because Journey had barely rung the doorbell when he answered.

"Ah, if it isn't my favorite feral pigs again." His grin was wide with nothing friendly about it. "Sorry. I meant to say federal."

"A comedian, I see." Journey broadened her stance, hands on her hips.

"No. I just pride myself on being a warm host."

Their self-proclaimed warm host did not, however, welcome them inside.

"What can I do for the two of you today?" Walter met Journey's and then Lucas's eyes, his toothy grin never wavering.

"You home alone?" Lucas shifted to glance over Walter's shoulder, but whoever he'd been speaking to at the window didn't appear in the entryway at his back.

"Who I invite into my house is none of your business."

Though his wide smile remained, Walter's gaze darkened. "Now tell me, why are you here?"

As Journey pulled out her notebook, Lucas stepped back to give the surrounding area a glance. To his relief, no one was sneaking up on them from around the house.

"Curious about your whereabouts last night, Mr. Albright. What were you doing around eight or nine o'clock?"

"Walter, please." He *tsk*ed and wagged a finger at Journey. "I would hope that since you're trying to frame me for murder, we'd at least be on a first-name basis."

"Walter." Journey wrote the name in her notebook with a flourish and held it up for him to see. "Did I spell that right? I'm just a simple federal agent, so I have to check my work."

Albright smirked. "What lovely handwriting you have."

This wasn't going as smoothly as yesterday's conversation, and that had hardly been a tea party.

Lucas eyed his partner, trying to guess her next move.

"Phew!" She slapped the notebook shut and stuffed it back into her pocket. "Hard to believe I graduated from Yale."

"You?" Walter raised an eyebrow as if he didn't believe her.

"Boola boola."

If that was the Yale fight song, Lucas was gonna give her some serious shit once they got back in the car.

Walter puffed his chest like the defensive posture of a gorilla. "I'm a Fordham man myself."

"I'm sorry to hear that." Journey's tone had switched to a disinterested monotone.

"And now you're standing on my doorstep insulting me." Albright's bravado deflated slightly. "Get on with your questions and go."

"But we already asked you a question, Fordham man."

Journey grabbed her notebook again and waved it. "Where were you last night between eight and nine?"

"As it is apparently so important a question, I'll tell you." He sighed. "I was at the Lodge with Bill."

Journey cocked her head. "You'll tell us that you were at the Lodge? Or were you actually there?"

"I was there." Walter's eyes bugged out as if he were on the verge of blowing a gasket, but he opened his phone and flashed it at them. "See? Time stamped photos."

Lucas leaned in for a look. It was the Lodge, all right. He recognized the back room immediately.

Walter flipped through several more pictures, which grew increasingly blurry. He and Wheeler were arm in arm, apparently singing or something like that.

Journey gave the images an unimpressed glance. "That's a lot of selfies."

"What can I say? That place brings out my inner teenager." Walter fished into his shirt pocket and withdrew a slip of paper. "My receipt. Check the time and date."

Lucas took the paper and gave it a quick once-over. Walter had paid his bill last night at eleven forty-two. A whopping four hundred and ninety-seven dollars. "The date's correct, but the time stamp seems pretty late. You could have arrived at ten or eleven."

"I just showed you the time stamps on my photos!" Albright's face reddened.

One advantage of having grown up with a lying, cheating, bully of a father was that Lucas didn't take anyone at their word. Not even at the word of their time stamped photos and receipts. His father's ability to talk his way out of nearly anything—like the time his dad talked his way out of a DUI by claiming he was in the early stages of Parkinson's—had etched deep skepticism into Lucas's bones.

"Tell me, Walter…" Lucas paused, using silence to

demand the man's attention. "Why so adamant about documenting your evening? Seems like a copious number of selfies for two middle-aged men, and you were awfully eager to show them to us. Especially considering you offered nothing of the sort yesterday when we asked you about your whereabouts during the previous crimes."

"Who do you think I called immediately after you left yesterday? My lawyer!" Albright blustered. "And I supplied him with ample evidence that the two of you are trying to blame me for murder."

"Uh-huh…" Lucas waited. *Never, ever fill in the details for the denier.* His childhood had taught him that too.

"My lawyer's advice was to document my activities to protect myself." He held up his phone again. "Want to smile for the camera?"

Lucas ignored the *snap snap snap* of Albright's phone.

"I'm just curious. Have you taken a photo of yourself at home today?"

Walter frowned and lowered his phone.

Lucas fought the urge to laugh. "I ask because yesterday, you told us you were at home during each of the time periods when the other murders took place. But then you didn't have any way of proving it."

"And?" The word came out as a growl.

"And I'd expect that if you're so convinced we're trying to frame you, you'd want to document your location at all times. When you wake up, when you wander out into the yard, when you go to bed. Instead, you've only documented last night." Again, Lucas paused for effect. "A very specific period of time in which a murder took place."

"Now, look here!" Albright stepped back and grabbed the door handle. "I've had enough of this. If you want to ask me any more questions, you'll have to go through my lawyer."

"Hang on." Journey stuck the toe of her boot on the

threshold just in case he tried to slam the door shut in their faces. "I have one last question, and I promise it isn't about you."

Albright studied her but made no move to close the door.

"The archery competition. Who else competed?"

Walter huffed and waved her off. "That's information you can easily get from the organizers."

"Yes. We have it. Only, that's just a list of names. We want to know your impressions. What did you think of the other teams?"

At this, Walter brightened some.

Lucas was impressed by his partner's ability to twist the conversation with such precision. Suddenly, the blustering Walter Albright looked pensive. He was being asked for his opinion, and Journey had accurately touched on the one thing an egotistical man couldn't resist…giving his authoritative thoughts on a matter.

"I thought the level of skill among my competitors was remarkable." He released his grip on the door and smoothed the front of his shirt. "The Allegheny County event has become one of the most competitive in the United States."

"That's what Mark Forester said." Lucas nodded.

"Yes, well, Mark's done quite an impressive job of developing the club." Albright smirked. "For years, it was little more than a field. Now it's getting the upgrades needed to turn it into the elite range it ought to be."

Lucas wondered if some of Albright's money lay behind those improvements.

"Any conflicts you were aware of?" Journey kept the conversation on track. "Between teams?"

Albright stiffened. "None that I can think of. General rivalries, certainly. It's a competition, after all. But nothing notable."

"Any youth competition?" Journey pivoted, and Lucas

knew where she was going with this. "I mean, apologies, but I don't know the hierarchy of the sport. In baseball, for example, there are the youth leagues, the minors, and then the majors. Anything similar in archery?"

"No. It's every archer for himself. Individual points become team points." He stopped and shook his head in frustration. "That's how we lost the previous year's competition. A bad round for one of your members can sink the team's chances."

Journey jotted a note in her notebook. "So feasibly, teenagers could compete against adults?"

"Absolutely. It's difficult, of course, for a kid to qualify. But as the sport grows, so does the diversity of talent. In fact, the team who took second place this year was a younger one. They looked like kids, but I saw that the team captain drove a brand-new Porsche. I think one of their names was Travis something. He was really tall."

"Wow."

"Exactly. But, like all overprivileged pricks, their sportsmanship needs a bit of fine-tuning. Money can buy everything from fancy coaches to the best gear, but it can't buy good manners or common courtesy."

Lucas stifled a laugh. That was quite the statement from a man, who, according to Mark Forester, was a poor loser.

"Pardon my language." Albright looked directly at Journey. "Let me rephrase my statement. Those boys are arrogant and obnoxious, but there's no denying their talent."

22

Leaving Walter Albright's house, Journey took the wheel again. "I'm going to drive out of the neighborhood and then find an empty lot. We can make some calls and check out what Albright just told us."

Lucas let out a breath. "Good plan."

A few miles down the road, Journey pulled into a deserted strip mall and drove around the back of the building. Chances were slim that Albright would get in his car to follow them. Even so, a bit of cover was always better than working exposed.

Journey slid the manila folder holding the archery club lists out of her bag. "I'll look over the list of contest participants. You call the Lodge to check out Albright's story."

Lucas nodded and pulled out his phone. Journey began to skim names.

In the previous year, the team that took first included Walter Albright, Harold Cubbins, Carson Steele, and Bill Wheeler. This, they knew.

Second place included Travis Butler, Gene Bannon, Joel O'Halloran, and Scott Whitman.

Journey had the names of the "overprivileged pricks" Albright told them about. Coming from him, that comment left her mighty curious.

Lucas dropped his phone into his lap. "Albright's story checks out. The server we spoke to yesterday confirmed Albright and Wheeler were there all evening. Even left her a hundred-dollar tip."

"You don't think that was hush money, do you? To maintain a cover story?"

"It's possible. But the receipt Albright flashed earlier totaled nearly five hundred dollars. A twenty percent tip is standard."

Journey whistled. "That's a lot of whiskey."

"Or, judging from what Bill Wheeler said, a little bit of the good stuff."

"Nothing can be that good." She knew she sounded like a miser, but come on. There was no need to spend that much on booze. "I got the names of the younger team, by the way. I'm looking into their backgrounds now."

"I'll help. Give me a few."

Journey opened the windows to let a breeze into the car while she worked. But with the tools on hand, she couldn't pull up much. None of those boys' names showed up on social media, which, of course, was impossible when adolescents were involved. There had to be some record of them somewhere.

With Lucas hovering over her shoulder, Journey continued searching, scouring the internet. No matches. However, Scott Whitman, a seventy-nine-year-old man, came up nearly every time she searched. Travis Butler gave Journey plenty of information on a deceased local man. And when she looked up Gene Bannon, a woman kept getting flagged.

Something was off. But without going back to the office to use the FBI databases, Journey couldn't confirm her suspicion. She tried one last time with Joel O'Halloran. That one showed an arrest record for a man who'd been in prison since 2011.

She locked eyes with Lucas. "Fake names, you suppose?"

He shrugged. "Could be."

"Why would a bunch of teenagers use fake names for a tournament?"

"I'm guessing that's the million-dollar question." His thumbs flew across his phone screen. "I'm giving Keller a heads-up, and I'll see if we can get someone in the office to double-check those names while we're on the road."

"Good idea." She put the car in drive. "Meanwhile, I think we should head back to the archery club. We need to ask Mark Forester a few more questions before we bury ourselves in paperwork. And maybe track down some photos of the event."

23

When she pulled into the archery club parking lot, Journey noted a marked uptick in activity from their visit earlier that morning. With the construction crews stopped for lunch, archers occupied nearly half of the target stations on the outdoor field nearest to the entrance.

Lucas checked his watch. "A little lunchtime target practice, I presume?"

That was how it looked to Journey. "See any teenagers out there?"

"A few, yeah. But most of the archers are prematurely gray and pot-bellied."

She headed for the same space where they'd parked before, driving the perimeter to get a look around. SUVs and trucks filled the lot.

"I was secretly hoping we'd see a car with a parking pass for one of the local high schools, but no such luck." Years earlier, while working a case, Journey spotted a truck bearing a window decal favored by members of a violent paramilitary organization. It was parked at the bar where a key witness worked. That decal went from a red flag to the crucial piece of information that split the investigation wide open.

"It was worth a shot." Lucas shrugged. Then he smiled. "Get it? Shot. Archery?"

"Boo."

Journey parked and stepped outside into the steamy midday heat. The humidity was stifling, like breathing in soup. Thankfully, Forester's trailer would be air-conditioned.

They knocked on the door, but this time, he didn't answer.

Journey shielded her eyes and scanned the surrounding area. Despite the pause in construction, the work had kicked up a lot of sawdust, and it stuck to her clammy face and neck. Much more of this and she'd smell like a lumberyard for the rest of the day. "How about we check out the indoor range? We didn't walk through there earlier, and I'm already overheating."

Lucas was three steps ahead of her. "Me too."

The indoor range reminded Journey of a cross between the Bureau's gun range and a bowling alley—a long row of shooting lanes, each facing a paper target, each of them occupied by an archer. The smell of fresh paint and perspiration hung in the air.

Journey scanned the faces of the archers between shots while they nocked their arrows and fixed their stances. At least half of them were women, and several of them were excellent shots.

Forester, however, was nowhere to be seen.

"Any guesses about where to look for him next?"

"Restroom." Lucas stood at the window, looking out onto the grounds. He pointed toward a quartet of portable toilets about fifty yards away near the construction area.

She grimaced. Mostly because she could only imagine

what they smelled like, standing out there in the heat. "I say we watch the doors from here. Spot him when he exits."

The investigation fairies must have been listening, because a minute later, Forester emerged, straightening his shirt.

Journey hustled outside to catch him, with Lucas following steps behind.

"Afternoon, Mr. Forester." Journey waved. "Sorry to bother you again."

"Mark. What can I help you with?" His face wasn't as ashen as it had been that morning, but his smile was obviously strained. "Did I miss something earlier?"

"First, thank you for your cooperation. The information you provided was helpful. We're back because we have reason to believe a team that competed in last year's event did so while using aliases."

"Who on Earth would do that? Why? What would be the point?" Mark screwed his face in confusion.

Lucas picked up from Journey. "We're not sure yet, though we have our suspicions. Mainly, it may've been an attempt to keep their identities as archers and criminals separate."

"We're hoping you have more information on them." Wishing she'd brought her sunglasses from the car, Journey shaded her eyes from the noonday sun. "Photos or copies of driver's licenses. Anything we might be able to follow up on."

He remained baffled. "Sure. Of course. Let's go have a look at my files."

Journey and Lucas followed Mark toward his office trailer.

"We're hoping to examine your photos from the event too. We presume you take pictures of the teams who placed first through third, at least?"

"Of course." He plopped into his desk chair and woke up

his computer, just as he'd done earlier. "First, second, and third-place teams, obviously. But we take competition and audience shots as well. You know, to show the size of the crowd and the excitement generated."

Mark's mouse went into overdrive, clicking through file indexes, deeper and deeper, folder after folder. It was a marvel he could remember such a complex system.

"Uh, well, this is embarrassing." Mark wiped sweat from his brow with the back of his arm.

Journey might have gotten her hopes up too soon. "Problem?"

"Give me a minute here. It should be here."

Journey caught Lucas's eye. *What's the issue?* Mark had obviously found the competition photos.

Leaning in for a better look, Lucas pointed at the screen. "We've seen this picture." It was the photo of Albright and crew they'd seen on the wall at the Lodge. "They took first place, correct?"

Mark nodded, but he appeared flustered. "But see…" He clicked. "The photos of the top three teams should all be here." Again, he clicked his mouse, but the file directory didn't contain any other photos. "There's no photos of the second-place team. The teens."

Journey leaned in, too, concerned the old man might try to pull a fast one on them. "Does this folder contain all the pictures from last year's event?"

"Yes."

"Do you have them in any other folders or locations?"

"Not to my knowledge." Mark clicked on another file folder and another with increasing frustration.

"Okay, let's just slow down." Journey knelt by his side and settled in. She didn't want to seem ageist, but she knew that computers and the elderly sometimes did not mix. "Take us through every photo, one by one."

Mark obliged.

Image by image, they examined every file. All seventy-plus of them. By the end, Journey's eyes burned from all the squinting.

And yet, he was right. A photo of the second-place team, the one with the teenagers, was missing. There were teenagers in some photos, but they were girls. A few young kids. Some of them looked as if they were in elementary school. Journey hadn't even considered there'd be competitors in that age range.

"I swear they were here." Mark dropped his chin to his palm, frustrated. "I've seen them with my own eyes."

Lucas straightened. "Do you happen to remember how many photos were in the file before? There are seventy-three now."

"More." Mark was emphatic. "I don't know how many, but definitely more."

Journey was beginning to share his frustration. "Could someone on your team have moved them? Your granddaughter, maybe? You said she was working toward taking over the business."

Mark grabbed a walkie-talkie from his belt. "Norma, hon?" The unit bleeped and crackled.

"Yeah?" A woman's voice crackled over the device's speaker.

Mark's face lit up at the sound of her voice. "Any chance you've reorganized or moved the photos from last year's Allegheny County event?"

"No, why?"

"Oh." Forester glanced at Journey, as if worried about saying too much. "I just can't find one I thought I remembered seeing. Must be imagining it."

Norma's voice crackled over the walkie. "Want me to come help you look?"

The line went silent as Mark considered. "No, no. I'll ask Rod."

"Who's Rod?" Lucas asked.

"Our assistant facilities manager. He sometimes prints blowups to hang inside the buildings."

Mark switched channels on his walkie-talkie. "Hey, Rod. I know you had some photos from last year's competition hanging around the clubhouse. Would you mind bringing them over to the trailer real quick? I'm trying to…" He hesitated. "Oh, you know. My old brain is struggling to put a name to a face."

The line bleeped and Rod came on. "Don't you have all those pictures on the computer?"

"Sure do." Mark grunted. "I just, um…"

Journey whispered her suggestion. "Password."

He nodded. "I lost the password to the drive we keep them on."

"Really?" Rod sounded surprised. "Well, I'd love to help you out, but I tossed those prints when we cleared the building out for construction. They were getting pretty beat up. It was time."

The photos they sought had gone missing.

"How about your computer system?" Journey looked the man in the eyes. "How safe are you from hacking?"

He hesitated for a moment but held her gaze. "I think we're well set up. This isn't exactly my area of expertise, though."

"The entire system?" Lucas shook his head as disbelief creased his brow. "In my experience, small businesses have better security on their financial files than anything else."

Mark's jaw clenched, and his face flushed. "I'm afraid that also describes us." He spun toward the keyboard. "But the company who installed our software assured me the system is top-notch. They're the ones who recommended putting additional safeguards on our financial files." He located the name of the security program and showed it to Lucas.

"May I?" He gestured toward the mouse, and Mark slid out of the way. Lucas clicked around for a few seconds, examining the structure of their setup. Then he straightened and pursed his lips. "So the company who sold you this system wasn't lying. You have a decent level of protection. Unfortunately, however, it's not impenetrable. We've seen this software get hacked before."

"But why?" Mark's face scrunched in confusion. "Why would anyone be interested in hacking our little club?"

"*If* that's what's happened." Nothing in their investigation was certain yet. "The good news is we can request the help of FBI Cyber Crimes specialists."

Journey made a note to call Cyber as soon as they left.

"For now, I'd like you to tell us everything you remember about the second-place team."

"Young." Mark didn't hesitate in his description. "No older than high school, I think. Incredible skills. High-end equipment."

"And their physical appearance?" Journey wrote everything he said.

"They were all white. Reasonably athletic, I suppose." He shook his head as if he were trying to loosen the memories. "I'm not sure what else to say. It was months ago. They were just normal-looking teenage boys."

"How about personality or attitude? What do you remember about that?"

"I recall they were competitive. I think I may have mentioned that to you before. They took the competition seriously." He snapped his fingers. "Oh, and I guess we had a bit of an incident. One member of their team physically shoved up against an archer on another team between rounds. I called him on it, but he claimed it was an accident.

Said he wasn't looking where he was walking. I found that hard to believe, but what could I do? The other man was angry but told me to let it go. That he didn't want to get into it with a kid."

"Do you recall who the other person was?" Lucas got up, returning Mark's seat to him.

Mark paused for a moment, rubbing his chin. "Someone on the first-place team, I believe. Both groups had mighty big egos."

Journey wondered why Albright hadn't mentioned any of this to them during their last conversation.

"Did those two teams have a problem with each other, would you say?" Lucas resumed his old seat. "If not physical, then verbal?"

"I suppose you could say that." Mark nodded. "But mostly in their attitudes. That incident was the only issue I'm aware of. And we pay attention because we have to be strict. No carelessness allowed. Not with safety at stake."

For the second time that day, Journey and Lucas thanked him and exited the trailer.

"Ugh, this heat." The humidity stuck Journey's clothes to her skin like glue. She pulled at her shirt, fanning her chest. "I'll drive if you wanna call Tim Cranz, that buddy of yours in Cyber, about the possible hacking."

"Yeah." Lucas slowed his pace for the last several steps to the car. "Our conversation got me thinking, though. If the perpetrators we're looking for are tech savvy enough to hack into a small business, they might shop the dark web too."

The idea hadn't struck Journey yet, but that was an angle worth exploring. "You think that might be where they got the fake IDs for the competition?"

"Maybe. But I was actually thinking about the juiced-up gunpowder."

"Ah. Right. I guess fake IDs are a lot easier to get than munitions."

He clicked open the driver's side door. "Put it this way. If you can buy a kidney on the dark web, you can definitely get your hands on explosives."

24

There were few things better than the exhilarating rush of power, and I couldn't get enough of it. With all the mayhem I'd orchestrated lately, I wasn't just powerful. I'd become the bringer of doom. A living nightmare, the hell master of demon puppets.

My soldiers acted on my command, and our prey fell dead at my feet. Or punctured onto a fence, like a butterfly behind glass, as Greg Thompson was last night. We'd done him after getting back from Aaron's cabin.

I knew what lay on the horizon for me, and it wasn't handcuffs or a courtroom or prison. It was fame. And followers.

The police and the Feds...they were gobbling up the crumbs I'd left, ten steps behind our crew and turning down whatever trail I dictated. Control was mine, and she was a sexy beast.

For the moment, I would kick my feet up and enjoy the hell out of my fifty-dollar cigar.

We were all at the bungalow, the four of us. The others

were amusing themselves in the corner, throwing darts, but not me. As their leader, I was making plans.

Thanks to the snowy owl feathers, I figured the FBI had connected our string of murders. Obviously, these were simple-minded bureaucrats we were dealing with, but I was still willing to grant them the benefit of the doubt.

I wanted them spinning their wheels with that backwater archery club's snowy owl feather logo and its excuse for a competition. I mean, come on. How could they not take the bait? All those competitors to weed through.

Sure, they were all pathetic asshats who considered themselves master archers. They all thumped their chests and behaved like cavemen, but those sorry bastards would never survive a life in the wild, let alone be capable of defending their own lives against attack. They were all talk—soft men who let their expensive equipment inflate their egos well beyond the stretches of reality.

Which gave the police and Feds plenty of people to point the finger at while me and my crew continued our hunts.

This was the rush of a lifetime. A chance to experience the hunt as it was meant to be. To watch a fool beg, to make him run, to hear the delicious *squelch* of arrowhead meeting flesh. And best of all, to drink up the fear in their eyes before the end. "*Why?*" one of them had cried. *"Why are you doing this?"* I hadn't answered because anyone worthy of survival already knew.

The predator hunted because the kill allowed him to live another day. *And only the apex predator will survive.*

Nature designed the mighty and powerful to stomp out the small and useless.

I knew what man's most powerful weapon was—deadly force and the skill to deploy it.

A hunter needed the right tools, of course. Cash could plug leaks and fortify defenses. In my case, it bought top-of-the-line equipment and gear, the time and means to travel and hone our skills, and respect.

Out of excess caution, I'd decided we needed to eliminate any image online that connected any of us with archery. Cracking that rinky-dink archery club's laughable excuse for cyber security hadn't required the brightest of criminal masterminds. And I didn't have to pay for it. Hound was a whiz at CS, and he was as loyal and dedicated as they came.

Aaron had thought that was a good idea. When we first started training at the cabin, it had just been about improving our archery skills. What I hadn't expected was that Aaron was going to open the doors to a new world filled with activists like myself. My kindred spirits.

The Chosen.

Before I'd met him, Connor Leopold had hooked me hard with his most popular lecture on YouTube, *Are they feeding you or starving you?* Aaron showed the video to us of Leopold expounding his theories over a series of apocalyptic images.

Leopold wasn't talking about food. He meant those who controlled us. The government and the ultra-rich tech oligarchs building fortified bunkers in places like New Zealand and Finland and Chilean Patagonia to hunker down after *The Event*.

Those so-called world-changers wore the mask of philanthropy while secretly hoarding the world's most precious resources for themselves. The men who preached the gospel of *one world* were literally stockpiling water, timber, and rare earth metals. Stealing from the rest of the world, they were eager to watch those left kill each other for the ever-diminishing share.

To survive the slow-motion genocide at the hands of the billionaire overlords, true warriors needed to do three things. One, wake up to their schemes. Two, thin the herd so that the truly awakened and committed wouldn't be weighed down by the weak and asleep. And three, prepare for the coming war.

We must be worthy of the fight and powerful enough to survive it.

Before we met, Aaron had told Leopold about our ongoing efforts of thinning the herd. About how I was ridding my community of those who only took. Those who would never rise in the ranks of the deserving.

Considering my background and economic status, it might've come as some surprise to him that I had firsthand experience with these parasites. Every few weeks, I made an appearance at a local food bank. I was there "volunteering." You didn't get into a top university without extracurriculars. The Ivy Leagues wanted to see that you "cared about your fellow man" or some such BS.

And I did care about my fellow man, just not in that fake, phony way colleges wanted someone to care. So while I volunteered, I scoped out my targets—the people who needed to be eliminated. Calling upon Hound's hacking skills once more to break into the food bank's database, I'd gotten the addresses we needed.

Before I actually met Connor Leopold, I truly believed we spoke each other's language, saw ourselves in the other. But, in person, he was just such a pansy.

My concern came from The Chosen's religious bent. Leopold was a Bible-thumping kook, and you didn't have to look further back in history than Waco to know God and the government didn't play well together. Besides that, he himself just wasn't it. He didn't have the raw power I had.

But I still believed The Chosen was an army of true believers. I suspected that with time and the right leadership, there were ways to migrate away from all the higher-power crap. Man was Earth's apex predator, and he couldn't stay focused with some ghost whispering nonsense in his ear.

It was the army I hoped we could soon have at our disposal.

But that problem could wait for another day. For the moment, I had a narrowing window in which to steer my men toward action, as Leopold had made clear. That was around when he told me they had tools that might expedite our work.

"We believe we can help each other. You continue your campaign of extermination while we provide a few tools to make your efforts increasingly fruitful."

At the cabin in the forest, he gave us a demonstration of the gunpowder's power. A few dozen grams of the stuff poured onto the hood of an old John Deere combine and lit with a long fuse.

After the *boom*, the vehicle lay in scraps of steel and rubber across the clearing.

I got hard at the sight of the old military munitions case full of black powder. When we brought it back to Pittsburgh, I noticed a note tucked inside the steel case.

Throwing in an extra pound, gratis. Show us what you can do with it.

I almost rolled my eyes when I read it. All the gunpowder he'd given us was free. But I was pleased by the show of faith.

Leaning into my cushioned chair in the bungalow, I inhaled a deep puff of the cigar into my lungs and then coughed it out. "He wouldn't have given me extra if it weren't the real thing. He wants us to impress him."

Buck was a little skeptical. "How?"

"That's what we need to figure out now, isn't it?"

That was yesterday, and all we'd thought about to do with our "gift" was to use it in a message for our law enforcement toadies. It wasted some of our stash, yeah, but they'd have to test it, and when they did, they'd discover just how much of a threat we'd become.

Here in the bungalow, however, I knew we couldn't waste any more time or product. Our next move had to be a big one. We had to scare the shit out of law enforcement but also prove that my merry band of brothers was worthy of collaboration with the growing army aligned with The Chosen.

I looked over at my crew, still trying to bust each other's asses for a few measly points at the dartboard. "Hey, shitheads. Time to conference."

Hound and Bull tussled with each other as they moseyed, a little bit drunk and their attention spans nearly nonexistent.

Buck, however, came right over and stood by my side. "What have you got in mind, Boss?"

"We all know our next move needs to be huge. To win the full-throated partnership of The Chosen and to show our simple-minded cop friends they don't have any idea how far we'll go in achieving our goals." And here was the trick. I knew exactly where we'd end up, but to ensure my team's full commitment, I needed the three of them to believe it was their plan. "I want to hear your ideas."

Bull was the first to speak. "Let's blow up the Fourth of July parade!"

Hound laughed as if that were the funniest idea he'd ever heard.

It was a shit idea. Terrorists went after parades. We were apex predators. But I knew better than to shut my team down too quickly. Instead, I faked a look of sincere curiosity. "How do you propose we do that?"

"With, you know…" Bull twiddled his thumbs. "The powder."

"Of course." I forced a smile onto my face. Sometimes the guys needed a little more guidance. "But would we smuggle it onto a float? Which one? What are you thinking?"

His face clouded as his enthusiasm dropped from one hundred to zero. "I dunno. We'd just…figure it out."

"Exactly!" Hound slapped Bull on the back. "We'll just figure it out!"

"But isn't that what we're trying to do now?" I couldn't be the one to shoot this idea down. They had to do it themselves.

"Too many complications, guys." Buck shook his head. "For starters, we'd have to figure out how to get a deadly explosive past security, which is bound to be tight."

"Oh, right." Bull's excitement waned by the second.

"I know!" Hound threw his finger in the air. "We pour the powder into balloons and throw them at people."

"You mean like water balloons?" Buck shook his head. "What the hell are you going to ignite it with, dumbass?"

I nodded. "Buck's right. We need a spark or a fuse to initiate the explosion." Then I held up my palm as if I were trying to think. "Maybe before we decide on a method, we should choose a target. Something that's not only vulnerable but matches our goals. Who do we want to take out, and where do they congregate?"

"Obviously, we need to keep targeting society's leeches." Buck crossed his arms, defensive but strong. "Like we've been doing. The people who aren't ever going to provide more to the world than they take."

"So the poor!" Bull sprang to his knees, his enthusiasm returning.

"I like it." I poured intrigue into my tone. "Tell me more."

Buck beamed. "When do they hand out welfare checks every week? There's got to be a line of people waiting somewhere."

Hound spoke up, but unlike the others, his excitement had yet to return. "My grandma was on housing assistance for a long time. They just mailed her vouchers. She didn't have to go anywhere."

I hadn't known about Hound's grandmother, which made me wonder if he was as committed to the cause as he professed to be. Descending from a poor family could warp his thinking.

He'd failed to fire a shot into our latest prey, after all, even though we'd gone out there just for him to get a crack at the experience. When that spineless *just take my car, man* bastard nearly made it over the backyard fence, Buck and I had loosed our arrows simultaneously. Hound's remained nocked to his bow.

So I pressed him. "What would you target, then?"

He studied me like he was debating whether he really belonged here. But like a good soldier, he fell in line. "A homeless shelter. Or…I got it. The food bank!"

"Yeah." I smiled. "You're right. The food bank's perfect." Hound had landed exactly where I'd hoped he would. And I knew just the one to target. "At the one we know, they line up every day at noon. You can see them outside on the sidewalk."

Buck and Bull smiled too.

"Let's put the powder in hand grenade shells," Bull said. "You can order them online."

Buck shook his head. "No. Let's shoot exploding arrowheads. Stick with our brand."

"I like that idea. But if we do it, we'll need larger arrow shafts." I already knew this, obviously. "And we don't have time to wait for shipping. We need to find them ASAP if we're going to move fast enough to impress The Chosen."

"What about Durham's?" Buck, apparently, was already formulating how to bring the exploding arrows idea to life. "Wouldn't they carry the sort of shafts we need?"

"Probably." I smiled, pleased to have brought my plan full

circle, and looked at Bull and Hound. "Are we all in? Make our next big move on the food bank?"

Bull threw a fist in the air. Hound stared, wide-eyed, but nodded.

I thrust my fist into the middle of our circle. "All for one."

Four fists met and four voices rose. "And one for all!"

God, it was just so easy. Less than five minutes, and I'd led them straight to my plan, all the while letting them believe they'd gotten there themselves. If I could accomplish that, maybe I ought to consider taking Leopold out too. An army of hundreds was a far deadlier weapon than a squad of four.

With all I've accomplished with my small team, imagine what I could do with a mass of robotic, single-minded, cult-member soldiers?

The possibilities were endless.

25

Journey pulled the Ford up to the field office shortly before two p.m. She and Lucas had stopped for a quick bite at their favorite deli nearby after both their stomachs had rumbled all the way from the archery range. They'd missed lunch yesterday—Journey wouldn't do so two days in a row for anyone.

Fully refueled, they were ready to work.

Journey held the front door open for Lucas and followed him through. "Where do you want to go first? Check in with Michelle about what she's found since this morning or head straight to Cyber Crimes?"

"Keller's assistant told me she's in a meeting until at least three." Lucas bypassed the elevator and opened the door to the stairwell, a habit Journey knew he'd only picked up after becoming her partner. He'd complained for the first few weeks, then finally surrendered to the stairs.

"Are you just saying that so you only have to climb to the second floor?" Journey elbowed him and sprinted up, two steps at a time.

Lucas dashed past, beating her to the landing by several seconds. "Want to ask me that again, slowpoke?"

"Show off."

They turned toward the forensic unit and found Michelle in her cubicle, hunched over her laptop.

"What's the word, nerd?" Journey tugged on her sister's black ponytail.

"I'm glad you're here." She sat up and rubbed her eyes. "I think I'm on to something."

Lucas pulled over two chairs from empty cubicles nearby, and the two of them sat, ready to hear Michelle's news.

"Since all the forensic information has been processed, I've had the time to take a closer look at recent crimes reported close to at least one of our four scenes. It's got me thinking the perpetrators were working their way up to murder."

"That would make sense." Journey pulled her notebook out of her pocket. "Serial killers rarely start with the main event. They have to get comfortable crossing smaller criminal boundaries first, like cruelty to animals, arson, breaking and entering. That sort of thing."

"Exactly. You can't break into someone's house to kill them if you're not even sure how to get in there. Not that they broke in. In each case, the victim's back door was open. Here, look at this." Michelle slid a few sheets of paper across the desk—a sketch that looked like a scatterplot, one big circle containing a smattering of dots. She pointed at the large dot at the center. "I chose one of our murder scenes and drew a one-mile search radius around it." She pointed at the marks scattered throughout the circle. "All these smaller ones are crimes reported within that radius during the three months prior to the murder."

Lucas picked up the first sheet to examine it. "Why the different colors?"

"I color-coded the incidents. Green is for B and E, blues are vandalism, red is arson."

Journey picked up her own sheet and looked for red, probably on instinct. She and fire had a history. "I don't have any arson on this one."

"I only found a few. One near the first murder…a man reported his car window had been broken, and there was fire damage to his front seat. There was also a small fire lit in an empty storefront." Michelle shuffled through the other two diagrams until she found what she was looking for. "Here. Near the last scene. A dollar store in a strip mall a few blocks away."

Journey took a few seconds to mull over the findings. "We don't know these are all the work of the same perpetrators, though, correct?"

"Correct. I've been looking for similarities, but I'm still trying to see if there are any patterns in the rate, location, or types of crimes."

"Found any?" Lucas dropped his diagram onto the desk.

"Possibly. Mainly in the rates." Michelle shuffled again until she found the diagram of the crimes surrounding the first known murder scene. The one in which Antonio White had his throat ripped. "I was curious about this one, given that it's so far from the other scenes. So I compared it to reports from neighboring communities and found their petty crime rates to be much lower than in White's vicinity."

"But why?" The location of White's murder still didn't make sense to Journey. "It feels like a long shot that the same perpetrators went all that way when the rest of their suspected crimes scenes were located twenty minutes south."

Michelle shook her head. "It's not so much about the location as the timing. The uptick in petty crime happened in the months *leading up to* the death of Antonio White. It's dropped off a cliff since then."

Lucas appeared to be thinking along the same lines because he'd leaned way in. "Like you said, they might've been building up to murder."

"Right. And before the two of you stopped by, I was creating a spreadsheet of the reports, sorted by date and type. So far, most of the easier crimes like vandalism happen early. Then come the B and Es, with the gap between those getting smaller and smaller. The weird thing is, nothing all that important was taken, and there didn't seem to be any apparent purpose for the crimes."

"Huh. Nothing taken, even though they escalate the timeline along with the complexity." Lucas peered at the spreadsheet, but Journey could see from where she sat that he was too far away and Michelle's laptop screen was too small. "Can you send us a copy when you finish?"

"Of course."

Journey sat back and folded her arms while she sorted the new findings in her head. "So we've got an uptick in petty crime in the months leading up to the first murder. The crimes go from easy to complex, then come faster on the heels of the last."

Slowly, Michelle rubbed her eyes. "Right."

Journey scratched her head. "We have reason to believe this is a group committing these crimes. And indications, such as the seeming impulsivity of the crimes, lead to the theory that the criminals are teenagers. But have you ever seen a group of teenagers capable of agreeing where to meet up for food, let alone commit something as organized and complex as murder by hunting bow?"

Lucas smirked. "Speaking as the only person here who was once a teenage boy, I can say from experience that my buddies and I were too hung up on girls and skateboarding to think about much else."

"But if you'd had a ringleader?" Journey gave him a

pointed look. She recalled what life was like when she lived undercover with The Chosen. Even though she was a trained FBI special agent, there were times when what Leopold had said just made *sense*. "Someone charismatic and persuasive?"

"We did have a ringleader, actually." Lucas cocked his head, suddenly reflective. "Gideon. He was the product of divorce and could manipulate his dad into buying him practically anything. As soon as he showed up with a Mad Circle board, we all had to have one. Only, he convinced the rest of us we couldn't handle it, that only he had the skills necessary to manage a board of that caliber."

Michelle rolled her eyes. "Mad Circles were mostly flash. Anyone with feet could've ridden one."

"Exactly. And Gideon was nowhere near the most talented rider among us. But that didn't matter. None of us thought we could handle one because he'd convinced us we couldn't. Wouldn't even let anyone touch it."

"Board fraud." Michelle rolled her eyes again.

Journey grinned. "But that's exactly what I'm talking about. Humans are highly impressionable, especially when we're young. I think we're looking at a group of wannabes here, and if we can catch the leader, the rest of them will crumble."

"I like it." Lucas smiled back at her, just as Journey's phone buzzed in her pocket.

"Hang on." She pulled the device out and answered. "Special Agent Russo here."

On the other end was Jed Durham, owner of Durham's Hunting Supplies. "You told me to call if anything strange or suspicious happened, and, well…"

26

Durham's Hunting Supplies was a sixteen-minute drive from the field office. Journey and Lucas arrived at three thirty to find a *Closed* sign on the front door.

Durham, however, must've been watching for them, because as soon as they jiggled the door handle, he came flying from the other side of the store and let them in. "Sorry. I didn't want to be distracted by customers when you arrived." He left the sign and ushered them away from the front window.

The man was acting a little too agitated, so Journey glanced around the shop, looking for anything that might explain why. "Mr. Durham, have you been threatened?"

"No." Durham pulled out three camp chairs and invited them to sit. "Nothing like that. I just got a bad feeling."

Lucas flipped open his notebook. "Why don't you tell us what happened? Start from the beginning."

"Well, it happened about a half hour ago." Durham took a breath and rubbed his palms against his rugged canvas pants. "A man I'd never seen before walked in. Something about him just looked off."

"Okay. Can you describe him?"

"Yeah." Durham nodded. "He was disheveled, hair needed combing, and he was wearing a long coat even though it's the beginning of June. I worried he was a shoplifter, so I kept a close eye on him. That was when I noticed his sneakers still had the security tag on them. It took me a minute, but finally I realized…he's not a shoplifter, he's homeless."

"Or maybe both." Journey had questioned more than her share of unhoused folks over the years. "Theft becomes a survival skill."

"Well, I wish he would've stolen some soap because he smelled awful." Durham stopped and suddenly looked ashamed. "I'm sorry. That was cruel."

Lucas reviewed his notes. "So when you realized something wasn't right, then what?"

"I tried to get him to leave. It was awkward. I didn't want to come right out and say he couldn't afford anything here, because I didn't want to insult him."

"What did you say to him, then?" Journey braced herself for another awful comment.

"I tried to herd him out the door, mostly. I'm sure I made an excuse." Durham waved his hands in the air. "Closing for lunch. Everybody out. And that was when he pulled out the cash."

"A lot?" That piqued Journey's curiosity.

"A stack of bills about a half-inch thick." Durham showed the height with his fingers. "I should've known better, but the salesperson in me took over, and I simply blurted out, how can I help you?"

Lucas nodded, his eyes on his notebook as he jotted down notes. "And what did he want?"

"Ain't that the million-dollar question?" Durham paused dramatically. "One hundred Day Six carbon fiber arrow shafts."

Journey didn't know enough about archery to understand the importance of those carbon shafts, but it was enough to have Durham seeing dollar signs. She played along. "I take it you don't have many people walking in here with the same request?"

"Not from a man with dirty fingernails, no!" Durham scowled. "They're fifteen dollars apiece."

For the moment, she'd have to take Durham's word for it that this was an unusual order.

"I tried to suggest a less expensive brand, but he flat-out refused. Then he fanned out his stack of cash, and I could see it consisted entirely of crisp one-hundred-dollar bills."

Lucas and Journey exchanged glances.

"I only had fifty to sell." Durham shook his head. "He cleared out my entire stock. Day Six isn't an average brand. They're incredibly strong, so they're typically used for heavier-than-normal heads."

"Can you explain that?" Lucas stopped him. "Do you mean arrowheads?"

Durham nodded. "Yes. The heaviest varieties of arrowheads."

"And what are they used for?"

"Many things." Durham took a breath and scrubbed his hand across his face before answering. "Large game like moose and bear. That's why I stock them. For my large-game hunters. Sometimes they're used for trick archery. But I can count on one hand the number of those sales I've made over the years."

Journey raised an eyebrow. "Trick archery?"

"Oh, you've seen it." Durham nodded. "Especially if you've ever attended a Renaissance fair. Flaming arrowheads that archers use in an attack. Or exploding heads. That type of thing."

"Arrowheads that explode?" Journey kept her face

carefully neutral, but the potential for escalation was increasing exponentially with every word Durham said. "Like hand grenades or something?"

"Yep." Durham chuckled. "Hollow broadheads. They're illegal for hunting in Pennsylvania, so I don't bother selling them, but they're available online. Or other stores might have them. Most of them, you insert a bullet, often a .357. Others, you fill with your munition of choice. Those are much more complex to employ, however. There's a lot of math required to match the weight against the trajectory against the spin."

And again, Journey caught Lucas's eye. Was he thinking about the gunpowder like she was?

Durham suddenly deflated in his chair. "Anyway, that's why I called you. It all just felt wrong. A homeless man with all that cash. The highly specialized arrow shaft, and especially the quantity he requested. But I saw the money and…" He rubbed his eyes. "I went profit blind. I'm ashamed to say it, but it's true."

Neither Journey nor Lucas spoke while he appeared to be gathering his thoughts.

"It wasn't until after the man left that I recognized the potential harm I'd just done. I heard about those families that were murdered. There was a segment on the news last night. Those poor folks shot to death with a hunting bow on their own property. It's a nightmare. And now I may have just sold supplies to whoever's out there killing these people!"

Lucas finished scribbling out a note. "I presume you have a security system in the store? Do you think it might have caught him on camera?"

Durham leaped to his feet. "Crap, I didn't even think of that." He hustled toward the back, Lucas and Journey hot on his heels.

They stopped at a desktop computer in the back room. Durham found the security application and scrolled. "Like I said, I think he was here thirty or forty minutes ago. Aha!" He pointed at the screen. "That's him. See the heavy coat and the messy hair?"

The agents leaned in. The footage was grainy, but at least it was in color.

"Darkish skin," Journey noted. "Age somewhere in his late thirties or forties?"

Durham nodded. "Wide-set eyes. And a chin dimple!"

Lucas took a picture of the paused footage with his phone. "Did you see where he went after leaving the store?"

"Out the front door and to the left." Durham pointed, even though they weren't anywhere near the front entrance. "I didn't follow him. I just wanted him gone and certainly didn't want to risk stirring up any conflict. But I know he headed left down the sidewalk toward the intersection."

Journey turned to Durham. "One last thing. How is business? Are you in any debt?"

Durham's face changed. He looked almost offended. "Debt? No, of course not. Do you want to see my ledger? I can prove it to you."

Journey smiled. "That would be fantastic."

Durham brought up his bank statements on the computer. He'd been telling the truth. His business accounts were firmly in the black.

They thanked him for the information. Before leaving, Journey repeated what she'd asked of him the last time they visited. "Thank you for calling, Mr. Durham. Please do it again if anything else comes up."

27

Journey stepped onto the sidewalk and headed in the direction Durham said the homeless man had gone. She and Lucas went all the way down the block, keeping an eye out and scanning the ground in case he'd dropped anything, like a fifteen-dollar Day Six carbon shaft or a hundred-dollar bill, however unlikely.

After finding nothing, they headed back to the car.

Lucas held out a hand for the keys.

She unlocked the car before tossing the keys to him. "You thinking what I'm thinking?"

"Which part? The fact that a guy wearing stolen shoes walked in with at least fifteen crisp one-hundred-dollar bills wanting a hundred arrows? That Durham actually sold them? Or that the arrows he wanted are strong enough to support mini-hand grenades?"

"All of it. But mostly, the mini-hand grenades." Journey hopped in. "I wonder if our perpetrators are planning to fill the hollow broadheads Durham mentioned with juiced-up gunpowder."

"That would definitely be an escalation, like Kurt Booker suggested."

Once in the car, Lucas pulled up the GPS on his phone. "Hold on to that thought. First, I'm assuming we want to head over to a few spots where unhoused folks are known to camp out?"

Journey nodded and recited the locations she was most aware of. "Under the 376 overpass near Mercy Hospital. There's also the south end of Emerald View Park."

"No. It's gotta be someplace closer. Those are too far to walk, and I doubt our guy's patron gave him a ride, given the smell Durham described." He scratched his head while scrolling the map of the nearby area. "There's that empty strip mall we stopped at yesterday. We might find something there."

"Hit it."

Journey waited for him to figure out their route before getting back to their previous discussion. "All right, let's talk money, because I suspect we may be dealing with some wealthy unsubs. Fifteen dollars for an arrow shaft doesn't seem wildly expensive to a novice like me, but wanting to buy a hundred of them? With cash? Not to mention the prints at the Bragg and Reaver scenes from insanely expensive hunting boots."

"I agree. There's a decent amount of cash funding these crimes." Lucas pulled into the pothole riddled lot. The mall wasn't more than a minute or two away from Durham's shop.

"Not likely for teens to have that kind of money, eh? Maybe we should give Albright and his crew a closer look."

"I'm not sure. You'd be amazed by the amount of money some parents let their kids throw around. I saw it all the time in White Collar."

Journey scanned the area and pointed for Lucas to drive

down the alley. "I think I remember seeing evidence of an encampment at the far end."

There was plenty of garbage in the area behind the stores. Illegally dumped furniture and decaying cardboard boxes.

"Is that a tent?" Journey pointed toward a thick cluster of shrubbery and trees several yards away.

"Unless someone's hung a large red dress in the trees to dry, yeah, I think so."

"There's less risk if we approach on foot." Journey was already unbuckling her seat belt.

After Lucas threw the Ford in park, they walked the last fifty feet.

The closer they drew, the more shelters appeared. As they approached, a woman came into view. She was seated on a low stool beside the red tent with a defiant expression on her face.

"Hello?" Journey took a few small steps forward and introduced herself and Lucas as special agents with the FBI.

"I got permission to be here." The woman glared, not moving from her spot.

"We're not worried about that." Journey raised her hands. "We don't have any issue with your camp here. We're hoping you'll look at a picture. Maybe tell us if you've ever seen the man in it."

"What he done?" The woman smirked, as if hungry for a bit of gossip.

"We're not sure yet." Lucas pulled out his phone and zoomed in on the photo he'd snapped from the security footage. He passed it to Journey, who was close enough to hold the screen up for the woman to see. "Does he look familiar?"

The woman pulled an old pair of glasses from her pocket. One arm had snapped off, so they drooped to the right side of her nose as she peered at the image on Lucas's phone.

"Don't think I've seen him around here." She shook her head. "But we keep our community pretty small on purpose. Less riffraff to deal with that way."

Journey returned the phone to Lucas.

The woman stood and stretched her back. "'Course, he could be one of them up near the old elementary school. The dugouts in the baseball field are good shelter when it rains."

"Which school?" Journey knew of a couple in the area.

"Woodrow Wilson over on Ash." The woman pointed. "I hear they's about to bulldoze the whole area. But there's lots more folk over there for now."

Lucas tapped on his phone a few times and held it up for the woman to see. "Two blocks west and one block north?"

"I don't pay no attention to directions. But that sounds about right." She pointed again.

Journey thanked the woman and turned to leave.

"Hey. You run into a gal named Harriet over there. Tell her I know she didn't just *borrow* my umbrella."

Journey waved as she hurried for the car. "Will do!"

It took them more time to get in and out of the car again than it took to find Woodrow Wilson Elementary. The building was a relic of its mid-century past and falling apart before their eyes. Crumbling brick and cracked windows. A large baseball field sat in the back, beyond the cement playground and its rusty monkey bars.

A line of tents was pitched along the walls of a dilapidated concession stand. Plastic tarps hung from the roofs of the dugouts, shading the inhabitants from the wind, rain, and sun.

Lucas took the lead and headed straight for the home team dugout.

"Hello?" He knocked awkwardly on the tarp.

He waited a second, but no one answered. "No one's home."

"Let's try over there." Journey pointed at the visiting team's dugout.

Lucas knocked again, and this time, he got a response.

A deep and definitely male voice issued from within. "I didn't do nothing."

Lucas introduced himself and Journey. "Sir, we're just here asking a few questions. No one's in trouble."

"Or at least not yet," Journey mumbled to herself.

"Can you please come out?" Lucas took a step back from the edge of the tarp. "We'd like to show you a picture of someone. See if they look familiar."

They heard a groan, and after a few moments, the tarp flap opened to reveal a squat man somewhere in his fifties. "I told you I didn't do nothing."

Lucas held up his phone. "Can you tell us if you recognize this man?"

Unlike the woman living behind the deserted strip mall, this man's answer came without pause. "Yeah."

Journey resisted the urge to dance a celebratory jig.

Lucas continued. "Does he happen to camp here? Can you direct us to where we can find him?"

"What do you want with him? He's not one of the troublemakers. They all took over the concession stand." He pointed in their direction.

"Sir, like I said—"

"Actually," Journey interrupted, shooting her partner an apologetic look, "we believe the man in the photo could've been scammed or taken advantage of."

She didn't know this to be the case, but she knew how highly unusual it was for an unhoused man to have fifteen hundred dollars in his pocket. Someone far less vulnerable than him had provided it, and the money could also have come with attached strings beyond the transaction at Jed Durham's store.

"If, as you say, he's not a troublemaker," Lucas added. "Then I assume you don't want him to get hurt, right?"

"Okay. All right." He raised a hand and hollered across the field. "Hey! Al. C'mere."

The tarp flapped over at the other dugout. For a moment, Journey spotted a male figure, but what little she saw disappeared behind the nylon sheeting.

"Thank you!" Journey called as she hustled back to the home team dugout with Lucas on her heels.

Lucas reached out to slow her down as they approached. "He's already spooked. Let's keep it cool."

When they got there, Journey covered the far end while Lucas took the closer side. "Sir? You're not in danger, and you're not in trouble. We just want to ask you a few questions."

"I shouldn't have done it." This man's voice was even deeper than the first guy's. "He was no good. I should've seen that."

Lucas took a step forward. "Can we ask you about him?" He reached for the tarp and eased it slowly aside. Journey stepped around to his side to peer in with him.

Al squatted like a frightened child in the shadows, his head bowed. "I'm sorry." Dark hair splayed every which way, and his oversize shirt was torn at the sleeves. A black overcoat hung from his hand, the hem dragging on the ground.

Journey lowered into a squat. His eyes were nervous but intelligent. Despite that, as soon as he returned her gaze, she knew. This was the man who'd walked into Jed Durham's shop with a wad of cash. "Can you tell us your name, sir?"

"You already heard it. Al."

"Can you tell us your full name?"

The man's gaze flicked between the two agents. He was

certainly skittish. Journey waited, not wanting to startle him or frighten him into silence. "Al Burczynski."

Journey really hoped she spelled his last name right in her notebook. He was far too sensitive for her to risk requesting a spell check.

Lucas crouched low, like Journey. "Were you at Durham's Hunting Supplies this afternoon?"

Al nodded.

"What brought you there?"

"He paid me three hundred dollars to do it." Al sighed. "Told me it would take five minutes. It seemed too easy to pass up."

Journey opened her notes, ready to capture everything Al could tell them. "Start from the beginning. How did you meet this man?"

"He just showed up here." Al dropped from his crouch and sat on the ground. "I wouldn't normally have even spoken to him in that ski mask, but he cornered me over by the fence."

Lucas glanced at Journey. "The man was wearing a ski mask?"

"Yeah. And I don't have nothing to do with the crazies around here if I can help it. But then he flashed the money and told me what he wanted. I knew if I didn't do it, then one of them over there would." He nodded toward the tents in the outfield.

"Money is always an excellent motivator." Journey nodded as she jotted the information down.

"I haven't eaten anything that didn't come out of a dumpster in a long time. Neither has Scoop over there." Al gestured toward the man they'd just spoken with. "We do our best to take care of each other. There's a few others who come at night, too, and they're worse off than us. I knew the money would go a long way for a long time."

Journey imagined he'd experienced plenty to know that was true. "What did the man in the ski mask ask you to do, specifically?"

"Go to that store, that Durham's. He was quite particular about that part. It had to be that store. And I had to buy one hundred Day Six carbon fiber arrow shafts. He made me say it repeatedly until he was sure I'd remember."

"And he gave you fifteen hundred dollars to buy them with?" Journey kept her prodding gentle.

"Bit more than that, but yeah. That's when he told me again that I could keep three hundred for my troubles." Al nodded, looking a little more animated. "Only now I know he would've probably scammed me out of my share. Those arrows were more expensive than he said. If the guy at the store would've had the full hundred, there wouldn't have been any money left over for me."

This didn't surprise Journey. The most vulnerable never seemed to get a fair shake.

"Can you tell us anything about his appearance?" Lucas prompted. "I know his face was obscured, but what about his clothes or the way he talked?"

"Uppity!" Al scowled. "He talked to me like I was dumb as a dog and he was my owner. I have a master's degree, you know. Just because I'm living here doesn't mean I don't have a brain."

"Of course not." Journey met his gaze, trying to show him she was listening. "What else? Did he have an accent of any sort?"

"Nah." Al shook his head. "But he sounded young."

"How young?" Lucas shifted a little in his crouch.

"Just not old, if you know what I mean." Al shrugged. "No smoker's cough, no roughness to his voice. He called the job our 'collaborative venture' instead of just saying 'job,' like he was trying to sound fancy or educated."

"How tall, would you say?" Journey flipped the page in her notebook and kept writing.

Al looked at Lucas. "Tall. Just about your height."

Lucas seemed to understand. "Six-two or thereabouts?"

"And built." Al patted his bicep. "Muscular arms and chest under his shirt. That fancy brand with the horse and rider logo."

"What color?" Journey jotted *polo shirt* into her notes.

"Dark blue. Red horse."

"Anything else stand out? Scars, maybe? Cologne? Shoes?"

"White sneakers." Al responded without hesitation. "Brown suede swoosh. But his jeans were just jeans. You know, average, I guess."

She'd secretly hoped he'd tell them he was wearing hiking boots. No such luck.

Lucas nodded toward the road. "You see his car?"

"Nope. I think he parked up by the school. That's the direction he headed when we were done. Can't confirm it was him, but soon after we talked, someone roared their engine. If I had to guess, it was a twin-turbocharged flat six."

Journey and Lucas both gaped at him in surprise.

Al grinned. "Told you I had a master's degree. I was a mechanical engineer at Chrysler for almost twenty years."

28

After speaking with Al—and giving him twenty bucks for a meal—Lucas and Journey checked out the fence where their unsub had waylaid him, but the ground there was all asphalt. No point in calling in forensics to check for prints. Back at the field office, they raced up the stairs to the fourth-floor bullpen and headed for their corner of the world.

Megadesk was ready and waiting. On it was the Bragg's case file, which confirmed that both Michael and Rose Bragg worked blue-collar jobs. He was a mechanic, while she was a cashier at a gas station.

Journey shut the file. "So we were right. There seems to be a trend that the perpetrators are targeting blue-collar workers."

Lucas nodded. "Let's get it up on the board.

Journey pulled out a thick stack of sticky notes and a marker from her drawer. At the same time, Lucas rummaged in his file cabinet until he found what they needed—an oversize map of Pittsburgh, folded into a neat square.

He handed her one corner, and together, they taped it

securely to the wall. The city's neighborhoods, intersections, landmarks, and parks looked suddenly large as life.

The locations of the murders went up first. Antonio White, the Bragg family, the Reaver family, Greg Thompson.

Three of the victims' houses formed a semicircle, but White's house was several miles north.

Next, Journey placed the locations of the hunting supply shop and the archery range on the map. The shop fell near the center of the semicircle of murder scenes. But Forest Cove Archery Club was located north and slightly east, beyond the city limits.

Lucas took a step back. "The range is the only location so far that's not in Pittsburgh proper."

"True. But remember, Forester told us they serve all of Allegheny County. Land was probably cheap up there in the eighties when he opened it."

"Probably so." He pointed at the map. "But look at this. We took the Roseland Avenue exit off Highway 19." Finding the exit with his finger, he traced it west. "It meets up with West View Avenue here."

Journey caught on immediately. "Antonio White lived on West View Avenue."

He beamed. "Just a few miles south of the exit for the archery club."

If what he was implying was correct, the perpetrators might have chosen White's house because it was on their route to and from archery practice.

"Nice find." She high-fived her partner. "Okay. Speaking of our perpetrators, after our discussion with Al, I feel comfortable concluding that we're looking for a group of wealthy teenagers."

"Teenagers, yes." Lucas held up a finger. "But we can't assume they're all wealthy."

"True." Journey nodded. "But as a group, they've got a good-sized bankroll."

"People with money often opt out of the public schools. Especially when Pittsburgh public schools are ranked among the lowest in the state. Most parents in the area who can afford to send their kid to private school do. Haven't you ever wondered about all the kids wearing private school uniforms?"

"I will now."

"Really, the state of public education is underrated. Hallie is doing great." Lucas felt a rush of pride. For all his issues with his ex, they were really succeeding as co-parents. "But if our teenage perpetrators are local, chances are high they're at a private prep school. Let's split up and identify everything in the area near our semicircle."

It took a bit of digging, but Journey narrowed the list of possible schools down to a handful. Several of them were religiously affiliated. One school, however, stood out from the others. Mockingbird Academy.

Journey stared at her laptop screen and scrolled. "Their website is like one long list of all the Ivy League schools their graduates attend."

Lucas looked over her shoulder. "Ranked as the best prep school in the state. And it gets better. Tuition is close to forty grand a year."

He turned and stepped over to the murder board, searching for the Mockingbird Academy address on their overgrown map.

His finger landed three blocks away from Durham's Hunting Supplies. "But do they have an archery team?"

"Yep. Found it. They call themselves the Mockingbird Archers."

"Any more information? A participant list or faculty sponsor?"

"Nope. Just the description and a photo."

Returning to her side, Lucas read over her shoulder.

Mockingbird Archers introduce novice students to the use of bow and arrow and provide experienced archers with a safe environment in which to further develop their skills. Mockingbird Archers may also elect to compete in regional competitions.

Above the description was a photo of a group of students in matching athletic outfits with the school colors. All of them held a bow above their heads in a kind of celebratory manner. Lucas didn't recognize any of the faces, but they certainly seemed happy.

That was to be expected, though. No school would post a photo of unhappy students on their site. He wondered if the diversity in the photo represented the actual demographics of the school.

"Give me the main number." Lucas returned to his side of the desk. "I'll call the school. See if someone there can tell us more."

While Journey continued exploring the website, looking for anything useful she might've missed, Lucas made the call. He knew that just because a school had an archery team, didn't mean it held murderers among its ranks.

And even if it did, those kids could've already graduated. Men could keep their teenage features into their twenties. They didn't automatically mature the moment they turned eighteen. So while getting their hands on the previous year's roster might be helpful, it could just as easily lead to nothing.

After speaking with the secretary, Lucas hung up and looked at his partner. "Okay, they put me in touch with the school principal. He said the archery club was formed last year and has been sponsored by the same teacher since its inception. His name is Jason Lansbury."

"It's Friday evening. He won't be teaching."

"No. But I got his home phone number. I'll call ahead."

29

Jason Lansbury lived on the northwestern outskirts of Pittsburgh, twenty minutes from the field office. His house was sizeable, but modest, situated within a newer development targeted at young families. Three or four bedrooms. Decent-sized yard but manageable with a push mower. Cookie-cutter facade. The kind of neighborhood where residents weren't rich, but not visibly struggling paycheck to paycheck either.

He was waiting for them and opened the door to his house before they were halfway up the sidewalk. "Evening." He was lanky and tall, dressed in a golf shirt and cargo pants, dark hair just visible beneath a Pittsburgh Pirates baseball cap.

Journey and Lucas presented their badges and introduced themselves.

When he was satisfied they appeared to be who they said they were, Lansbury ushered them through the door.

The family room was just off the front entrance, and Lansbury directed them to take a seat. "After you called, I asked my wife to take the kids to the pool. We have the house to ourselves for about an hour." His tone was polite with an undertone of concern.

Pulling out her notebook, Journey took one half of the couch, while Lucas took the other. As he'd been the one to contact Lansbury, she let him take the lead.

"Hopefully, this won't take that long." Lucas leaned forward, elbows on his knees. "We're investigating a series of murders in which the weapons used were bows and arrows. Our colleagues in the behavioral unit have developed a possible profile of the killers, and it indicates that the suspects may be a group of teenage archers. Further evidence in our investigation appears to support that theory."

Journey watched the man slump farther into his chair with every word.

"Can you tell us, Mr. Lansbury, about your history at Mockingbird Academy and with the archery team?"

He was silent for a moment before responding. "I just finished my tenth year of teaching there. Biology. Last year, a group of students came to me needing a faculty sponsor for a new archery club, so I agreed to do it."

Lucas followed up with a nod of understanding. "What does that involve?"

"Not much." Lansbury shrugged. "The team captains have to meet with me at the beginning of each season with their membership roster and schedule for the year. I'm also responsible for collecting the dues. If they need funding for something extra, like a new competition, I introduce them at the administration meeting, and they plead their case. Or I can help them coordinate and run a fundraiser."

Journey narrowed her eyes in disbelief. "You don't have a regular hands-on coaching role?"

Lansbury sighed and ran his fingers through his hair. "No. It's student led, and only the school's official sports teams get enough funding for coaches and uniforms."

"Did the academy provide practice grounds?"

"No." Lansbury shook his head. "They had to take that off-site. For insurance reasons. There are a few different regular places. There's a state park about a half-hour from the school with a range. There's also Forest Cove, I think it's called. But that's a private range with a fee. I don't think they ever went there. Again, the club doesn't get much funding, so if they go there, it's not in any official capacity. Members have to pay their own way."

"The academy obviously enrolls many students of wealthy families." Lucas paused, as if planning his next question. "Does that entitlement ever intrude on your authority as a teacher?"

"My friends and family ask me the same question all the time." Lansbury laughed. "Yeah, there are some mighty spoiled students at Mockingbird. When I saw kids turning up in brand new Porsches my first year, I couldn't help but think, *what the hell did I get myself into?*"

He seemed lost in his memories for a second. "With time, though, I learned those kids had many of the same issues as public school kids. Sure, they don't want for material things, and they don't go hungry. But their relationships with their parents are just as rocky, if not more. And their insecurity is often off the charts. They compete over everything…the most exotic vacations, the best SAT scores, acceptance into only a handful of *acceptable* universities."

Journey understood the folly inherent in the belief that anything not Harvard, Yale, Stanford, or MIT was an embarrassment.

"In fact, as soon as I saw these kids for what they were, real kids with genuine concerns, I grew to love being their teacher." Lansbury spoke with sincerity. "Some amazing young people pass through my classroom every year."

Throughout her education, the quality of a teacher had

made all the difference in what Journey took away from her class. More than that, a great teacher could change a person's life. If it weren't for her Criminal Forensics professor at Yale, Journey wasn't sure if she'd have even pursued a career as an FBI agent. But that recommendation plus the niggling suspicion about her family's death had propelled her forward the way nothing else could.

Lucas sat back in his seat, visibly pivoting to his next question. "Let's talk about some of those kids. I told you we have evidence to support the theory our killers are most likely teenagers or just slightly older. Did anyone from the archery club let their insecurity and need to compete take it too far? Maybe become violent?"

"No. Not a one." Lansbury was shaking his head before Lucas could finish the question. "I can't imagine any of them would be capable of murder. Nothing like that has even crossed my mind, ever."

Journey cleared her throat to signal to her partner she wanted to jump in. "Let me ask it this way, then. Was there a member who you may have considered a ringleader? Someone charismatic, a natural leader, a person who others naturally gravitated toward."

"Well, sure." Lansbury scoffed. "Building leadership in its students is one of the academy's core tenets."

"Just take a second." Journey held up her hand. "Think about whether some members stood out from the rest."

The request appeared to make him uncomfortable, and he shifted in his seat, crossing and uncrossing his legs.

"Okay. Yeah. One guy." At last, he sighed. "Chad Brooksby. The kind of kid who looks like he could've walked out of a movie. Handsome. Knows how to charm just about anyone. Skilled socially. Definitely influential among club members. And with girls always on his heels in the hallways. You know the type."

Journey and Lucas nodded.

"I didn't have reason to dislike him. He never tried to pull something over on me. Always polite whenever discussing the Archers. But between you and me, I found him smug, maybe a bit narcissistic. Only, I try hard not to let my personal impressions get in the way of how I treat Academy students."

"Anything you can tell us about his archery skills?"

"Yeah." Lansbury nodded. "Like I said, I didn't go to practices, but I knew Chad and a couple of other club members were competing at a big event over at Forest Cove. It was Chad Brooksby, Brayden Willingham, Jenson Buckley, and Trent Tucker. I went to watch them, of course. Support my team and all. I was shocked, frankly, at their level of skill. The whole team was great. They took second place, and Chad was the best shot of them all."

Journey's brain worked overtime to weave the small details together. "Is he still at Mockingbird?"

"No. Well, he just graduated." Lansbury sat up straight, his eyes clear of the doubt clouding them just seconds before.

"And what about the other boys on that team?"

"They were in the same class. I'm sure you can get their contact information from the school."

Lucas, however, was already sliding his phone from his pocket. Journey watched out of the corner of her eye as he googled *Chad Brooksby*.

30

The Brooksbys lived behind the walls of a gated community. A luxurious fortress of socialites and elites, complete with a guard responsible for checking every car and passenger that tried to enter.

But when Journey flashed her badge as she pulled up to the iron gates, the guard waved them through.

She turned to her partner as she stepped on the gas. "See everything, say nothing. Must be their motto."

"Oh, I'm sure at least one resident has bribed a guard or two for especially juicy gossip."

"Think a visit from the FBI qualifies as juicy?" She was being sarcastic. *Of course it did.*

"Definitely."

At the crest of the hill sat the redbrick Brooksby mansion with four individual chimneys peeking out of a slate-tiled roof. The home looked as if it had been airlifted off a Kentucky horse farm. The kind of farm that bred Derby winners. They even had a lawn jockey.

As she stepped out of the car, Journey sensed eyes peering out at them from every window on the block. Their FBI-issue Ford sedan stood out among the luxury cars parked along the street, and Journey's off-the-rack suit blended in about as well as a Prius at a monster truck rally.

It wasn't as if she hadn't spent a lot of time around wealthy folks—her years at Yale certainly exposed her to the top one percent of the country's most well-off. And she knew that, for some, her Ivy League credentials placed her in that same "elite." During her time in New Haven, however, she'd liked the fancy people she went to school with. She didn't feel she was lesser than her richer peers—she was invited to plenty of swanky parties.

And she didn't mind standing out. After all, she had her special agent's badge. Even if she hadn't earned her pedigree, that was a ticket to just about anywhere.

At the door, Lucas stepped forward and rang the doorbell.

They waited a minute, listening to the pealing of bells echoing inside the mansion.

After no one came, Journey jabbed at the doorbell, then again.

Lucas cast a wary glance round the yard. "Ring again? Fourth time's the charm."

Before her finger could touch the button again, the door opened, and a petite woman with salon-blond hair blinked, taking them in.

"I don't know you." Her expensive clothes hung off her body like rags, and the cut crystal glass in her hand clinked with ice and a liquid that wasn't water. "You're at the wrong house."

Journey took a step back to avoid the vodka fumes emanating from the woman's mouth. "Mrs. Brooksby?"

"Yeah. S'me, Jillian Brooksby." She held her glass up like she was ready to give a toast. "And you are on my property...why?"

"I'm Special Agent Journey Russo, and this is my partner, Special Agent Lucas Sullivan." Journey lifted her badge for Mrs. Brooksby to see. "Is your son Chad home?"

Mrs. Brooksby's eyes narrowed as she leaned forward and glared at Journey's badge. "Why?"

"We'd just like to speak with him." Journey smiled as she put her badge away.

"I don't think he's home." Mrs. Brooksby stood still for a moment before turning away from them, as if ready to close the door. She then paused, not looking back. "But I'll check."

"Thanks, we appreciate it."

Leaving the door ajar, she walked into the cavernous foyer. "Chad!" Her voice seemed to echo into nothingness as she shouted for her son. She turned back and smirked at the agents. "He hates it when I do that." Mrs. Brooksby shouted her son's name up the stairs again, but he didn't appear. "Consuela, our old housekeeper, used to keep an eye out for him. I've been utterly helpless since she left."

"Can you call his cell phone, please?" Journey held her phone up in case Mrs. Brooksby needed a visual clue.

"Hold, please." She laughed at her own joke as she swayed and pulled her phone from her back pocket. "Doop, doop, doop." She made the sound of the buttons as she dialed.

Journey shot Lucas an *is this lady for real?* look. "Ma'am…"

Mrs. Brooksby held the phone up on speaker so the agents could hear for themselves that the call went straight to voicemail. *"This is Chad. Text me."*

Lucas stepped forward. "Sounds like his phone is off. Do you know where else he might be?"

"Oh, he and his dumb-dumb friends are always out doing God knows what." Mrs. Brooksby took a healthy sip from her drink. "Try the country club. They love to run up my husband's tab there."

"Which club?"

Mrs. Brooksby opened her mouth as if about to answer, then shook her head. "No, not until you tell me what you want with him."

Journey tapped her pen on her notebook in feign irritation. "Has Chad ever been in trouble?"

Mrs. Brooksby took a sip of her drink. "No, no, nothing like that. He's a good boy."

Journey narrowed her eyes. "What about his friends? Are they all as good as he is?"

"Well, you know, boys will be boys sometimes."

Journey made a show of scribbling that down in her notebook. "Sure…boys will be boys, great. And do you know where your son is right now?"

At that, Mrs. Brooksby grew flustered. "I, um…at the park maybe?"

"Not the country club?" Journey raised an eyebrow. "So that's a no…mm-*hmmmm*." She scribbled some more in her notebook. "Why not?"

"I don't know! What is all this about?"

Lucas's face was cold as stone. "Mrs. Brooksby, we're investigating some crimes committed by archers, and we would really like to speak with your son Chad."

"Oh, for shit's sake!" Mrs. Brooksby's face drained of color as she stammered out her response. "You don't think Chad was involved, right? You just want to talk to him about bows and arrows."

"Right now, all we're doing is talking. But it would be helpful if you could tell us what club Chad is at."

"Westerfield Country Club." Mrs. Brooksby downed the remainder of her glass.

"Thank you. And just one last thing. What shoe size does your son wear?"

She looked offended. "How the hell would I know that?"

"Just asking, ma'am." Journey pulled her card from her

pocket and handed it to the woman. "Please call us immediately if you hear from your son."

As they turned for the car, Chad's mother stood in the doorway, hollering. "I don't think you realize who you're dealing with. We're the Brooksbys. We're an important family in this community, and Chad is a good boy."

31

Journey pulled through the Westerfield Country Club gates onto a half-circle drive lined with Italian cypress trees. Each one was like a long green finger pointing to the sky. Dusk had not yet fallen, but the day's hot sun had relaxed, casting fading shadows across the expansive estate.

"You ever been out here?" Journey eased the car down the lane, avoiding the golf carts crossing the road as they were heading out toward the rolling bunkers that stretched to the horizon.

"Once. During my White Collar days." Lucas gazed out the passenger's side window, taking in the grounds. "We had a potential witness who was a member. Funny…he didn't like being approached by the FBI in the same clubhouse where he negotiated business deals."

Journey snickered as the entrance of a massive early twentieth-century stone mansion came into view. It featured a covered front porch that could have comfortably seated fifty.

As Journey rounded the half-circle driveway and came to the large porte cochere, a valet in a blue polo shirt and pressed khaki golf shorts descended the steps to take their car.

She rolled down her window. "We're gonna need to park this ourselves. Can you direct me to the lot?"

"The valet team services all members and their guests, ma'am. If you'll just put your vehicle in park—"

"FBI." Journey flashed her badge. "As much as I would like to leave the car, valet parking is not an option in this vehicle. Just point me to the lot, please."

He flushed and directed them to a lot behind the clubhouse. Their car looked like the ugly stepsister among aisles of Mercedes, Porsches, and Land Rovers.

At least it'll be easy to find when we leave.

Journey hopped out, and she and Lucas headed inside and straight for the welcome desk.

A blond receptionist met them with a thousand-watt smile as they approached. "Welcome. Are you here for a tour, or are you being sponsored by a member of the club?" Her ponytail brushed her shoulder with every perky bob of her head as she spoke.

"We're here to speak to one of your members. Chad Brooksby." Journey smiled and held up her badge. "FBI. Special Agents Journey Russo and Lucas Sullivan."

"Oh, um. Of course. I..." The receptionist continued to stammer while anxiously scanning a laminated list of phone numbers she pulled from a drawer. She dialed and turned her back to the agents, cupping the receiver with her hand—though not well enough to muffle her conversation. "Yes, sir...I'm certain...here at the welcome desk..."

Her face looked like a strawberry by the time she hung up and turned around again. "Mr. Winthrop will be right out. Would you like to take a seat while you wait?"

She'd barely finished speaking when a forty-something

man in a white sport coat that emphasized his sun-bronzed skin hustled out of the adjoining dining room.

Lucas extended a hand while pulling the badge from his pocket.

Just seeing it made the man rush forward and bark in a whisper. "What do you think you're doing flashing that around in here? It's bad enough you're standing in the lobby for all to see." He waved at them to follow.

Journey and Lucas exchanged familiar, amused glances. Being greeted by strangers as if they were a turd in the punch bowl was nothing new.

They walked the length of a short hallway and arrived at the man's office. The plaque next to the door read, *Robert Winthrop, President*. The agents each took a seat at a round mahogany table at the center of the room while Winthrop closed the door behind them.

"It ought to be against the law to do what the two of you just did." Winthrop resumed his less-than-friendly reception, not yet choosing to sit. "Parading around a public area, announcing yourselves and flashing your badges. Your mere presence could ruin the club's standing in the community. Though I'm sure that was part of your plan."

Lucas crossed his hands in front of him on the table and leaned forward. "We're sorry if you feel inconvenienced by our presence, Mr. Winthrop."

Winthrop ran a finger around the inside of his shirt collar. "The decency of a heads-up phone call is hardly too much to ask."

Journey opened her notebook and jotted a note about Winthrop's extraordinary concern for the club's reputation.

Lucas met Winthrop's gaze. "While investigating a string of recent murders, we were led here."

"Here." Winthrop's response came as more of an accusation than a question.

"Are you familiar with the Brooksbys? I believe they are members of your club. Mr. Jeffrey and Mrs. Jillian Brooksby."

Color drained from Winthrop's face. "Of course I am."

"Including the Brooksbys' son Chad?"

Journey noticed the tiniest twitch at the corner of Winthrop's eye as he considered his response.

"Chad is here often. Full of piss and vinegar, that one. Good stock." Finally taking a seat at his desk nearby, Winthrop folded his hands on the surface, mirroring Lucas.

Journey watched Winthrop's knuckles turn white as he clenched his fingers tight.

Lucas continued. "What does Chad like to do when he comes? Golf? Swim? Maybe archery?"

"Archery. What would make you say that? Westerfield doesn't have an archery range." Winthrop's eye twitched faster. "Chad doesn't avail himself of our numerous amenities. He comes with a group of friends. They congregate in a bungalow on the property."

Journey imagined something like an upgraded shed, a place to store golf clubs and racquets and whatever gear was required for a day at the country club. "What's the purpose of these bungalows?"

Winthrop's eyes narrowed. "I don't know how residents choose to use the space. Our members value their privacy, and we honor that. I can tell you that each bungalow is equipped with a wet bar, a sitting area, and a bedroom."

"And Chad," Lucas cut in, "and his friends regularly use the same bungalow?"

"That's correct." Winthrop shifted in his seat as he nodded.

"But you aren't aware of, or concerned with, what they do inside?" Journey noted the president's discomfort as she continued to scribble into her notebook.

Color rose to Winthrop's cheeks. He seemed more agitated with this line of questioning. His indignation made Journey's blood boil. This man might be harboring murderers in his club, but all he seemed to care about was that his guests weren't disturbed at the golf club or the spa. What an asshole.

"It's a matter of privacy," Winthrop snapped. "We have rules forbidding illegal activities on our property, and we presume the upstanding members of our club adhere to them, on the honor code. I don't care for your insinuation."

"We're not insinuating anything, Mr. Winthrop." Lucas's calm tone contrasted Winthrop's agitated voice. "But we are eager to learn how Chad and his friends spend their time while on the club's premises."

Journey bit back a smile. She enjoyed watching how Lucas's subtle reminder to Winthrop seemed to sink in. By law, the club could be held liable for activities that took place on the property.

Winthrop's emotions were on full display as he silently went from anger to fear, and after a few moments, he deflated.

With a heavy sigh, he nodded. "Normally, we wouldn't allow members' children free rein over any part of the club, especially a bungalow. I personally made an exception in this case, however. Chad's father is exceedingly generous in his support of the club's capital improvement campaigns and other special projects. His firm also sponsors our big golf event every year."

"Any theories why?"

"The Brooksbys have been members for generations. Families like theirs understand the value our club provides, and they want to see it continue for their progeny. Despite our members' profound wealth, you might be surprised how difficult it is to raise the necessary funds for special projects.

But Jeffrey knows that if someone of his stature kickstarts the campaign, other members will follow. As for his company's sponsorship, I'm sure he sees it as a great image for his firm to be affiliated with Westerfield."

Lucas nodded. "So given Jeffrey's financial generosity, you allow Chad a certain amount of leniency when it comes to club rules."

"I have broad discretion as president to assess each situation and make exceptions." Winthrop flexed his fingers and returned them to his lap. "In that vein, I've allowed the young men to push the boundaries of what is acceptable. The fact of the matter is that we prefer they remain in the bungalow. They've developed a rather unsavory reputation."

"Can you elaborate?" Journey flipped pages and continued to write in her notebook. "Who are they? I'll need the names of the other boys, too, please."

"Chad Brooksby is a member because of his parents. And the other boys…" Winthrop turned to his computer and clicked a few keys on the keyboard. "Brayden Willingham, Jenson Buckley, and Trent Tucker. They all sign the guest list whenever they're on the property with Chad."

"Thank you." Journey found the names in her notebook from the interview with Lansbury earlier. "So please, continue. What did these boys do to earn their unsavory reputation?"

"Annoying the waitstaff," Winthrop grumbled. "Hijacking golf carts and driving them recklessly, taking liquor from the bar, disrupting rounds of golf by wandering out onto the greens. Of course, any damages are simply added to the family's tab."

Journey suspected the list in his head was much longer than the one he recited out loud. He clearly wasn't a Chad Brooksby fan. "Would you be willing to show us the Brooksbys' bungalow, Mr. Winthrop?"

"Please, call me Bob." He sat back as he considered her question. "The rental agreement gives club management the authority to enter the bungalows in circumstances deemed urgent or threatening." He stressed the last word as he looked directly at Journey.

Journey recognized the position Winthrop was in. Members would balk if he appeared to violate their highly coveted privacy. But it appeared he wanted to comply. He just needed a good reason.

"Bob, we understand our request puts you in a delicate position with your members. So let me try to help." She leaned forward, dipping her chin slightly. "Chad and his friends are persons of interest in an active case we're working. If we come back with a search warrant, we'll also have to bring additional agents and possibly even SWAT. But we can potentially avoid the dog and pony show, if say, you as the property owner representative, unlock the bungalow and allow us to discreetly look around."

Understanding filled his eyes, and he slapped both palms down on the mahogany desk before getting to his feet. "I'll drive you there in my cart."

Bob Winthrop might have been prickly, but Journey realized it was probably from years of dealing with entitled elitists.

He drove them to a line of small gray-and-brown stone bungalows behind a grove of trees shielding them from the thirteenth tee. The Brooksbys' was the farthest away, separated from its neighbor by a small sand trap. A narrow metal sign on the door announced the bungalow as St. Andrews Cottage.

Winthrop pulled a band of keys from his pocket, opened the door, and stepped aside to allow them access.

Journey took in the Scottish Highlands decor—leather armchairs, stone fireplace, trophy elk head mounted above the mantel. This was a far cry from the glorified shack she'd pictured earlier. It smelled of smoke. "Is that fresh cigar smoke?"

"I'm hardly surprised." Winthrop sniffed the air and wrinkled his nose. "Private bungalows are one of the only places members are allowed to smoke on the property. But what's that…?"

Winthrop was right. There was another smell. And it was foul. Covering her nose, Journey knocked open a door with her foot. It was a bathroom. And in the toilet bowl was perhaps the largest turd she'd ever seen. "Gross."

Luckily, Lucas appeared to be handling the smell more professionally. He moved toward the wet bar, which consisted of an ivory marble countertop, stainless steel sink, bar shelves, and a narrow wine refrigerator. "When's the last time you recall seeing Chad and his friends here?"

"This afternoon. One of our groundskeepers had to chase them off the eighth hole. Frankly, I thought we might find them in here now."

Journey headed to the opposite side of the room, where two leather chairs and a couch formed a sitting area facing the fireplace. A single sock lay on the carpet. Several empty lowball whisky glasses lined the hearth. Past the fireplace in the corner, a dart board was mounted on the wall, and the plaster and faux wood timbers surrounding it were pocked with holes.

Spotting the damage, Winthrop stiffened.

"Lucas." Journey pointed at the darts clinging to the board as she pulled a pair of latex gloves from her pocket and put them on. "Let's collect these for prints and possible DNA. The drinking glasses on the hearth too."

"What about this?" Lucas's voice gave off a tinge of excitement, enough that she spun around to look at what he'd found.

It was a brown rubber mask lying on the strip of wooden floor beneath the bar counter. It appeared to be a dog, complete with ears, whiskers, and a flat, black nose.

"A dog mask?" Journey hustled over, then looked at Winthrop for an explanation. "Has the club held any sort of costume party recently?"

Winthrop appeared less bothered by the mask than the damage to the wall. He sighed as his gaze swept around the space, surveying the destruction. "No. Not since our annual Black and White affair back in February. It's an elegant masquerade ball, and all the gentlemen wear tuxedos in either black or white." Noticing the rubber mask on the ground, he huffed his disgust. "No one would wear a mask like that to our gala."

Journey and Lucas knelt for a closer look. Mentions by neighbors of a dog running from the Reaver and White scenes briefly sprang to Journey's mind, but this was just a mask. And a rubbery, clownish-looking one at that.

Lucas stood. "I'm calling forensics right now. This whole place needs to be examined."

"Agreed." Journey eased the mask into an evidence bag before standing, her knees cracking as she straightened. She reached for the counter, tempted to stretch her muscles, but caught herself, knowing better than to touch anything even with her gloved hands. "Holy crow. Look at this, Lucas."

Right where she'd have put her fingers, a thin layer of black powder dusted the marble countertop.

He paused while dialing his phone. "You think it might be…?"

With Winthrop in the room, neither one of them said the word *gunpowder*.

"Let's see what forensics can tell us."

32

I paced the old hangout—our spot in the woods behind Mockingbird Academy—lit up with adrenaline and rage. By the time Bull, Hound, and Buck found me, I could've jumped out of my skin.

"Are you sure you weren't followed?" We'd met here plenty of times before I got my hands on the bungalow, but out in the open like this, we risked exposure if people weren't careful. "And you didn't tell anyone where you were headed, right?"

All three swore on their mothers' graves they'd followed my instructions exactly. Buck even doubled down, vouching for everyone. "We came here first thing after we saw your text, but I made sure I didn't have a tail. Switched up our route, watched our six, the whole thing. Here's your burger, by the way." He tossed me a greasy little paper bag.

I swatted it to the ground. "Like I give a fuck about a burger right now."

But I had to admit, the news calmed me down somewhat. Buck was good for his word.

"All right." I scanned the woods for unwelcome company one last time before dropping the bombshell. "So it's confirmed. The Feds found the bungalow."

"Holy shit." Their reactions came in unison.

"Yeah. Thanks to Hound clogging the toilet with another one of his gigantic shits, we had to get out of there to air it out. I had to go back to my car, anyway, to get those new carbon shafts to show you guys. That's when I saw old Leather Face unlocking the door for a couple of nerds in suits."

Hound was always clogging up the toilet, but today was so bad, it was atrocious. I told them to go grab us something to eat while the bungalow was airing out.

I had to roll my eyes. "Little did I know Hound's ass would end up saving ours."

Bull gave Hound a high five. "Nice timing!"

"Feds?" Buck's eyes widened. "You said they were wearing suits."

"Yup. They weren't in there more than a few minutes before they called in a team. And those assholes were wearing suits too. Hazmat suits. Plus, a couple more nerds wearing FBI windbreakers rolled in."

"Shit." Buck dropped his ass onto a nearby stump.

I took a seat on the old log next to him, leaving Bull and Hound with the choice of dirt or dead leaves for their seating pleasure.

Buck leaned forward, covering his face with his hands, and began to rock. "Shit. Shit. Shit."

He was starting to spiral. If I didn't act quick, he'd pull the other two down with him.

"How the hell did they find us?" Bull picked up a rock and threw it deep into the trees. "Seriously, man. We wore the masks, the gloves, took our arrows, everything."

Hound didn't say anything. Just stared at me, eyes blank with panic.

"Listen up." I got stern without getting mean. "The bungalow was a convenience for us. That's all. We keep our bows and shafts at home like we've always done. As far as the parents know, we're the same teenagers we were last summer. Archery by day, hanging out by night."

"But the Feds!" Buck whined through his hands. "Something blew our cover!"

That fact didn't sit with me any easier than it did my crew. But I kept my head cool and my face steady. "The Feds don't have anything on us because they don't know what we're planning next. We're still miles ahead of them."

I decided it was time for the great reveal. Nothing like a surprise to make the world look sunny again. "Wait 'til you see what I brought." I stood and walked behind the tree where I'd stashed the box. The weight of it thrilled me every time I picked it up. Power in pounds.

Setting it on the ground between us, I pulled open the cardboard flaps. "Feast your eyes on these beauties, fellas."

The fifty high-performance shafts I'd paid a homeless animal to buy lay in a gleaming silver line across the top of the pile inside.

"Holy shit, dude." Buck recognized the shafts immediately, picking one of them up to examine. "These are top-of-the-line. These are for the food bank?"

"I'll explain all the details in time." I patted Buck on the shoulder. "Just know that tomorrow we'll make The Chosen stand up and notice how effective our little band of brothers really is. We'll show them how much they need us."

If everything went smoothly, my crew would do more in one afternoon to rid the community of its bloodsuckers and weak links than The Chosen had achieved in its entire history.

After meeting him, I recognized that Connor Leopold was smooth, obviously. And persuasive, and he had a certain amount of charm. But that voice? That fucking ponytail? And what had he really achieved? Once we pulled my plan off, Leopold's blind devotees would see that The Chosen was doing nothing to change the future. At least, not with Connor Leopold at the helm.

I peeled back the layer of shafts and revealed the second surprise underneath—the explosive arrowheads, each filled with Leopold's gunpowder—letting them look through it all for themselves. Buck was speechless. Bull could hardly contain himself, rolling one expletive after another off his tongue.

"I don't know, man…" Hound refused to touch a thing.

He looked terrified enough to run.

I leaned close, eye to eye with him. "You are ready, Hound. With this arsenal, we have the power of a hundred men at our fingertips. Our attack is a ten-minute operation, and its effects will change everything…our standing, our influence. Think of how much we'll accomplish. Tell me you don't want to be a part of that."

Hound stared at the ground, driving a stick into the dirt as if stabbing at his fear.

"You know I'm never sloppy." I softened my approach to reassure him. "You've seen me work and know how exacting my standards are for my crew. And don't forget, you may be our newest member, but I chose you. Which means I don't have any doubts about your abilities. About how strong and deadly and determined you are."

His stick stabbed at the dirt until it snapped. The sound came so suddenly, Hound startled. "I can't. It's too much."

"Too much?" Rage bubbled up my throat, but I disguised it as laughter. "Too much? Think about what I went through to get this arsenal. I walked through homeless camps that smelled like piss and shit, filled with people ready to spread every type of disease my way. Was that too much for me to endure? No. I stayed until I found my mark. The one guy in a hundred capable of doing what I told him. He was nothing but a dirty piece of meat, and I handed him several hundred dollars. Because that was the plan, and I executed it to perfection."

Hound shook his head. "I don't know, man."

I picked up the broken stick and pointed at him. "You want to know my one regret about meeting that homeless dude? That drain on society?"

Hound's mouth hung open. He still didn't look at me.

"That I didn't kill him when he was done."

"Yeah!" Bull punched a fist in the air.

Buck cocked his head. "Why didn't you?"

"Too many people around." I shrugged. "Even though I was wearing a ski mask, there would've been witnesses."

Buck and Bull seemed to understand. They nodded.

Hound still sat there, mouth gaping stupidly.

I kicked his toe. "Hound, the choice is yours. Decide now. You in? Or are you out?"

Bull didn't hesitate. "I'm all in, man. One hundred percent."

Buck nodded. "Me too. You know I'm in."

I locked my gaze on Hound, waiting for his answer. "You're already in deep with us. You were at every one of the killings."

He snapped back to the present. "I haven't killed anyone."

"Like that matters to the Feds? The way I see it, it's either show The Chosen we're worthy of their partnership and protection or spend the rest of your life living like a filthy animal in its cage."

"Prison, dude." Bull laid it out plain, as if Hound didn't

understand. "Think about what happens to guys like us in there."

Hound was silent for a long time. After what felt like a full minute, he nodded. "Okay. Let's do this. Let's blow some shit up."

33

The enemies were closing in, and fast.

Blam!

Lucas zapped them. But he wasn't through yet, not nearly done. He'd probably have hours left in this campaign.

Snap! There was another squadron. *Ker-blam!* Lucas smashed through them.

Phew. That was close.

Suddenly his screen changed. It was Journey calling.

Looks like Candy Crush will have to wait.

He answered the call. "What's going on, partner?"

"Hey, Lucas." Her voice sounded subdued, almost melancholy. This was unlike her. "Good time?"

Lucas surveyed his living room, where he was currently lounging with his feet up on his black leather mid-century modern sofa. A few plastic containers of *tteokbokki*, *gopchang*, and *bimbimbap* lay strewn across his coffee table, beside a half-drunk bottle of Heineken. "Well, you just screwed up my level."

"Oh, I'm sorry. It's no big deal. I'll see you tom—"

Lucas sat upright. "No, no. This is a great time. Literally just playing Candy Crush. What's up?"

There was hesitation on Journey's end of the line. "I wanted to ask you sort of a personal question."

A strange and unpleasant twinge erupted in his chest. "Is everything okay?"

Journey exhaled so loudly into the mic that Lucas had to hold the phone away from his ear for a moment. "Well, it's just that…I've been thinking…"

The bad feeling in his chest only got worse. He recognized this feeling. It meant he was about to get his heart broken, in some form or fashion. "C'mon, spit it out."

Journey coughed, clearing her throat. "After what happened to you in Alaska, about what you saw. You went to therapy, right?"

A wave of relief washed over Lucas, followed immediately by a pulse of concern. "Yeah, of course. Saved my life. That was how I got back to VC, to tell you the truth."

"So it really helped?"

Lucas stood and began to pace. "It really did. I can tell you all about it, if you like. Are you thinking about going?"

Again, there was only heavy breathing on Journey's end of the line. "You know what? It's okay. I'll see you in the morning."

The call ended as abruptly as it had come in.

Lucas stared at the phone in his hand. The Candy Crush screen had replaced the caller screen. But now he was in no mood to keep playing. Those pesky confections would just have to wait for another time.

Troubled by the phone call, he strolled over to his window and looked out. The street outside his town house was quiet and usually was at this time. But behind each of those other windows that looked back at him was a person working through their own issues, as his partner appeared to be doing.

Struck by an idea, he scrolled through his contacts to the letter *M*. It was Michelle's number that he called as he sat back down on the couch.

Her bright voice cut onto the line after the fourth ring. "Hey, Lucas, *¿qué pasa?*"

He rubbed his forehead. "Oh, y'know, not much. Just dominating Candy Crush, as per usual." A wave of embarrassment hit him. "Oh, jeez...I can't believe I just admitted all I do at night is play Candy Crush."

Michelle laughed. "Ummm. I'm so disappointed. I assumed you spent your free time listening to opera and painting elegant watercolors of still lifes...as I do."

Lucas shook his head. "Yeah, not so much." He could hear water splashing on Michelle's line. "Are you at a pool or something?"

She laughed again. How had he never noticed how lovely and silly her laugh was? It was low and guttural, sort of like a cute version of *Beavis and Butthead*. "Actually, if you *must* know, I'm in the bath right now."

Water splashed again. His dad brain turned on. "I hope you're being careful, answering the phone in the bath like that. You could hurt yourself."

"Okay, Mom."

Instantly, Lucas's face heated. *You're such a dork.* Thankfully, there was no way she could see him.

"You ever hear of a little something called Alexa? All I have to do is say, 'accept call,' then my Tori Amos turns off and you're all I can hear."

You're all I can hear. He liked the sound of that.

Were they flirting? This definitely seemed like they were flirting. It wasn't wrong to flirt...or was it? On the one hand, he was single. But on the other, maybe this was crossing some line, what with Michelle being Journey's sister and all.

He thought back to when he saw her walking into the office. She was so smart and funny and just ridiculously good-looking.

An image filled Lucas's mind of Michelle naked in the bath. Her long hair, sopping wet, fanned out over the surface of the water and clinging to her full, soft breasts. The dew on her smiling face, like freckles on her cheeks. The laughter coming out of her gorgeous mouth. For him—

"Lucas, buddy. You there?"

He shook his head, and the image went away. "Yep, sorry."

A hot feeling of shame burst up his spine. *Get it out of your head, Sullivan. Nobody in the history of romance has ever called the object of their affection "buddy."*

"Okay, weirdo." He could tell she was smiling, even over the phone. "So what's up? Not that I mind just chit-chatting. But I do have some sweet tunes to get back to."

Lucas remembered why he was calling in the first place. "Oh, yeah. Have you chatted with your sister?"

Michelle snorted. "Like, ever? Yeah."

"No, I just…I just spoke to her tonight. She seemed a little out of sorts."

Once more, Lucas could hear the water splashing in the background. This time, it had none of the previous effect. Rather, it sounded like Michelle was sitting up.

"About therapy?"

Lucas wasn't sure if he wanted to betray his partner's confidence. But then again, if he couldn't express his concern about Journey to Michelle, then there was no one he could express it to. "Exactly."

Suddenly, she spoke to him like they were at a crime scene. All business. "It's all good, Lucas. I spoke to her tonight, too. I think she's opening up to the idea, which I'm all in favor of, by the way. She's just taking proactive steps, being responsible for her health. That sort of thing."

Relieved, Lucas let his head fall back against the sofa cushion. "Okay, wonderful. Good to hear."

Michelle's voice softened. "But you're sweet for asking."

There was that burning in his face again. "Stop."

"No, you." She snorted. "Good night!"

Once again, Lucas was left with the dead phone in his hand, but this time also with a pleasant pounding in his heart.

What was it with those sisters and not saying proper goodbyes?

34

Journey and Lucas stood in the hallway outside the forensic analysis lab, waiting for Michelle's results on the powder residue she'd collected at the Brooksby bungalow. It was seven thirty in the morning, and Journey was feeling the temporary sugar rush from her vending machine breakfast. She'd had coffee and Peanut M&Ms, plus a stick of fruit leather to lessen her guilt. At least she could tell herself she'd tried to have a serving of fruit.

Lucas was pacing, arms swinging, eyes to the ceiling.

"You okay, partner?"

He changed direction. "I'm trying to keep myself ready."

Late nights and early mornings were common. Investigations didn't follow a nine-to-five schedule. But they did eventually take a toll on the body and mind. This case had been full speed ahead since the discovery of the Reaver murders three days ago. And with perpetrators in possession of a supply of explosives and the means to use them, there was no slowing down until Journey and Lucas caught them.

Journey leaned over, trying to stretch her knotted up back muscles. A spot between her shoulder blades tended to hold her tension, and over time, that tightness always ended up wrapping itself around her spine, all the way down to her tailbone.

She was standing folded over in a forward bend, face at her ankles, when Michelle emerged from the lab with news.

Journey straightened up so fast her head swam. "Is it a match with the gunpowder found at the Thompson scene?"

Michelle nodded. "I'd like to know how the hell these kids managed to get their hands on this stuff. And how they haven't blown themselves sky-high while handling it."

Lucas stopped pacing to join the conversation. "We suspect they may have sourced it on the dark web. We've been in touch with Cyber."

"This is powerful stuff, and whoever mixed it knows what they're doing." Michelle pulled off her hairnet and ran her fingers down her scalp. "Journey, you know me. I don't use hyperbole. You have to stop these guys before something catastrophic happens."

Journey thanked her sister for the quick results and pulled out her phone to call Keller and update her on the recent developments in the case.

"Keller here." When she answered on the second ring, Journey put the phone on speaker. "What's up, Russo?"

"We found traces of highly explosive gunpowder in a bungalow at Westerfield Country Club used by the four individuals who we believe may be responsible for the Reaver, Bragg, and Thompson murders."

"Is it a match with the powder found in Thompson's kitchen?"

"Exact. Michelle just confirmed it."

"Any DNA or fingerprints?"

Journey began pacing, with Lucas attempting to keep up. "We're waiting on rush testing of items found in the bungalow. A dog mask was discarded there, and that's being tested as well." She stopped in her tracks. "And there's this. Witnesses from two different murder scenes reported seeing a dog running from the homes. It's still just a theory, but due to varying cognitive impairment by those witnesses, we think they may have actually seen one of the perpetrators fleeing wearing the mask we found."

Lucas chimed in over Journey's shoulder. "The president of the country club told us Chad Brooksby, Brayden Willingham, Jenson Buckley, and Trent Tucker were on the property yesterday afternoon. Their signatures were logged in the guest registry at three, specifically for the bungalow."

"What do you mean, 'for the bungalow?'"

"Well, all guests not only have to sign in, they have to specify what they're doing at the club. And get this, all four boys were also previous members of the Mockingbird Academy Archery Club."

"That'll do it." Keyboard clacking started on Keller's end. "We need to bring them in for questioning. I'll get a BOLO out while we confirm the DNA. We've got to make their photos public. If anyone has seen these boys, we need to know that ASAP." More keyboard clacking. "And I'll work on getting a warrant, based on the gunpowder and feathers and Al Burczynski's witness statement."

"Yes, ma'am." Journey nodded. "I suspect these guys might be lying low. When forensics gets to a scene, they don't really keep a low profile. Anyone at the club would have seen the activity. So let's assume word got back to them."

Lucas shooed Journey in the direction of the stairwell. "We're going to talk to the suspects' families. See if anyone will tell us where these guys are."

"Perfect. Go." Keller hung up.

35

The Brooksby residence was the first on their list, and Lucas pulled up to the house shortly after eight thirty. He pointed at a green Jaguar in the driveway. "That wasn't here yesterday, was it?"

"Nope. And something tells me it's not the gardener's."

They approached the front door and rang the bell. The same melodious chimes echoed in the hall, but this time, they only had to ring once. A sharp-nosed man in a tailored navy suit greeted them alongside Chad's mother, the woman they'd met yesterday.

Lucas took the lead. "Mrs. Brooksby. Good to see you again. And are you Mr. Brooksby?"

"Come inside." The man threw open the door and ushered them in. "The last thing we need is to be the topic of neighborhood gossip. They're jackals, every one of them."

Journey and Lucas obliged and, once in the privacy of the Brooksby home, produced their badges and introduced themselves.

Mr. Brooksby grumbled but extended a hand. "Jeffrey Brooksby. You've met my wife, Jillian."

Mrs. Brooksby smiled, looking perfectly sober compared to their last visit.

A second man appeared in the entryway. He also wore a suit that only expensive tailoring could buy, and his tan looked cultivated by a lifetime of leisure.

"This is our family lawyer, Jim Partridge." Mr. Brooksby pointed at the new arrival. "He will handle the discussion today."

Partridge offered his business card instead of a handshake. Journey and Lucas reciprocated in kind.

"Any questions you have for the Brooksbys, now or in the future, are to come through my office." He flashed a smile so white it looked ice blue against his tanned skin.

"Is Chad home?"

"He's not."

At Journey's side, Lucas kept his face pleasant and his tone light. "We hoped to speak with the family this morning, actually."

Partridge put up a hand. "And I will be here to make sure everything is aboveboard."

Journey snuck a glance at the parents. Mr. Brooksby appeared resolute, determined to let his attorney earn his bill rate. Mrs. Brooksby, on the other hand, shuffled her feet uncomfortably and darted her gaze between Lucas, Journey, and her husband. The one person she didn't look at, however, was Partridge.

Mrs. Brooksby huffed. "What is the harm of answering their questions if it helps clear Chad's name?"

"Jillian…" Mr. Brooksby's tone elicited an unspoken warning. *Stop talking.*

Mrs. Brooksby looked at her fingernails, twisted the bracelet on her wrist, smoothed her shirt, and glanced toward the kitchen.

Which gave Journey an idea. "I hate to trouble you, but

may I get a glass of water?" She touched her throat gently with her fingertips and cleared it. "My allergies are acting up this morning."

"Of course." Mrs. Brooksby perked up. "Right this way."

Partridge cleared his throat. "Mrs. Brooksby, perhaps she might fetch her own water."

The lady of the house shot him a quizzical expression. "Of course not. She'll get lost." She turned to Journey. "Follow me."

The lawyer clapped his hands. "Well, I'm coming with you."

In the kitchen, Journey stood by quietly, allowing Jillian Brooksby a moment. If she was tempted to talk, pressing too quickly might cause her to clam up. The lawyer took out his phone and looked at it intently.

Mrs. Brooksby flung open one cabinet after another, seemingly flustered, until she landed on the one with the drinking glasses inside. "I've been in such a state since Consuela left. Every new housekeeper I hire moves things around, and now I can't find anything. Including a decent replacement for Consuela."

Journey marveled at the enormous kitchen. Her entire apartment could fit into it. "I'm sorry. Who is Consuela?"

She noticed that when she spoke, Mr. Partridge stopped looking at his phone. But apparently the subject of the conversation—women talking about domestic help—wasn't of sufficient interest to him. He returned to his scrolling.

"Our long-term housekeeper and nanny." Mrs. Brooksby grabbed a tall, crystal glass from a shelf and thrust it against the ice dispenser on the refrigerator door. "She'd been with us since Chad was a toddler. Ran this whole house. Kept Chad's and my schedules from falling apart."

Journey wanted to ask when that had happened, but the woman kept talking.

"I mean, she did everything." Mrs. Brooksby filled the glass with water and added a slice of lemon from the fridge. She handed Journey her drink. "I didn't even realize how much until she up and left."

Journey, seeing her opportunity to keep Jillian talking, *tsk*ed sympathetically. "That must be difficult."

"The last maid I hired was here for such a short period of time, I didn't even learn her name." Mrs. Brooksby slumped against the counter and crossed her arms. "I blame Consuela, honestly. She trash-talked our family to every decent agency in the area, and now, no one will come here. Every name my friends suggest, the agency says, 'No, everyone is fully booked. Sorry.' I know they're lying, because let's face it, when was the last time any of these people had the luxury of turning down extra work? And for good money!"

These people? Journey forced her jaw to unclench.

"I can see you have an impressive household to run." She took a sip from her drink. "And if Consuela had been with you since Chad was a toddler, she must've felt like family in a way. What a loss."

"Absolutely! Thank you." Mrs. Brooksby's face softened, as if enjoying the fact that someone would finally listen to her. "Fifteen years is a lifetime. And we made sure she knew we appreciated her. Like family, as you said. A distant cousin, maybe, something along those lines."

"She was both your housekeeper and nanny?"

"Well, we hired her as Chad's nanny originally. He'd just started walking, and he was driving me insane…getting into absolutely everything. I told Jeffrey that if I didn't get someone who could handle him, I was going to lose it. He, of course, thought I was just being hysterical, but he told me to do whatever I thought was best."

"Good for you. Knowing what you needed and acting on it." Journey didn't have to believe the words she was saying.

Pretending was part of the job, even if it did make her feel slightly icky. But sometimes, it was necessary to get the information she needed.

"Right? Then Consuela proved so competent that I gave her more and more responsibility. Especially after Chad started preschool. What else would she do with her free time? We were paying her, after all."

"Of course." The relationship with Consuela sounded less like family the more Mrs. Brooksby spoke. "What else did she take on? You mentioned giving her more responsibility."

"The housecleaning, of course." Mrs. Brooksby mused, tapping a manicured nail against her lip. "Although for a long time, I had a maid who did the lion's share of that work. But Consuela had complete charge over everything concerning Chad. She took care of his clothing, kept his room, got him back and forth to school. Eventually, she even became his tutor."

"His tutor?" Journey hadn't expected that.

"Yes. Surprising, I know. But she was really smart. And Chad resisted everything about school. It was all an absolute nightmare for him."

Yet Chad's archery sponsor had referred to him as charming and popular.

"Ahem," Mr. Partridge looked up from his phone. "No questions about Chad."

"Um…" Mrs. Brooksby drew in a deep breath and straightened.

"I didn't ask any questions." Journey kept her tone carefully neutral. She didn't want to startle Mrs. Brooksby or push Mr. Partridge. It was a fine line.

But sometimes, when interviewing someone, the best policy was to simply stay quiet and let the other person ramble on. Journey held her silence.

Then, as if struck by lightning, Mrs. Brooksby's posture

went rigid.

Journey touched her arm. "Are you okay?"

Her face had grown pale. "You know, until you just asked that about Consuela's responsibilities, I never even considered the fact that his lack of stick-to-itiveness might've been her fault. Why was she letting him mess around when she should've been helping him find his passion and learn to persevere? And then to just up and quit on us like she did. Talk about turning your back on your loved ones. I feel incredibly betrayed."

"Do you have Consuela's contact information?" Journey hesitated, choosing her next words carefully. "Perhaps she knows some information that could vindicate Chad."

Mr. Partridge chimed in. "I don't recommend that, Mrs. Brooksby."

"But someone has to defend him, and she could do that." Mrs. Brooksby seemed quite taken with the idea, and Journey wondered if there wasn't a bit of a breakfast champagne-and-orange-juice in her system. "I don't see a problem with them speaking to the help." Mrs. Brooksby stared at Journey for one last second, then grabbed a slip of paper and quickly wrote Consuela Castillo's contact information.

Journey slipped the paper into her pocket and followed Mrs. Brooksby down the hall to rejoin the others, Partridge in tow.

"You better drive me straight over to the drug store to pick up some allergy medicine. I'm miserable." Journey touched her throat again, giving Lucas a telling glance. She smiled at Mrs. Brooksby. "Thank you for the water. I think that helped."

Lucas nodded, catching the hint that it was time to leave. "Since the Brooksbys are unwilling to speak with us, I think we're done here."

36

As soon as they pulled away from the Brooksby mansion, Journey gave Lucas the lowdown on Consuela and everything Jillian Brooksby had revealed in the kitchen, including how little she seemed to know about her own son.

"Nice work." Lucas flashed her a smile from behind the wheel. "I knew you were up to something."

"Mrs. Brooksby is a talker. And desperate for someone who will listen to her."

"Well, you got more than me. All I got out of Jeffrey was a pretty serious staring competition."

Journey pulled Consuela's phone number out of her pocket and flashed it at him. "Pull over, and let's give the maid a call."

"On it, partner."

Moments later, in the parking lot of a coffee shop that Journey intended to patronize as soon as she hung up, she dialed Consuela's number and put the call on speaker.

After several rings, a woman with a Spanish accent answered.

"Ms. Castillo?" Journey used her friendliest tone.

"*Sí?*" Consuela's drew out the one-syllable word, a tremor in her voice.

Journey decided her best shot to get through the woman's nervousness was to get straight to the point. "My name is Journey Russo, and I'm a special agent with the FBI. We're investigating a series of recent murders. I'd like to speak with you about Chad Brooksby."

"Chad?" Consuela's voice pitched. "He has not been killed, has he?"

What a strange opening question.

"No, ma'am. But he is under investigation."

"*Acchh!*" Whatever concern she had about Chad's safety quickly turned to anger. "I don't have anything to say about that boy. And I don't have time to talk. I'm at work, and I should not have answered my phone."

"Please." Journey suspected she had no more than a few seconds to get Consuela to cooperate. "We'll come to you. We'll even assure your boss you're not under suspicion. In fact, we could tell him how helpful you are, sort of put in a good word. But it's crucial we speak to you, ma'am."

Journey paused, hoping her plea would prove convincing. Mrs. Brooksby had said she quit angrily and without notice, so if Consuela had a bone to pick with the Brooksby family, Journey hoped she'd see this as an opportunity. Talking to the FBI about Chad could give the former nanny and housekeeper a chance to drive that bone sliver directly into the Brooksby family's heart.

Consuela remained silent but didn't disconnect the call.

Journey switched tack, appealing instead to the woman's humanity. "You need to know that Chad is a suspect in a series of murders, and we're obtaining an arrest warrant for murder." She paused, letting the news sink in. "Consuela, you may have information about him that could save countless lives."

"That child…" Consuela's voice shrank to a whisper. "He is *el diablo*."

The devil? A chill slipped down Journey's spine at Consuela's appraisal. "Please, will you help us find him?"

After a painful silence, Consuela finally agreed to meet. She gave them the address of the hotel where she worked in housekeeping.

Before leaving the parking lot, Journey contacted the hotel's head of housekeeping, who promised to make Consuela available for as long as they needed her. She would even have a private space for their interview ready when they arrived.

The hotel was part of a mid-priced national chain popular with retirees and families for its free breakfasts and generous loyalty program. Consuela's boss met them just inside the lobby and escorted them to a small conference room.

Consuela was there, waiting, and stood to greet them, her hands shaking as she fidgeted with the material of her uniform. She was a petite woman, barely five feet, with black hair threaded with silver and eyes that burned with intensity. Journey guessed she was in her forties, but when asked, Consuela said she was fifty-one.

Journey took the lead on the interview. "As you know, we'd like to speak with you about Chad Brooksby…"

"El diablo." Consuela grimaced. "That boy is the devil."

"Yes, you said that when we spoke on the phone." Journey nodded. "Why the devil?"

With the upright posture of a debutante, or at least fifteen years of being in service to one, Consuela began her tale.

"I came to the Brooksby family when Chad was twenty-one months old, and I could see right away his mother didn't know anything about nurturing a child. Always using the television to babysit that little boy or leaving him with the country club childcare so she could go off to drink all afternoon with her lady friends."

"What were your responsibilities as his nanny?" Journey got her notebook out.

"Nanny? *Pfft*." Consuela flicked the notion away. "I did everything...cook, clean, care for that little boy. Mrs. Brooksby couldn't keep help. The maids never stayed long. So I had to pick up their work. If I didn't cook, the boy didn't eat. If I didn't clean, he would live in a pigsty. You see what I mean?"

"So while you did the extra work, primarily for Chad's benefit, it helped the entire family."

"Of course." Consuela's dark eyes became saucers. "What's good for the family is good for the child. And what is good for the child...it goes both ways. But did Mr. or Mrs. Brooksby thank me or pay me extra for my time and effort? *Nunca*."

Consuela's laughter echoed against the bare beige walls.

Journey peered at her. "Then why did you stay?"

"For the boy, of course." Consuela met her question with consternation. "He was awful when I came. Spoiled to the core. Everything he wanted, he got. And there's only one reason a child acts like that. Do you know what it is?"

"I don't have children, so no." Journey didn't give Lucas the chance to guess, even though he was a father. They didn't need this interview to become a quiz show.

"The parents. They gave him things instead of attention. Showed their love with money and possessions." Consuela's voice pitched, but her body didn't move, remaining rigid and straight in the chair. "Also, I had my own children to raise, and without the Brooksby job, there was no money. For years, I fooled myself into thinking that taking care of them allowed me to care for my own family."

"Were you able to make progress with Chad?" Lucas

leaned forward over the conference table, the opposite of Consuela's perfect posture. "Did he respond to your care and attention?"

"As a young child, yes. He began to say *please* and *thank you*. Smiled and laughed when we played games. Called me Miss Consuela."

"But that changed?" Journey prodded.

She scowled, seeming to recall unpleasant memories. "Yes. When he started going to school, he began to lie right to my face. Always with the lies. 'My teacher says homework is only for the dumb kids.' Or he would tell me he did his work at school. He made me feel…" She made circles around her temple with a finger. "Crazy, you know? Impossible to know what was real and what was false."

"And how long did this continue?"

"Years. Always. He told me lies, and then Mrs. Brooksby would get a call from the school, saying his grades were bad or he was missing projects. And she'd blame me. Chad always acted like an innocent angel." Her voice went high pitched as she quoted him. "'Consuela didn't remind me to do that. Consuela didn't put it in my backpack.'"

"And his parents believed him?" It seemed odd to Journey that a family so willing to blame the nanny for their child's troubles would then turn around and make her his tutor.

"His parents didn't want to know the truth. Heaven forbid they have to pay attention to their child or take the time to understand what is happening." Consuela shook her head. "No. It was easier to blame me and return to the country club or the airport or wherever they went so that they didn't have to deal with the boy."

To Journey, it seemed ignorance was Jillian Brooksby's preferred parenting style. "If he was struggling in school, and they blamed you, why did they hire you as his tutor?"

Consuela laughed again. "Who else are they going to hire?

Everyone who started quit. I was the only one left willing to deal with him. I tried to tell the Brooksbys. He doesn't listen to his teachers or me. But they didn't care about excuses, they wanted results. Told me I had to change my approach." She stopped laughing. "At that point, I probably would have just gone along with it. The money was good. That was until…"

Journey was on the edge of her seat. "Until what? What happened?"

The housekeeper's face grew grave. "*Pobre conejito.*" She wiped her eye. "I was preparing dinner. I remember exactly what I made that night. Broiled chicken. Rice with butter. Peas. It was Chad's favorite meal, and my kids' too. I made it all the time. Anyway, dinner was ready, and I walked out onto the back patio to call for Chad. I always had to call for him for dinner, since he was always outside doing whatever he did. That's when I saw it."

"Saw what?"

"This little rabbit, just lying there on the stone. An arrow was sticking right out of its eye. It was so horrible." Consuela shook at the memory. "And then Chad came downstairs, wiping his hands, as if he'd just washed them. Which he never did, by the way. He was a very dirty young man."

"And so you thought Chad killed the rabbit?"

"I'm sure of it. But I confronted him about it, and he said no, he didn't do anything."

"But that was normal for Chad, correct?"

"It was. But for some reason, I couldn't take it anymore. I got so angry." Consuela took a deep breath and raised her hand to the sky. "Finally, I said enough. I was not crazy. My children were obedient, respectful, hard workers who got good grades. Chad Brooksby took responsibility for nothing. Whatever he could get away with, he did. He is el diablo. And I wanted nothing to do with him."

Journey couldn't blame Consuela. "How old was Chad when you quit?"

"Seventeen, almost eighteen."

"And that's when you took your job here at the hotel?"

"No. I took this job because it was all I could find. After seeing what tutors were charging, I wanted to make that kind of money. And I had plenty of experience with Chad, of course, but with my own children too. But Mrs. Brooksby… she was angry when I left. So vindictive. She destroyed my reputation. No one would hire me as a tutor or a nanny or even a maid. Thankfully, here, I work with nice, friendly people who don't use their money as a weapon."

"I have to ask…" Journey put down her pen and folded her hands. "Mrs. Brooksby asserts you destroyed her reputation among your colleagues. Says she can't get anyone to work for her and the ones who do…quit."

"Are you surprised?" Consuela rolled her eyes. "How could I let anyone else walk into that crazy house only to be taken advantage of and underpaid? And those who do anyway figure it out on their own and leave."

Journey didn't judge, only jotted the answer in her notes and sat back. She glanced at Lucas. *You take it from here.*

Lucas nodded as he laid out the series of murders, then explained the gunpowder discovery at both the Thompson scene and in the bungalow. "We suspect Chad might be planning to escalate and hurt a lot of people."

Consuela's gaze went darker than black.

"We need to be able to predict where he might strike and when. As you seem to know him better than his own parents, can you tell us about any people or groups he may have held hostility toward?"

She thought for a moment. "So much of what he said to me was offensive. It is hard to narrow down. Chad always considered himself better than everyone. Nothing was ever his fault, as I said. But if other people had troubles, oh. Then they must have deserved it. Those less fortunate than him were just lazy. Homeless people were trash who needed to…" She pursed her lips. "This is his language, not mine. But he would say they needed to 'get their shit together' or be 'removed from draining society.'"

"So victim blaming. Even classist?"

"Sí. He used to roll down his window when we were in the car and mock the students outside the public middle school that was on our route to his fancy academy. He would call them losers and a drain on society. I would shush him and roll the window up. It was mortifying."

She stopped talking and held up a finger as if to say *pause*.

Journey raised an eyebrow. "What?"

"I had forgotten about this, but maybe it is relevant. The Brooksbys did not pay well, and money was often tight. Sometimes, I had to turn to the food pantry to keep my family fed."

Journey's heart twisted. She had volunteered at one during college and saw families just like Consuela's.

"Eventually, I learned that the best food came in on Saturdays at noon. That meant that it was always busy on that afternoon, and the line would be out the door. The wait was long, but worth it. If Chad's parents were out of town, I had no choice but to bring him along. But I also hoped that maybe going with me would teach him an important lesson. He needed to see that not everyone was as fortunate as his family."

Journey found Consuela's dedication remarkable, even as she noted that today was Saturday.

"Unfortunately, he took no lesson from it at all. I still remember his hateful words. One day, he called me a crazy old witch and said I was guilty of child abuse for forcing him to look at 'all these worthless people.'" She cleared her throat.

"He also said the government ought to put them out of their misery instead of letting them bleed the rest of us dry."

The room went quiet, and the hair on Journey's arms rose.

Lucas reiterated what they'd just heard. "So you brought him along with you to the food bank to get food for your family, and one day while you were there, he told you that anyone who needed food assistance should be killed."

She nodded. "Sí."

"Was it always the same food bank that you went to with Chad?"

"Sí. Oh, and then he started volunteering there. He did it for college, to get into a fancy one."

Journey pounced. "Can you tell us the name and location of this food bank? It's important. I think that boy has something big, and terrible, planned."

37

The food bank was in a shopping forum downtown and it was closed when they arrived. "This is going to be a long morning." Journey picked up her cup of coffee from the center console and took a sip of the still steaming-hot brew. She stared at the beige brick-and -lass building. No lights were on, no big signs announced the building's reason or purpose.

To find this food bank, a person would have to be introduced to this food bank. Otherwise, there was no way to know what it was.

After leaving the hotel and Consuela to her work, they'd stopped for coffee and called in their findings to Keller. Journey had wanted to brainstorm a sting operation, as the food bank seemed a ripe place for the teen boys to target. It was empty now, but in a few hours, there would be dozens of people who Chad Brooksby would consider "drains on society" just lined up, right there for those sociopathic young men to pick off.

Keller, however, wasn't willing to pull the trigger on a full-out operation. "You don't have any concrete evidence that Brooksby or any of his companions would focus on this food bank. There are dozens of food banks and soup kitchens throughout Pittsburgh. If what you say is true, any one of them could be a target."

"They would pick a spot personal to them." Journey leaned closer to the phone speaker, as if proximity could drive her point home. "And the food bank is well within their geographic range. This makes the most sense. It's personal to Brooksby."

"You don't know that the other boys haven't volunteered elsewhere. All of these guys would be focused on building academic résumés. They could select another space. And we don't know that they would be making any moves today, tomorrow, or next week. Without that kind of information, we can't build an operation."

Journey could practically hear Keller rubbing her forehead. She knew the SSA wanted to approve a sting, could feel Keller thinking through the steps to justify one.

"We need more information." In the background, Journey heard Keller's keyboard clicking. "You and Sullivan take the primary target. Stake it out, see if you can get a sense of its pattern and who goes in and out."

"If we're here, who is hunting down the suspects?"

Keller sighed, but it was more like a huff of frustrated air puffing through the phone. "I'll send a couple teams to their addresses and see if we can locate them. If they're not located within the next couple hours, we'll up the number of eyes on your food bank."

It was a small comfort, but Journey would take it. "Thanks."

"I'll ask the PBP to send a couple patrol cars to back you up," Keller continued, "and then see if they can increase patrols around as many nearby food banks, soup kitchens, and charity works as they can."

"Can you run background checks on the other teens and see if they did volunteer? Then put focus on those as backup." Lucas leaned forward so Journey's phone speaker would pick up his voice. "But I agree with Russo that this will probably be the place."

They'd disconnected and done a sweep of the exterior of the building.

There were four points of ingress and egress—one front entrance, a side door, and two rear doors. Journey and Lucas were currently at a spot catty-corner to the building, so they could see the front and side.

"Your parking leaves something to be desired." Lucas gazed out the windshield, sipping his own coffee.

The body of the Ford crossed three parking lines.

"Your face leaves something to be desired." Journey set her cup back down on the console, not looking away from the empty lot in front of her. "My parking strategy was to see as much of the building as possible. My strategy is a success."

"Your strategy will also bring extra police presence. They'll come to tell us to move our vehicle."

"Then we have an added bonus for backup."

Journey checked her watch. It was almost eleven. They'd been at the building for forty-five minutes now. She anticipated the volunteers who ran the place to show up any moment.

A paper coffee cup tumbled across the parking lot. If that was the most action they saw today, Journey would count herself lucky.

She couldn't help disagreeing with Keller's decision, though she saw the SSA's point. There were a lot of logistics to cover. The thought made her feet itch.

"Let's walk the perimeter again." She couldn't bear to stay in the car another minute.

"You got it."

Her phone buzzed with a text message from Keller.

None of the suspects are accounted for.

She handed her phone to Lucas and watched his face as he took in the news.

All four teens were in the wind. That could be significant. Maybe each one of the four had a separate appointment on a Saturday morning—anything was possible—but she doubted it.

No, these four fuckers were together somewhere.

And they were a dangerous pack.

38

I told the crew to meet in the woods behind the academy at eleven a.m. sharp, and not a single member let me down. All three of them arrived dressed and prepped before the top of the hour.

We weren't going to wear the animal masks this time. We needed to blend in. So I brought some hats and t-shirts from the gas station. I also brought some of my mom's makeup from home and told the boys to smear it on. We needed to look grungy.

That didn't mean they were ready. In fact, a couple looked downright terrified. Especially Hound, who kept fiddling with that mole on his face.

"Hey, guys." I wasn't frightened. I was so ready to go, I could barely keep still. "If you're feeling unsteady, consider that a good thing. It's all energy, so use it. Take everything running through your mind and focus it on one thought. Success."

That was what we learned at Mockingbird. One of the few lessons that was useful. I looked at my number two. "What are you picturing in your head right now?"

"Success." Buck tried to sound strong, but there was an edge of hesitation in his voice.

"What does it look like? Tell me. Be specific. Imagine the outcome."

Buck snapped to attention. "Bodies. On the ground. Blood everywhere. Arms and legs torn from their torsos."

"What do you see when you look into their eyes?"

"Nothing." Buck answered without missing a beat. "Just death."

"And what do you hear?"

"Alarms blaring. Screams. Panic. Chaos."

"You're ready, soldier." Buck was as good a lieutenant as they came. I patted him on the cheek, grabbed him by the chin. "Do you feel it?"

"Yes. I'm ready. Let's go."

I turned my attention to Bull. "You. Tell me what you're doing during all that chaos."

"I'm looking for prey. Aiming. Shooting."

"Yeah, you are." I couldn't help but smile at these soldiers I'd created. "How do you see through the smoke? It's black. Thick. Blurring your line of sight."

Bull looked up at me as if he'd never considered the possibility. "Uh…"

I grabbed him by the shoulders and shook. "Use your instincts!"

"I keep firing until I'm out of arrows."

"Yes, you do." I patted Bull on the back. "The goal is success. The goal is to kill. Kill the weak. Thin the herd."

"I'm ready!"

"I like what I'm hearing, soldier."

Now I had Hound to deal with, and he was so scared, he was wheezing. We were only as strong as our weakest link, so I needed to whip him into shape, like the great leader I was. And he required a gentler approach.

"Hey." I placed a steady hand on his shoulder and lowered my voice. "Tell me what's in your head. What's got you shaking?"

He dropped his gaze to the ground, avoiding my eyes. "I just…"

"Tell me what's spinning in that head of yours."

Like magic, he saw it. Named it. Looked me in the eye. "The killing. I don't want to kill anyone."

That was exactly what I *didn't* want to hear.

"The killing." I repeated it for his benefit, hoping hearing the words back might wake him up to the fact that killing was the whole reason for today.

"Yeah. You guys are good at killing people." Hound's voice shook. "But I don't want to do it."

So I'd trained a killer who didn't want to be one. It made no sense. But what was I gonna do? Still, after his reluctance yesterday, I'd prepared for the possibility that he might change his mind. "The good news, Hound, is that I've got a job designed just for you. One where you don't have to kill anyone. You wanna hear what it is?"

I always gave my crew a choice. That way, they couldn't blame me for pressuring them when they knowingly chose to walk through the door themselves.

"What would I have to do?" Hope lit Hound's eyes.

"We'll wait for the right moment, and when it comes, I'll give the signal. That's when we'll need our diversion. You'll set off the first round of smoke grenades. It's nothing more difficult than dropping a few cans on the floor and walking away. Meanwhile, Buck and Bull and I will put on our gas masks and attack." I clapped Hound on the shoulder. "Then you can be our getaway driver. You'll have to get us out of there safely, man. Do you think you can do that?"

"Yeah." Hound nodded, almost gratefully. "I can do that."

"Are you sure?"

"Yeah." His head bobbed up and down so hard, I wondered if it might snap off his neck. "Definitely. I'll get you all out of there, away from the chaos."

That brought a smile back to my face.

"I trust you, Hound." I patted him on the back. "I trust you with my life. With all our lives."

He gobbled up my praise like a starving man at Thanksgiving dinner. "I got you, man. Don't worry."

"I never worry. Take some time now and figure out exactly what route you're going to take to get us out of there. There won't be any time to second guess. Afterward, we're going to collect at our spot and then on to Aaron's cabin, where we'll hide out until all this dies down."

Now, with my crew committed and focused, there was nothing more to do but move.

"Everyone clear on the plan?"

They all nodded.

"Great. Now I have a little something for you guys." I handed them their backpacks, each of them individually prepared by me.

Each of them loaded for war.

39

Journey anxiously watched the clock above the front doors that led out to the parking lot.

11:58.

11:59.

God, she hoped her hunch that this place was the target was wrong. But also right. If it was, they could stop these sickos before they took more lives.

"Agent Sullivan, how's looking out there?" Journey spoke into the hands-free radio connected to the earbud in her ear. When the PBP backup arrived a few minutes ago, in the form of Detective Lonnie Gutierrez and a patrol officer, they'd all radioed up.

Lucas was outside, positioned around the corner of the building from her, watching for the perpetrators' approach. She'd taken the front of the building.

During their last hour in the car, they'd memorized the teens' social media pictures in order to recognize them. She doubted they would approach such a busy place and time with masks on—too obvious to spot.

"All clear."

"Copy. Same here. Gutierrez?"

"Back is clear."

"Copy. Stay alert."

Everything was as it should've been, and that was the problem. Everything was so freakin' normal. She took a peek through the front window. Groups of families huddled together in the line inside, waiting for hot food. And there were clusters of people sitting on eight long rows of fold-out tables.

We've got to keep them safe.

She didn't expect the potential perpetrators to start blowing the place up—or whatever the heck was about to happen—at twelve on the dot. As a general rule, criminals weren't exactly known for their punctuality. Especially if the criminals in question were a bunch of overprivileged, teenage prep school jerks.

But still, the waiting was the hardest part. After waiting almost two hours already, pacing the sidewalk entrance felt torturous.

Her palms were clammy. She always felt a rush of nerves before action. And she sensed something was about to go down. Every sign pointed to it. Her instincts blared at her like a foghorn.

And when things went down, she felt so freaking calm, it was crazy.

Another potential thing to talk about with a therapist.

An additional PBP patrol car pulled into the parking lot, right next to the FBI Ford. To Journey's astonishment, a patrol officer—a young woman who didn't look old enough to have graduated high school—got out, looked around, and then wrote a ticket, tucking the piece of paper under the windshield wiper.

It was everything she could do not to yell at her. But she didn't want to call attention to herself.

Journey wore a pair of worn gray sweatpants and an oversize shirt—borrowed from the food bank's lost and found—to cover the vest beneath. Though vests were little good against both arrows and explosions, she felt better with the protection, slight as it was. The goal was to blend in as one of the bank's typical patrons, so they didn't draw the attention of Brooksby and his crew. At least, not immediately.

The best they could do at the moment was study each face carefully to ensure they didn't miss any of their perpetrators. If Brooksby showed, they assumed he would take a place in line, though he could always enter as a "volunteer" too.

The clock struck twelve.

Lucas's voice ripped through her earbud. "Heads-up. Potential suspect heading toward the building. White male, orange hat."

Less than a minute later, Journey spotted the young man coming around the corner. He wore an orange baseball cap pulled low and looked down at a grocery sack in his hands. But the mole on his chin, despite his grimy face, was distinctive.

Trent Tucker.

Showtime.

As Journey stepped forward, all her anxiety melted away, utterly focused on what needed to be done. She shuffled toward Tucker, not wanting to blow her cover immediately, but also trying not to attract his attention.

Not that it really mattered. The young man wasn't paying any attention to her, nor anyone else for that matter. He appeared to be mumbling.

Journey shuffled closer. With the parking lot now full of cars going in and out, she was too far away to hear what Tucker was saying. About fifteen feet too far.

"Suspect at the rear—"

Boom!

Gutierrez's sentence was cut off.

The noise came from just outside the building.

Before she could respond, Tucker pulled a gas mask from his grocery bag and strapped it on.

Journey sprang at him, identifying the perpetrator to fellow officers, no longer worried about blowing their cover. "Man in the orange cap!"

Tucker was already reaching into his bag again.

He was palming two grenade canisters in each hand.

"Trent Tucker! This is the FBI. Freeze."

Trent dropped the canisters and sprinted toward the door. Instead of an explosion, the front entrance and sidewalk filled with smoke, cloaking Trent in a thick, gray haze. But Trent was already running away alongside the building.

From the smoke, an arrow whizzed through the air, hitting the food bank wall, exploding on contact.

The wall held, but mayhem erupted inside.

40

Journey crawled, inches from the front door, keeping her head below the smoke as best she could. It was already dispersing, but she could barely see above her. Her ears rang from the explosion.

From somewhere behind the building, she heard shots fired.

"Suspect moving around the building." Lucas's voice sounded tinny in her ear. If she didn't miss her guess, everyone was headed toward the front, toward her.

Toward the exits where civilians were trying to get out.

"Get back inside!" she yelled, but it was like trying to command the ocean.

Above the commotion, she heard a second arrow whiz by. Dimly through the smoke, she saw it connect near the first arrow, lodging in the side of the building.

Boom.

Just as Jed Durham had warned they could, they'd loaded their arrowheads with explosives.

Again, the wall held.

Better lucky than good.

And just like that, the food bank descended into chaos. The air quivered with terrified screams. Half of the people inside tucked beneath the foldout tables. The other half all seemed to be struggling to get out the side and front doors—the entrances available to the public.

The smoke cleared, its purpose of creating chaos and confusion apparently completed. As it did, their suspects became more identifiable. They were the only people wearing gas masks. The killers hadn't run away, they'd just moved back into the parking lot.

Three young men now stood shoulder to shoulder in the lot, just in front of the FBI's crookedly parked Ford, blocking any escape. Each held a hunting bow to his chest.

Only the archer in the middle seemed to be nocking arrows onto his bowstring, though. Chad Brooksby. *It must be.* Journey had memorized his description and knew he was six-three, several inches taller than all three of his criminal crew. Though the gas mask concealed his face, his height, build, and hair color confirmed his identity.

She raised her weapon, but her eyes were watering from the smoke. She saw the trio in duplicate. Blinking, she cleared her vision.

Brayden Willingham and Jenson Buckley stood beside him, not only shorter but seemingly frozen. The dissipating smoke and ventilator masks blurred their finer facial characteristics, but through the transparent shield, Journey saw their eyes, gaping black pools of fear. One of them held an arrow loosely dangling from his fingers. The other had his fist locked on the grip of his bow.

Journey had no cover. Staying low to avoid explosive arrows and choking smoke, she army-crawled across the ground as quickly as possible to improve her vantage point and get a clearer shot.

"Backup to front." She knew she said the words, but

didn't know if anyone could hear her. Her own ears were ringing.

"On our way, Russo."

Nearby, the PBP officer who'd just written the FBI a parking ticket knelt, shielded behind her vehicle. She raised her gun, taking aim.

Brooksby beat her to it. In rapid succession, he notched another exploding arrow and released.

Boom!

His arrow hit the hood of the patrol vehicle. Glass shattered everywhere. The crunch of metal was deafening.

The patrol officer was thrown back, slamming into a nearby telephone pole. For a moment, Journey thought she might be dead, but she stirred and blinked. The woman would be seeing stars for days, she was sure.

Journey didn't cover her head. There was no time to wait. She positioned herself so that her bullets would not pose a threat to fellow officers.

Even though she didn't have a great angle, she took aim at the perpetrators and pulled the trigger. Her shot was echoed by two others. Lucas and the rear PBP officer fired from the corner of the building. The shots echoed through the space, the sound leaving no doubt that this was no longer a one-sided battle.

The archer farthest from the door—had to be Brayden Willingham, based on the brown hair and muscular arms—cried out as he dropped, grabbing for his thigh as he went down.

Journey's aim shifted, focusing on the gap.

When the young man fell, he'd left her with a view of Chad Brooksby. She just needed to move another inch or two.

But Brooksby didn't give her the opportunity. He collared

the guy to his right, the blond Jenson Buckley, and pulled him tight to his chest, diving behind a nearby Toyota.

Brooksby was using his guy as a human shield. Lucas, Gutierrez, and the PBP officer maintained fire.

"Cease fire. Pursuit on foot." The gunfire stopped, and Journey jumped to her feet, sprinting in pursuit. Rubble from the patrol car explosion lay strewn everywhere, complicating her path forward. She vaulted over a fallen bumper.

Brooksby fled toward a silver Porsche parked down the street.

She leaped over Willingham, who writhed on the ground, and burst around the Toyota to find Jenson Buckley a crumpled heap on the sidewalk in front of her, bleeding from a gunshot wound to the head. That was when she saw Lucas sprinting toward their vehicle and waving her over.

"Come on!"

41

Lucas gunned the accelerator of the FBI-issue Ford while Journey, in the passenger seat, radioed HQ as they pursued the fleeing criminals. Their siren rang out as their tires screeched on a hard right out of the parking lot onto the street, leading a small fleet of PBP squad cars behind them.

"They got here fast." She was impressed.

"Detective Gutierrez called it in when I called out Tucker."

The parking ticket stuck under their windshield wiper flapped in the wind as they chased the Porsche.

Journey's gaze hardened as she spied the orange cap atop the driver of the silver Porsche. Trent Tucker. He drove with abandon—weaving and dodging like a maniac, proving he was no professional, just a kid who'd probably only ever experienced high-speed chases in video games.

The Porsche swerved dangerously between lanes. Horns blared from the other cars on the road. Two cars in front of the Porsche blocked the sedan's way. Tucker leaned on the horn, making a terrible racket that accomplished nothing.

He swerved to the left, across the yellow lines, and

nearly caused a catastrophic head-on collision with an oncoming van. He shifted to the far-left lane just in time. Then sped up and crossed back over the left lanes, overtaking the two cars in the right lane that had hemmed him in.

"Two suspects moving south on Perry toward Rochester Road." Journey practically squawked into the radio as Lucas slipped around the offending vehicles. "Driver is becoming increasingly erratic."

Before anyone could respond, Brooksby stuck his head out of the Porsche's sunroof and fired an arrow at them.

"We're taking fire!" Journey shouted into the radio. Lucas yanked at the steering wheel, barely avoiding the shot that whizzed past them and exploded in their rearview.

It hit one of the cop cars behind them. The vehicle flipped back and sailed through the air.

"They got one!" Journey shouted into the radio for paramedics. "Get this road closed! And set up some blockades."

In rapid succession, still standing out of the Porsche's sunroof, Brooksby fired off two more arrows like Legolas at Helm's Deep. He dropped back inside.

Lucas veered onto the shoulder as those arrows exploded against the road, sending up an eruption of asphalt and gravel.

With the considerable destruction of the road, the cop cars behind them were forced to stop. They'd have to find a detour.

"That kid is not taking my head off today!" Journey rolled down her window and leaned out the opening, setting the sights of her gun on the area just above the sunroof. She was ready to fire as soon as the bastard showed himself again.

The Porsche's brake lights flashed red up ahead as the car swerved wildly across lanes of oncoming traffic. Once again, it nearly crashed into a white sedan but for some last-second maneuvering from the driver.

In her peripheral vision, Journey watched the white sedan skid off the road and tumble into a ditch.

Lucas stayed on the Porsche's tail.

Gun still aimed at the car, Journey called in the location of the crash. "Accident with possible injuries. Paramedics needed."

Two blocks later, the Porsche turned south again, this time forcing a mother crossing the street with her toddler to dive for cover.

"He almost killed them!" Lucas had kept his cool through the chase, but even the most experienced driver could make a mistake under pressure.

Journey provided constant updates to all responding officers regarding their position on each turn of their pursuit while tracking the route of the Porsche. "Despite his attempts to lose us by cutting through side streets and residential neighborhoods, he still keeps heading south." She searched her mind for possible destinations in that direction.

"Where do you think they're going?" Lucas was breathless.

"Not sure…somewhere they feel safe. Somewhere comfortable…" She caught a glimpse of an elementary school as they sped past. She didn't get a good look at the name, but seeing the school gave her an idea.

"Hold on. They might be headed for the school, Mockingbird Academy." She grabbed her phone and found the location on her navigation app. It was three blocks away, directly south.

When she turned to update Lucas, his eyes had become mere slits beneath his eyebrows. Sweat streamed down his forehead and temples, matting his hair to his face.

"Almost there, partner." Journey needed to keep him

focused and safe for a few more blocks. Grabbing the radio, she reported the suspected destination to HQ.

"Backup headed that way," came the reply.

Like a chorus of angels, she finally heard sirens blare, the cacophony closing in on the Porsche from every direction.

The convoy that'd had to detour had found their way back, ready to avenge their fellow officers.

42

Journey's instincts were spot on. Just as the entrance gates of Mockingbird Academy came into view, Trent Tucker swerved the silver sedan, jumping the sidewalk and driving straight for a wooded area on the backside of the campus. Despite his erratic driving, the Porsche had handled the chase with speed and agility. At least, on the asphalt.

But on the grass, its tires spun and struggled for purchase, the vehicle swerving and fishtailing down the long hill toward the trees.

"He's only got momentum because of the slope." Lucas wasn't having nearly as much trouble with the Ford, overhauled as it had been with all-wheel-drive and V6 engine.

Journey looked over her shoulder and spotted a PBP SUV behind them, maneuvering the terrain with ease. "One of us should be able to overtake them."

Tucker had gained just enough speed on the hill that, when he hit the flat at the bottom, the silver sedan spun out of control. The Porsche drifted sideways to the left, then right, turning ninety degrees and crashing the rear passenger side door broadside into a tree.

"That's gotta hurt." Lucas hit the brakes, and their Ford began a controlled slowdown.

Before they could get there, the driver door of the Porsche flew open, and Tucker dashed for the trees. Brooksby, scrambling over seats, followed quickly behind, his bow and quiver of arrows over his shoulders like a backpack.

"That kid in the front is one lucky son of a bitch." Lucas came to a stop. Before he could put the Ford into park, Journey leapt from her seat and barreled after in pursuit. Her partner followed right behind her.

The PBP officers had parked their SUV and were running with them in pursuit as well.

"Stop right there!" Journey set her sights on the boys. Brooksby was about fifteen yards ahead, while Tucker led five yards ahead of him.

Tucker turned back. When he saw her on his trail, gun raised, he stopped and threw his hands in the air.

Brooksby saw his partner give up the chase. "Hound! You worthless, fucking coward!"

"I'm not your fucking dog, Chad!" Tucker yelled back in a rage.

"You said my name, you damn piece of shit!" Still sprinting, Brooksby took an arrow from his quiver, nocked it, and let it fly toward Tucker, who dove out of the way.

The ground behind Tucker exploded.

"Serves you right!" Brooksby just kept running into the cloud of dust.

Lucas overtook Journey and caught up with Tucker before her. The young man lay sprawled on the ground. He dove onto Tucker's back and pressed his chest down onto the dirt before cuffing him. Meanwhile, Brooksby continued to dash for the cover of the deeper trees.

"You stay here! I'll take Brooksby!" Journey yelled over her shoulder as she streaked past them.

As she ran, Trent Tucker yelled a muffled warning. "You'll never catch him. He knows these woods too well."

Maybe that was true, but Journey wasn't giving up. She watched Brooksby's black shirt disappear behind a tree.

But then she lost sight of him. He wasn't running anymore, but he wasn't standing still either. Twigs snapped as he moved.

She heard the crunch of twigs and leaves behind her. The PBP officers had caught up with her, and she put a finger to her lips and silently pointed them to where she'd heard movement. She directed them to split up, believing that if Chad Brooksby kept moving, they'd be able to surround him and cut off his escape.

And if he shoots another arrow, he'll only take out one of us at a time.

The fates, however, weren't playing along. As soon as the officers moved, she heard the swish of branches several yards behind her in the opposite direction. She turned but saw nothing. The officers had heard it, too, and looked to her for a command.

Stay close, she signaled. *He's nearby.*

Journey's heart and mind pumped with adrenaline.

She crouched low and sprinted from behind a shrub offering sparse cover then slid around a large oak with a trunk you could park a smart car in. It looked old and large enough to have been there since the beginning of Mockingbird Academy nearly a century ago. The tree made for great cover.

From nearby came a thud, the unmistakable sound of a rock hitting dirt. Brooksby remained close, and now he was toying with her, trying to make her believe he was on the move.

But she had no sense of where he was, exactly.

She was exposed, and Brooksby was an expert shot.

Journey thought of him using Jenson Buckley as a human shield. Of him taunting Trent Tucker, who'd gone into battle with him and rushed him away from the food bank disaster via high-speed chase only to be called a fucking coward and become a human target in the end. She thought of Consuela, tormented by Brooksby for years with his mind games and gaslighting.

He was a malignant narcissist. But Journey knew something people like Chad Brooksby or Connor Leopold didn't even understand about themselves. A narcissist's greatest weakness was weakness itself.

"Hey, Chad!" Though raspy and raw, her words rang loud and clear. Her strategy had better work because she'd just given away her location. "Hey, genius!"

No response came. Perfect. The forest was oddly quiet now, the only sound her own breathing. Just as she'd hoped.

"How smart do you feel now? We knew your plan, and we foiled it. Filled the food bank with undercover officers. Took out two of your buddies. And your last buddy, Trent? He's in custody. He'll be spilling the goods on you soon enough and being treated like a king for his cooperation."

She felt certain elevating his foot soldier like that would piss Brooksby off. But there was no answer forthcoming. That was the problem with a gambit. Sometimes they didn't work, and you overplayed your hand.

Even so, she stayed the taunting course. "It's pathetic for you, really, how easily the people around you folded. We even found the man you paid to buy your arrows, and he just wouldn't quit talking about you."

She paused to let him stew. Her biceps flexed as she gripped her weapon.

"Oh, and nice hideout, by the way. In a public bungalow? That took us all of five minutes to figure out."

There, she'd driven in the knife. Now it was time to twist.

"You're a lazy fool, you know that? Weakened by one of the seven deadly sins, *sloth*. We've all been talking about it. Officers across the city see how lazy, weak, and pathetic you truly are. You're kind of a joke among law enforcement."

The scorn landed just where she'd aimed, at the dead center of Brooksby's ego.

And then, from up in the branches of the giant oak, came a roar of rage.

In a flash, her gaze darted up to the tree. There was Brooksby, clinging to a branch, aiming an arrow right at her. He shot. Journey dove forward. The arrow landed behind her, right into another oak tree.

It exploded into kindling a second later.

The smell of gunpowder filled Journey's nose, but no smoke blocked her vision. Finding Chad's position again, she met his gaze and grinned.

With steady hands, she lifted her service weapon, aimed, and with one shot, Chad tumbled from the tree.

43

Journey and Lucas sat facing each other across the board table in the fourth-floor conference room, sorting through the details of the case. They'd already surrendered their weapons and were finishing up some paperwork before they were officially placed on administrative duty.

Chad Brooksby was in the hospital, being treated for a gunshot wound through the shoulder. Brayden Willingham was also hospitalized, currently listed in serious condition. He'd undergone surgery, and doctors were ultimately forced to amputate the leg Journey shot. There was too much nerve damage. Doctors said it was a miracle he survived at all.

Jenson Buckley hadn't been so lucky. Paramedics declared him dead on the scene. A bullet from Lucas's gun went straight through his brain as Brooksby turned to run from the building with Buckley still wrenched in front of him.

The only one of the four to come away physically unharmed was Trent Tucker, despite the explosive arrow Brooksby fired his way. Still, he remained in police custody and faced a world of legal trouble like the other two. The survivors would never grow up to live the privileged lives their parents had envisioned.

The agents had spent the morning speaking with the boys' families. Brooksby's mother and father continued—despite all evidence to the contrary, including the DNA evidence found on the apple at Greg Thompson's house—to deny that their son had anything to do with the crimes of which he was accused. Not the attack at the food bank, not the high-speed chase, and most certainly not serial murder.

"This case will be the end of your careers and a monumental humiliation for the FBI." Mr. Brooksby's face had gone tomato red as he blustered at them. "Our lawyers will destroy you, and I'm going to enjoy watching every minute."

After they left, Lucas turned to Journey. "Their son's crimes will never be real to them. They'll never account for all the devastation and bloodshed he left behind."

Journey felt the truth of that like a stone in her heart. "I don't know if I'll ever cease to be amazed by what people can convince themselves of, no matter how many times I've seen it for myself."

Their next interviews did nothing to dissuade her.

Brayden Willingham's father Rob claimed Brooksby had brainwashed his boy. That his son owned a hunting bow but was not proficient. "Couldn't hit the broadside of a barn." And as for the archery trophy? Until the FBI had an indisputable photo or video proof that Brayden was a participating member of the second-place team, he didn't believe a word of their claims. Trent's testimony that Brayden had killed Claudia Reaver fell on deaf ears.

More astonishingly, Jenson Buckley's dad, Carter, refused to answer questions directly, speaking only through his lawyer. The attorney even had the nerve to end the interview by threatening a wrongful death lawsuit on the family's behalf. "You don't have any evidence that Jenson killed anyone, let alone evidence that he inflicted injury or harm. He was being held hostage by that madman, Brooksby, and yet it was Jenson you murdered."

There was nothing these families wouldn't do or say to exonerate their offspring.

The only parents to stray off script were Trent's mother and father, Lisa and Ben Tucker. Journey and Lucas scheduled the discussion with them for four o'clock, and they arrived right on time.

Lucas introduced himself and Journey, then invited the couple to sit down.

"Actually…" Ben, a tall, muscular man with the shoulders of Atlas, put a hand on his wife's back. She was half his size, with the bright-blond highlights of a woman fresh from the salon. Both of them remained standing. "We'd like to meet with Special Agent Russo."

"She's right here." Lucas had already introduced her, but he smiled congenially.

"Alone, I mean." Ben turned his attention to Journey. "We very much intend to make it worth your time."

To Journey, this edged too close to a bribe for comfort. She held up her palms. "Special Agent Sullivan is my partner. We've worked this case together from the beginning and will continue to do so." What she didn't say was that, after the pressure of this morning and the frustration of this afternoon's conversations, she barely had the patience to stop herself from walking out the door.

Ben folded his arms, his biceps spilling from his shirt sleeves like oranges from a bag. "I must insist, Agent Russo. We are aware of your professional history, and we plan to talk to you alone. It's about The Chosen. If that's not possible, we won't be talking with the Bureau at all without a court order."

Journey's ears pricked up at the cult's name, but she looked to Lucas for a signal. If this was what it took to hear what Trent's parents had to say, she was willing to do it. But not without her partner's consent.

He raised his eyebrows as if to say, *You okay with this?*

She nodded, and Lucas took his leave, closing the heavy door quietly behind him.

Journey leaned back in her chair. "What would you like to speak to me about?"

Lisa's eyes brimmed with tears while she shredded a crumpled tissue in her hands. "What will happen to Trent? He's only seventeen. Still a minor."

This was what they excused Lucas for? If their next question wasn't a whole hell of a lot better, Journey would be pissed.

She answered them anyway. "What happens next is up to the judicial system, frankly. It was our job to find the perpetrators of the murders and the attack planned for the food bank, and we did that. Unfortunately, your son was involved in both. We found a mask containing Trent's DNA at the bungalow, and we have eyewitnesses who can likely connect it to at least two of the murder scenes. Yesterday, he set off the smoke bomb grenades and later led law enforcement on a high-speed chase that led to injury and destruction of property."

"But he didn't murder anyone." Lisa's voice was pleading. "He swore it to us, and we believe him."

Journey pinched her thigh to keep from losing her cool. "Mrs. Tucker—"

"Lisa, please."

"Lisa, even if that is true, Trent is still implicated in heinous crimes. Please, take that seriously."

Ben placed an arm around his wife and pulled her close. "I assure you, we understand the gravity of our son's situation." He briefly caught his wife's eye, then returned his attention to Journey. "Which is why we'd like to ask if there's a possibility of exchanging information related to another one of your cases for leniency in Trent's."

This didn't surprise Journey as much as they probably thought it did. Information quid pro quo was a common tactic among defendants, even though the intel they promised rarely lived up to its hype.

"Well, before we continue, I must tell you, I'm not able to make any promises. And Lucas and I have the same title, so I'm not sure what you think I can do. What happens with Trent from here on out is solely up to the district attorney. But frankly, in the vast majority of situations like this, the information offered isn't nearly as valuable as people believe it to be. Are you prepared for that possibility?"

"We are." Ben nodded curtly. "But I suspect you won't find us to be a part of that overestimating majority."

Journey reached for her phone. "I'll need to record this."

"I understand."

She studied their faces, scrutinizing their sincerity. After a moment, she pressed record and began by stating the date, time, and location of the interview. Ben and Lisa Tucker both added their verbal consent on record.

Ben began. "My wife's uncle, Aaron Harris, has been a member of The Chosen for decades. As far as Lisa can recall, he joined the cult when she was in high school and remains active today."

A tingle of suspicion raised the hairs on Journey's neck. Her involvement in The Chosen investigation was not known to the public.

And why wasn't Lisa telling the story? Journey kept her reaction in check so he could continue.

"We have credible evidence that Aaron was directly involved with at least one of the cult's financial scams. We also have reason to believe he was associated with several murders. He's been living off the grid for some years, but we believe we know where he is. In a cabin in the Allegheny National Forest."

Few cases consumed Journey the way The Chosen had, and the possibility of taking down another member of the cult's criminal enterprise made her mouth water.

But she knew that if its top players were as easy to find as Ben had made it sound, they'd have been prosecuted years ago. And regardless, she was miles away from trusting a couple of strangers who clearly didn't even have their finger on the pulse of their child's life.

Even still, the idea that these random people had information of her, which they couldn't have known without some inside information, sent alarm bells clanging in her head.

"Why haven't you come forward to law enforcement before this?"

At last, Lisa answered for herself. "I come from an important family with a long, influential history in Pittsburgh. For decades, none of us has wanted to be associated either privately or publicly with Uncle Aaron. His name isn't even spoken at family events anymore."

Good grief, these families. Ostriches, every one of them.

Journey took a second to consider what they'd said. "If what you claim proves to be true, it could be an important lead in the ongoing investigation. But I'll need more information. Tangible evidence of what he was involved in and where he's living."

"Of course." Lisa beamed.

"That's not all. We'll also need confirmation that your uncle will cooperate. Just knowing that you have an uncle who did bad things does nothing to lessen the penalties against Trent."

Ben stood and extended a hand to Journey. "We're prepared to get our hands on anything you need as long as it makes a difference for our son."

44

Lucas exited the conference room and headed for the bullpen. If he was lucky, his fellow agents would be making a commotion, talking loudly, printers whirring, phones ringing. Given enough noise, he might just be able to drown out the chaos in his head.

His colleagues, though, weren't in a rowdy mood. Most were out in the field or hidden away in meetings, their absences unsettling. He sat down at their megadesk and cradled his head in his hands. Everything ached—joints, muscles, head, back. His skull felt as if it were compressing, a vise ratcheting ever tighter.

The investigation was over. They'd found the killers. Deciphered an unfolding plot and prevented a tragedy that might've left dozens dead and a community reeling. But none of it felt good. Theirs was a success without celebration.

Bottom line, he'd killed a kid. Jenson Buckley was eighteen, an adult in the eyes of the law. But Lucas knew that a number meant nothing. At that age, it took Lucas five minutes to fall in love and another five to fall back out again.

Back then, Taco Bell was authentic Mexican food. And if he just played his cards right, his future wouldn't be nearly as painful as his past.

Jenson Buckley was only three years older than Hallie. Lucas would never be able to view the kid solely as a criminal. Becoming a father had changed his perspective forever.

"Lucas!" Journey's voice floated across the void to his listless ears.

He watched her jog over but didn't stand, incapable of matching her sudden enthusiasm.

"The Tuckers wanted to trade information for leniency. And they asked for me because…get this…Lisa Tucker claims her uncle was behind one of The Chosen's financial scams. They even claim he was involved in multiple alleged murders."

That perked Lucas up. "Which scam?" During his time in White Collar, he'd spent years peeling back the layers on The Chosen's many financial crimes.

"That's not clear yet. But they also believe they know where he's living. Off the grid somewhere in the Allegheny National Forest."

The Tuckers' cache of evidence would have to prove accurate. But if it did, this might be the first meaningful lead against The Chosen he'd heard about in years.

"Fantastic, Ace. Truly." Though Lucas meant every word, his enthusiasm fell flat.

"You okay?" Journey cocked her head. "I mean, thanks, but I thought you'd be more excited."

"I am." He rubbed his raw, dry eyes. "I'm just too exhausted to sound it."

She smacked him playfully on the arm. "You're allowed to be exhausted. I am too. But our tireless work just might be about to pay off."

"Then we better get some coffee. Sounds like there's more work to be done." Lucas stood and stretched his arms wide.

"Sleep first." Journey patted Lucas on the shoulder. "The D.A. has to get involved before we get our information. And when that happens, I need my favorite partner to be in fighting form."

"Favorite? Really?" That made Lucas smile.

"Don't pretend you don't already know. I'm so lucky to have an amazing partner like you."

"Yes, you are."

She sneered, then playfully stuck her tongue out.

Lucas held up his hands in mock surrender.

Journey laughed. "Go. Sleep. Hug Hallie. And hopefully, when you come back, we'll be armed with info to take down The Chosen."

"Yes, ma'am."

There was a knock on the door. Lucas looked up to see a harried looking SSA in the frame. Keller seemed out of breath. "Good, glad I caught you both together."

"What's the word, boss?"

But Lucas already knew.

"I just wanted to say great work today. *But* because of all the exploding and gun discharging, you're both relieved of duty pending an officer-involved shooting investigation."

"Saw that coming."

45

Two weeks of administrative leave was almost enough time for Journey to consider committing murder so she could have something to solve. Just one more day of nothing left. She and Lucas had been cleared.

It was Saturday, and for the fourteenth straight day, she had nothing to do. Journey slept until ten a.m. before dragging herself to the couch to guzzle coffee and watch mindless TV.

By noon, she was thoroughly bored. She needed… something, so she strapped on her shoes and went for a long run. The sun beat hot on her skin, bringing the sweat down her back and neck in streams, taking what was left of her stress hangover with it.

Keller had told her to go home and not come back until the bags had disappeared from beneath her eyes. She was doing her best, but she could only take so much rest before it sent her mind reeling.

After the run, she took a long, hot shower. Then, for good measure, she sprayed bathroom cleaner on the tile and wiped it clean. The sinks and toilet too. Might as well, since she was on a roll.

In the kitchen, she scrubbed the countertops, then pulled out the contents of her refrigerator and threw out everything that was stinky, moldy, or expired. Once done, she prepped five days of dinners from everything she had left.

She vacuumed, but she'd hardly been home enough recently to dirty the carpet, so it took ten minutes.

What now?

And then, her phone rang.

Keller.

"You don't know how good your timing is."

Keller cleared her throat. "You may not think that when you hear what I have to say. I need you and Agent Sullivan to come in. We've got a new potential serial killer case. Young girl found mutilated on the boundaries of the Allegheny National Forest. Joint task force with Clearfield County and the National Parks Service."

Journey's heart fluttered. Keller had just offered her the exact salvation she needed.

Work. "Count me in. I'm on my way."

The End
To be continued...

Thank you for reading.
All of *Journey Russo* series books can be found on Amazon.

ACKNOWLEDGMENTS

How does one adequately express gratitude to all those who have transformed a shared dream into a stunning reality? Let us attempt to do just that.

First and foremost, our families deserve our deepest thanks. Their unwavering support and encouragement have been our bedrock, allowing us the time and energy to translate our collective imagination into the words that fill these pages. Their belief in our vision has been a constant source of strength and inspiration.

As coauthors, our journey has been uniquely collaborative and rewarding. Now, with Mary also embracing the additional role of publisher, our adventure has taken on an exciting new dimension. This transition from solely writing to also publishing has been both a challenge and a joy, opening doors to share our work more directly with you, our readers.

We are immensely grateful to the entire team at Mary Stone Publishing — a group who believed in our potential from the very beginning. Their commitment extends beyond editing our words; it encompasses the tireless efforts of designers, marketers, and support staff, all dedicated to bringing our stories to life. Their expertise, creativity, and passion have been vital in capturing the essence of our tales and sharing them with the world.

However, our greatest appreciation is reserved for you, our beloved readers. You took a chance on our book, generously sharing your most precious asset—your time. It is our fervent hope that the pages of this book have rewarded that generosity, offering you a journey worth taking and memories that linger.

With all our love and heartfelt appreciation,

Mary & Amy

ABOUT THE AUTHOR

Mary Stone

Nestled in the serene Blue Ridge Mountains of East Tennessee, Mary Stone crafts her stories surrounded by the natural beauty that inspires her. What was once a home filled with the lively energy of her sons has now become a peaceful writer's retreat, shared with cherished pets and the vivid characters of her imagination.

As her sons grew and welcomed wonderful daughters-in-law into the family, Mary's life entered a quieter phase, rich with opportunities for deep creative focus. In this tranquil environment, she weaves tales of courage, resilience, and intrigue, each story a testament to her evolving journey as a writer.

From childhood fears of shadowy figures under the bed to a profound understanding of humanity's real-life villains, Mary's style has been shaped by the realization that the most complex antagonists often hide in plain sight. Her writing is characterized by strong, multifaceted heroines who defy traditional roles, standing as equals among their peers in a world of suspense and danger.

Mary's career has blossomed from being a solitary author to establishing her own publishing house—a significant milestone that marks her growth in the literary world. This expansion is not just a personal achievement but a reflection of her commitment to bring thrilling and thought-provoking stories to a wider audience. As an author and publisher, Mary continues to challenge the conventions of the thriller genre, inviting readers into gripping tales filled with serial killers, astute FBI agents, and intrepid heroines who confront peril with unflinching bravery.

Each new story from Mary's pen—or her publishing house—is a pledge to captivate, thrill, and inspire, continuing the legacy of the imaginative little girl who once found wonder and mystery in the shadows.

Discover more about Mary Stone on her website.
www.authormarystone.com

Amy Wilson

Having spent her adult life in the heart of Atlanta, her upbringing near the Great Lakes always seems to slip into her writing. After several years as a vet tech, she has dreams of going back to school to be a veterinarian but it seems another dream of hers has come true first. Writing a novel.

Animals and books have always been her favorite things, in addition to her husband, who wanted her to have it all. He's the reason she has time to write. Their two teenage boys fill the rest of her time and help her take care of the mini zoo that now fills their home with laughter…and yes, the occasional poop.

Connect with Mary online

- facebook.com/authormarystone
- x.com/MaryStoneAuthor
- goodreads.com/AuthorMaryStone
- bookbub.com/profile/3378576590
- pinterest.com/MaryStoneAuthor
- instagram.com/marystoneauthor
- tiktok.com/@authormarystone

Printed in Great Britain
by Amazon